CONSULAR TIMES

ROBERT M. KERNS

Published by Knightsfall Press
PO Box 280
Mineral Wells, WV 26150

ABOUT THIS BOOK

New Job. New Faces. New Challenges.

Wyatt has settled into his role as Alpha of Godwin County and the town of Precious. Lyssa has moved to Precious full-time, only traveling to Chicago for Shifter Council meetings. Life is good.

But Wyatt's peace shatters when Miles arrives and says, "Lad, we need to talk."

Join Wyatt as he uncovers a truth that will change the shifters' world forever.

Get your copy today!

P *ANG! PANG! PANG! PANG!*
A hammer struck a baking sheet with the regularity of metronome. It might not have been so bad, but the baking sheet sounded like it was right beside her head. And the evil bastard hitting it with a hammer just wasn't stopping.

"I swear if you don't stop beating that metal with a hammer I will arrest you for assaulting a federal agent." Even inside her own head, her voice sounded rough, a mixture of a parched throat and disuse.

When no one responded and the hammering didn't cease, she forced her eyes open and immediately closed them against the bright white *everything*. The curtains around her. The ceiling tiles and fluorescent lights overhead. The sheet and blanket that covered her. Everything was pure white and too damn bright.

She heaved herself into a sitting position and found she sat on a hospital bed in one of those horrid hospital gowns, and then, the stringent smell of antiseptic hit her harder than that damned hammering. It hit her so hard her nostrils and lungs burned.

Her body felt like it needed a stretch, like she'd been immobile for too long. But that wasn't her focus. She looked for the source of the hammering, but there wasn't anyone in sight. It made no sense. *Something* hammered against metal, and it was so close.

She endured another few strikes until tiny motion caught her eye. She watched a drop of water fall from the faucet and strike the metal sink with the same headache-inducing noise.

"What the hell..." she muttered as she forced herself to stand... and clutched at the hospital bed when the room spun and heaved around her like a rowboat in a hurricane.

The sensation soon passed, and she tried to stand on her own once more. Success. Her legs trembled a bit as she took cautious steps to the metal sink, but they steadied soon enough. Her sole mission was to stop the faucet from dripping, but when she stood at the edge of the sink, her thirst claimed her. She turned the faucet on full-bore and leaned down to swallow as much as she could.

When an automatic door swooshed open somewhere behind her, she paid it no mind as she maintained her focus on quenching her thirst, and it wasn't until someone pulled the curtains aside that the memory of being in a hospital gown forced its way through her single-minded focus on the faucet.

She jerked a wet hand back to hold the gown closed just as a man said, "Well, it's nice to see you up and around."

She spun and found a man in blue jeans and a blue-and-green-checked shirt underneath a white lab coat. He looked like he was in his mid-40s.

"Hi. Most people around here just call me Doc. I run the infirmary. Can you tell me your name?"

She blinked and fought the urge to grimace. She *hated* her name. "Edwina Eustace Burke."

Doc smiled and nodded once. "Good. Do you hurt anywhere?"

"No... at least... I don't think so."

"Also good. Now, tell me the last thing you remember."

She turned and shut off the faucet, making sure it was all the way off and wouldn't drip. Then, she crossed to the bed and sat, all the while searching her mind.

"I think... I think... I was shot and Special Agent Hauser was carrying me out of some kind of control center. We had been captured while looking into the black ops group that had been hunting Sloane Martinez. We were in a hallway, and I think I passed out."

Doc smiled again. "Excellent. From what Agent Hauser tells us, that should have been your last memory. You were unconscious when Alpha Wyatt arrived and saved your life."

Her eyes shot up to lock on his. "*Wyatt* saved my life? How?"

"Really, Agent Burke... do you have to ask? You were seconds from death. How do you *think* he saved your life?"

She fought a wholly irrational urge to grin like a child. If Wyatt saved her, he did it by turning her into a shifter, and Wyatt was the first feline primogenitor in recorded shifter history... a Smilodon. The memory of running her hand through his fur came unbidden to her mind, and a slight smile escaped her control.

"So, I'm a Smilodon shifter now, huh?

Doc shrugged. "If the process holds true, yes. But there is much... well... we hardly know anything about primogenitors. If the process held true, Alpha Wyatt would've been a cougar, or mountain lion if you prefer. So, while I want to say you're a Smilodon shifter now, I—like everyone else in town—am waiting for your first shift. That will tell us beyond all doubt. Now, if you will excuse me a moment, I

3

shall contact Agent Hauser and Alpha Wyatt to inform them you're awake."

"Wait, please," Burke said. "How long was I out?"

Doc looked over his shoulder, answering, "Seven days. We were beginning to worry a bit."

Burke sat back on the hospital bed, trying to wrap her mind around that. It was almost impossible to believe she'd been unconscious for a whole week. She didn't feel hurt or sick or injured in anyway. In fact, she felt better than she ever had in her life. In the distance, she heard Doc talking to someone, and she guessed he was on the phone telling Hauser or Wyatt that she was awake. That meant she would be leaving the infirmary soon, and she needed clothes that were not bloody rags or a hospital gown.

Another cursory scan of her surroundings did not reveal the presence of her personal effects, which led her to wonder if anyone had found them in that black ops base. It wasn't such a big deal to replace her driver's license or voter registration card, but she despised the thought of dealing with her bank and credit cards.

Since she was a shifter now, would she have to move to one of the shifter territories? What would happen to her job? Burke reached behind her and pulled the sheet and blanket around her as she tried to organize everything in her mind. After chasing that rainbow for several moments, she realized that she had no way of knowing just what would change in her life now. She didn't like that. She didn't like not knowing. She didn't like not being in control.

While she ruminated on her new situation, she heard automatic doors swoosh again, followed by almost running footfalls. Before Burke fully lifted her head, Winnifred Hauser charged through the open curtain and almost leaped to enfold her in a hug.

"I was so worried," Hauser whispered.

Burke felt like her friend's primary goal was to compress her ribs until they would fit inside a soup can, but she didn't mind. Not yet, at least. They had become very close during the time they spent as prisoners of the black ops organization.

It seemed like they had only just begun to hug when the automatic doors swooshed again, and soon Wyatt stood at the curtain's perimeter. He smiled at seeing them hugging each other, and he moved to lean against the wall to wait them out.

Burke whispered to Hauser, "We have an audience."

Hauser jerked back from Burke and spun, her eyes wide and cheeks red from embarrassment. "Hello, Wyatt. I didn't see you there."

Wyatt grinned. "That's okay. Burke did."

Hauser's blush deepened. "Yes… well…"

"Don't worry about it," Wyatt replied. He righted himself from where he was leaning and reached behind him, producing a pair of flip-flops. He tossed them onto the hospital bed. "There you go. Even if your clothes were not a bloody mess, I doubt they wholly fit anymore. I know mine didn't, and the fit was off just enough that it bugged me like a low-grade toothache. Hank, at the general store across the street, is waiting for you; his wife will help you with your new measurements, and I expect you to walk out of there with clothes for at least two weeks. It's on me."

"Oh, no… I couldn't," Burke demurred. "That wouldn't be right, especially since I'm a federal agent."

"Yes… about that. You might be a federal agent out in the greater United States, but you're in Godwin County, which is shifter territory. And you're a shifter now, too. So, while I have no authority over Hauser as such, you are another matter entirely. Besides, Hank will just deduct the price of the clothes from his monthly administration fee, so it's all good."

Hauser frowned. "Administration fee?"

"Yeah... it kinda threw me for a loop when Alistair and Gabrielle told me about it. Apparently, shifters don't do taxes the way humans are used to thinking of taxes. Instead of quarterly taxes or annual taxes, all the shifters in a given territory pay a portion of the previous month's income to the Alpha. The Alpha then, in turn, handles all the 'normal' taxes and uses what's left over for maintenance, a personal salary, and things like that. So, Hank will tally whatever clothes or items you pick onto a form that he will then submit with his administration fee. I will then forward a copy of that form to the state and the IRS, when I handle our taxes... because nobody wants to piss off the IRS. Oh, and before I forget, I've arranged for a room to be waiting for you at the hotel, so once you get settled, find me. We have a few things to discuss, and I highly recommend you not put it off. I'd like to make your transition to the wonderful world of shifter life a little easier than mine was. But... that's up to you."

With that, Wyatt waved goodbye and left the infirmary.

Burke sat on the hospital bed, feeling a tad stunned. "He didn't even let me thank him."

"It's not like you won't have the chance later. Can you forgive me for having him bite you?"

Burke smiled and pulled her back into a hug. "Of course, I forgive you. I'd rather be alive than dead, and honestly, I'm wondering if I'll be a Smilodon, too. I'm a little anxious to find out."

"I know. I've thought more than once over the past week about asking Wyatt to turn me, too." Hauser looked around the space as if she wasn't sure what else to say. Then, she brought her eyes back to Burke. "Well, you ready to get out of here?"

Burke nodded, and Hauser grabbed the flip-flops, dropping them on the floor. Burke pushed off the bed and slipped her feet into them before following Hauser out of the curtained area.

"Doc, I'll bring the gown back as soon as I finish at the general store," Burke said as she followed Hauser out of the infirmary.

Doc never looked up from the book that held his focus, but he did acknowledge her with a wave.

Minutes later, Burke stepped out of the infirmary building and into the sun of a clear, cloudless sky about midmorning. The air smelled fresher, somehow, and she couldn't hold back a smile at the sheer joy of being alive.

As she followed Hauser across the street, Burke noticed Wyatt talking with a woman and a boy on the cusp of early adolescence. They stood beside a blacked-out SUV sporting US Government plates, and three or four people in suits and sunglasses—whose posture and mannerisms screamed protective services—stood near them. With a little effort, she forced her curiosity to release the idea and made doubly sure she had a tight grip on the seam of her hospital gown. She eagerly looked forward to wearing normal clothes again. Then food. Lots and lots of food.

2

A beautiful day greeted me when I stepped outside the infirmary building, the breeze still carrying hints of the heavy rain earlier in the week, and I smiled as I closed my eyes and focused on the smells wafting along with the wind. I loved a good rainstorm, especially how the air smelled fresh and clean in the wake of it.

The sound of engines rolling to a stop nearby pulled me from my reverie, and I opened my eyes to see two blacked-out SUVs across the street. The lead vehicle sported government plates, and I assumed the chase car did as well. The moment the engines shut off, every door on the SUVs opened. A woman and man in suits and sunglasses exited the front driver and passenger sides, respectively, and a woman who looked about twice my age stepped into the sun from the rear door on the driver's side. She shared a quick word with the driver before she started to cross the street, her eyes locked on me.

I started across myself, and we met on the yellow line that separated the lanes. It was a slow day, and their SUVs were the first vehicles the street had seen in a couple hours.

"Hello," the woman said. "My name is Mina Vickers. President Williams charged me with establishing and overseeing the American consular office here in Precious. Am I correct that you are Alpha Wyatt Magnusson?"

I smiled and nodded. "Yes, I am. Let's step over to the sidewalk beside your vehicles. It's been a slow day in town, but that could change at any minute. I also understand you may have something of a personal request for me."

Mina blanched. "How... how did you know that?"

"My sister Vicki told me about the situation with your son."

"Oh... uhm... what are your thoughts on the matter?" Mina asked, still seemingly rattled by my knowledge of her son's situation.

I shrugged. "How old is he?"

"He's thirteen."

"I'll be honest. I'm very new to all this; it's only been about sixteen weeks since I became a shifter. But... from what the born shifters tell me, the greatest risk in changing a human lies at the extreme ends of his or her life, so the further into childhood or old age they are, the greater the risk that they won't survive. Most shifters won't even consider trying to change someone who isn't through puberty yet, but I understand waiting would not be in your son's best interests."

Mina shook her head. "No, it would not. The longer we wait, the worse his condition will become."

The rear passenger door of the lead SUV opened, and a boy with red curly hair hopped out and ran to Mina's side. She put her arm around him as he hugged her.

"Noah, this is Wyatt."

I crouched to put myself at his level and smiled as I held out my hand. "Hi, Noah. How are you?"

He took a half-step out from behind his mom and gave

9

me an acceptable handshake for a thirteen-year-old. "I'm okay, I guess."

"Well, it's nice to meet you, and welcome to Precious." I gave him my best welcoming smile, then stood and turned to his mom. "I think the first step is getting you and your people settled at the hotel. Then, we can discuss both topics further. Maybe later today or first thing tomorrow?"

Mina nodded. "That sounds good. I think we're all still on East Coast time. My body is screaming that it's lunch time."

I pointed over my left shoulder with my thumb. "Then, you want to visit Gladys's diner right away. Since most of us get all our meals at the diner, we don't really have a true grocery store in town. Oh… and if you do visit the diner, you should ask for the human menus."

"Human menus? Why is that?"

"Let's just say the portion sizes are radically different, and they need to be aware that you can't put away food like the rest of us."

Mina blinked. "Oh, wow… seriously?"

I just nodded. "One of the most difficult adjustments to… my new situation… is that six thousand to eight thousand calories per day—and most of that protein—are normal for me now. That's how much it takes for one of us to be healthy."

"So…?" Mina's voice trailed off as she flicked her eyes toward her son and back.

"That would be a matter to discuss with Doc, but like I said, let's get you settled and fed. Then, I'll get Doc and Alistair to meet with us in the conference room to discuss the situation. Once we have that moving, we can discuss your consular office."

Mina grimaced. "We should focus on that. After all, it is the main reason I'm here."

I shook my head. "Nope. Don't worry about what the

government wants just yet. I'm still working on sorting out where the consular office will be. I'm thinking of taking First Avenue and turning it into a kind of Embassy Row, because the Magi Assembly decided to follow suit and will be establishing a consular office here, too."

"Oh... I wasn't expecting that," Mina replied. "Do you think they would be amenable to talks for establishing an American consulate with them?"

"Who knows? But probably. In terms of their consulate with us, Vicki pushed the idea through the Assembly just so that I would always have access to Magi certified to create portals and assault rifts; she was afraid that I might call her someday for one or the other when she was too tied up in other matters to hop over here for me."

Mina's expression made it clear to me that she had no idea how to process that. "Your sister wanted you to have Magi available to support you, so she forced a measure to establish a consulate here in Precious through the Magi Assembly?"

"Yeah. We're twins, but she has always looked out for me like an older sister. Besides, she will inherit the family seat on the Assembly one day, so Grandpa has been including her more and more in Assembly affairs."

"I think I have a lot of catching up to do. I didn't pay as much attention to the supernatural briefings as I should have, and that decision is coming home to roost with a vengeance."

I smiled. "Don't worry. We'll help you ease into it as best we can. But for now, let's get you checked into the hotel, so you and your people can get some food."

I LEFT Mina and her people in Melody's capable hands and headed back to the infirmary. I wanted to help her son if at all possible, which meant I needed to discuss the situation with Doc. There was also the issue of Moira MacCallan, but so far, she seemed content to keep pretty much to herself and treat her stay in Precious as some kind of vacation. It seemed odd that the idea of shifters didn't surprise her at all, while she presented no indication of being supernatural herself, but I had bigger things to worry about. I decided to make a point of checking in with her at least once a week and otherwise leaving her to her own devices, which meant it was probably time to invite her to lunch or something and see how she was doing.

These thoughts carried me into the ward room where Doc seemed to spend most of his time waiting for the few patients he ever had. I found him sitting at his desk, focused on what appeared to be a medical journal of some type. He looked up as I entered the room and smiled a welcome my way.

"Ah, Alpha Wyatt... what brings you to my corner of town?"

"I have a bit of a sticky situation on my hands, Doc, and I'd like you to weigh in on the matter."

"Of course, of course! Pull up a chair, and tell me all about it."

I grabbed one of the ubiquitous wheeled chairs that seemed to be in every doctor's office and hospital everywhere, pushing it over to a friendly conversation distance before sitting. "So, President Williams decided to establish a consulate here in Precious with the whole point of regularizing relations between shifters and Uncle Sam. I tried to get her to put it in Chicago where the Council meets, but Lyssa shot that down like a flak cannon. Anyway... the person President Williams named to run the new office is Mina Vickers, and her son has been diagnosed with Batten disease.

In fact, I'm almost certain her son's condition is *why* Williams chose her."

Doc nodded his understanding. "I see, and you want to offer to turn the boy into a shifter to cure the disease."

"Correct. So, what kind of minefield am I walking into? He's thirteen now, and from what little the internet told me about Batten disease, he may have at most another ten years or so, if he's especially lucky, with a progressive decline in his condition."

Doc grimaced. "All other things being equal, I'd counsel you to avoid changing the boy. The human body goes through enormous changes during puberty, and the added stress of becoming a shifter during that time is often more than a body can bear. I would like to conduct an exam and evaluation of him prior to embarking on this path, and if I feel the risk is too great, I would like for you to refuse to turn him. Yes, that's borderline cruel, but what would be worse? Going through an agonizing death now, or experiencing a progressive decline over the next ten years? That will be the question facing you and the boy's mother."

"And what if she says she wants to risk it, despite your recommendation?"

"I… don't know. Wyatt, you have to understand; I swore the Hippocratic Oath just like every other medical professional, and I believe in it down to my very bones. I'm not denying he's been dealt a bum hand in life, but I simply cannot sanction making him worse, essentially killing him. Honestly, it's a horrible situation and an excellent example of why we do our best to keep the greater world unaware of our existence. Can you imagine what it would be like to turn away parents with children too frail to survive the change as they beg and plead for you to try anyway? I *never* want to live through that."

I leaned back against my seat and sighed. "You have a

point, Doc. A very good point, to be truthful. So, what should I do? What's the best outcome here?"

Doc puffed out his cheeks as he heavily exhaled. "Damn, Wyatt... why put that on me? I suppose the best outcome would be that he's healthy enough to survive the change and comes out the other side, hale and whole. But what about his mom? I mean, are we going to tell him that becoming a shifter means he'll outlive all the humans alive today, even newborn babies, and probably their great-grandchildren? That's a lot to put on a child. Most people that age are not ready to confront mortality, theirs or anyone else's. I think the best way to go about it will be to have a meeting with the parents first, and I mean just you, me, and the parents. Say... you haven't said anything about the dad; what does he think of all this?"

"I have no idea, Doc. Mina never mentioned the boy's dad, so that's something we should discuss with her when we have the initial conversation."

Doc grimaced as he shook his head. "You never pull the easy ones, do you, son..."

"Nope. Mina and her people are getting settled at the hotel, and I think they're going to the diner afterwards. I'll see when she wants to have the first conversation and get back to you."

"That would be best." Then, he gestured to the otherwise-vacant infirmary wardroom. "I have so much work on my hands that I need to schedule my time, you know."

I could not hold back the grin and reached over to the medical journal. Flipping it open, I revealed a smaller golf magazine tucked inside it. "I wouldn't want to interfere with your brutal regimen of continuing education."

Doc shrugged as embarrassment tinged his cheeks a faint shade of red. I grinned and clapped him on the shoulder as I stood and returned the chair to its former place. Doc and I exchanged goodbye waves as I left the infirmary.

I once more basked in the pleasant day as I transitioned from the building to sidewalk and looked at my watch. The thought occurred that I wasn't completely certain what the day's agenda was supposed to entail, which meant I should probably visit the admin building.

EVEN THOUGH LYSSA was still settling into the move from Chicago to Precious, she insisted on being productive and useful, and since the Shifter Council only met for a week three times per year—unless exigent circumstances arose—she had a lot of time on her hands. Time that she decided to spend becoming my executive assistant.

There was no doubt in my mind that someone more indoctrinated into the 'shifter way' of doing things would've seen it as an affront or major disrespect, but the fact of the matter was she saved my fur nine ways from Sunday. She had many, many years of experience as one of the feline councilors—not to mention being a born shifter—so she understood all the ins and outs and minutiae of administering a shifter territory. She brought all the major decisions to me, of course, but in the days since she became my assistant, all the minor administrative tasks that I found too annoying to care about vanished from my list. For that small mercy alone, I wanted to kiss her all over, not to mention all the other ways she complemented the three of us—meaning Gabrielle, Karleen, and I—while enriching our lives.

The young receptionist working the admin building's front desk greeted me as I entered the building, and I returned it, making a mental note to stop and check in with him on my way out. I did care about all the people who looked to me as their Alpha, and it seemed like I'd been

ROBERT M. KERNS

running off and handling everyone else's problems too much lately. Maybe I should take a walk around the town later, too...

Lyssa's office was empty, and I found her standing at my desk with her back to the door. Her black pencil skirt and white blouse looked very nice on her, and I had to take a moment to clear several non-work thoughts as I approached her.

I was halfway from the office to the door when my willpower failed me, and I enfolded Lyssa in a hug as I kissed her cheek and then her neck.

"Well, hello to you, too," she said, her voice almost a purr.

"Hi," I replied in between kisses. I continued to hold her tight as I asked, "Do we have anything major on the agenda today?"

"Hmmm... nothing significant. Why?"

"The delegation to establish an American consulate arrived today, and President Williams named Mina Vickers as the ambassador or whatever the appropriate term is. Once they've had a chance to get settled and eat, I was going to call a meeting to discuss the situation with her son, because I can't stand knowing he's in a bad way if there's something we can do to help him."

Lyssa turned to face me, a warm smile brightening her whole expression. "That's one of the things I love about you, Wyatt... how much you want to help others."

I gazed into her eyes and wanted nothing more than to take my time expressing just how much I loved her in return, but... we didn't have that kind of time. And my office in the admin building probably wasn't the best venue, either. At least not during 'normal' business hours.

I stole another, longer kiss before releasing her and stepping back. "Do you want to be in the first meeting with Mina about her son? I care more about addressing that than sorting out the consulate."

Lyssa nodded as she smoothed her blouse. "Yes, I think I would. I would say we should invite Karleen and Gabrielle as well, but they took off on a hunting trip shortly after you left this morning. They *might* be back by nightfall, but probably not."

"Okay, then. If you don't mind, think about who else should be in the meeting. I'm on the fence about Alistair, not whether he should be in the meeting but whether we should bother him with it."

"Inviting him is not a bad idea. With all he has seen, I'm sure he has some experience to offer. Shall I discuss it with him?"

"Yes, please. I think I'm going to go for a walk around the town in the meantime. I feel a little disconnected after all the trips lately." Lyssa's expression fell, and I realized my mistake. Helping her sister by recovering her niece was one of those recent trips. "No. Don't think for even a moment that I begrudge the trip to Kansas. I would've been very unhappy if you had hired Gabrielle and left me out of it."

Then, just to be sure I reinforced the idea, I sniped another two kisses.

"Go on, get out of here," she said. "You have a town that needs walked around."

She pushed me back as she fought to contain her smile, and I left her in my office, an insouciant grin dominating my expression.

3

The builders or architects of the hotel in Precious styled it after the ritzy, up-scale hotels of the early twentieth century, favoring the overall Old West theme that seemed to run through what Mina had seen of the town so far. A pleasant wall of cool air kissed her cheeks to the accompaniment of an old-time, physical bell over the double doors that jingled every time one of them opened.

The lobby and an associated parlor that seemed large enough to accommodate all the guests at maximum occupancy continued the old-fashioned theme with period-appropriate furnishings and lighting fixtures. Mina blinked at seeing what looked like an old gas lamp on the wall and smiled when she noticed the contours of a lightbulb inside it; it seemed someone engineered fixtures to meet the theme while still affording modern conveniences.

A twenty-something woman with red hair almost the color of copper stepped out of a back room to stand behind the front desk and offered a welcoming smile to the group.

"Hello, and welcome to the Precious Hotel. I'm Melody. How can I help you?"

Mina extended her smile to the young lady. "Hi, Melody. I'm Mina Vickers, and I'll be overseeing the establishment and operation of the American consulate to the Shifter Nation here in Precious. Does the hotel have sufficient availability for me to book a few rooms for my people for the short term, until we can sort ourselves out?"

"Why, of course, ma'am. This isn't one of our higher-traffic seasons. How many rooms do you need?"

Over the next few minutes, Mina and Melody handled the temporary accommodations, and after moving all the luggage into the hotel, it was time to visit the diner Wyatt had recommended. Leaving the hotel, Mina led her son and a few of her people up the sidewalk before crossing the street to the diner's entrance.

Another bell overhead heralded their arrival, and the ambient noise level dropped as the diner's patrons took in the new arrivals. Before the moment could become too awkward, a woman who looked to be in her mid- to late-fifties smiled a welcome as she carried an almost overflowing tray to a nearby table.

"Hi, I'm Gladys. Please, seat yourselves, and I'll be right with you."

Mina chose an empty table and led the way to it. She and her people quickly assumed their seats, and each retrieved a menu from a collection in the center of the table. She was still looking over the options when Gladys arrived at her elbow.

"So, what brings you folks to Precious?" Gladys asked.

"I'm here to establish an American consulate to the Shifter Nation," Mina explained.

Gladys blinked, then looked all around like she expected a surprise. "You're not... what do the youngsters call it... pranking me, are you? It doesn't really make sense for the government to establish a consulate inside its own territory to its own people, does it?"

Mina shrugged. "The current administration feels the relationship between the Shifter Nation and the United States has not been maintained as well as it should have been, especially given the treaty between us, and desires very much to correct that."

Gladys regarded her in silence for several moments before giving an exaggerated nod. "Fair enough, then. Have you folks decided what you'd like to drink?"

They gave their drink orders, and Gladys bustled off to see to them. As she returned her focus to the menu, Mina couldn't help but feel Gladys had been just one short step from openly laughing in her face over the consulate idea. If she were completely honest with herself, she wasn't sure how she felt about that. On the surface, she agreed with Gladys; the idea was ludicrous, and to top it all, she didn't even have any formal diplomatic training. She was a lawyer, most recently a federal judge prior to her short-lived appointment as Attorney General. She was *not* the person for this post, and she knew beyond any doubt that President Williams chose her to establish and lead this mission just to give her the opportunity to save her son. She didn't like that and, more than once since she left the capital, felt like she should resign. But if she did, what was she supposed to do? Especially after resigning from her post as Attorney General? The idea of hanging a shingle in Precious as an attorney occurred to her, but was there really that much of a need? How much business would she have?

Almost before Mina realized it, Gladys was back with their drinks. "Have you settled on what you'd like?"

"I probably should have mentioned this when you took our drink orders, but Wyatt said something about asking for the human menus," Mina said.

"Oh, lordy me... I am so sorry. Of course you'll need the human menus. One second..." Gladys dashed over to the register counter and snagged a number of menus from beneath it before returning to their table. "Here you go, folks, and I apologize for that. The menu items themselves are the same; it's just that the portions are radically different."

Mina returned her menu to the center of the table while the rest of her party did likewise. Upon opening the new menu, the first thing that leapt out at her was the difference in prices. These numbers were much lower than those in the other menu.

"Don't get a lot of humans visiting the diner, huh?" Mina asked, adding a smile.

Gladys shook her head as she made a note on her order pad. "We surely don't. So... what would you fine folks like to eat?"

Each person at the table gave her an order, and Gladys nodded once she double-checked that she had everything correct. "Alrighty. This should be out in no time. Flag me down if you need anything."

Mina fought the urge to let her earlier doubts resume their hold on her. It was difficult, and she felt like she was losing ground until her son saved her.

"Mom, why does everyone around here act like they're not human?" he asked in a voice just loud enough for her to hear over the ambient noise. "And what was all that about Ma... Magi earlier? What were you talking about?"

"Honey, that's something we should probably discuss back in our room at the hotel, but the short answer is that the world isn't as simple as we thought it was. Is that okay for now?"

He shrugged. "Yeah, I guess so."

Mina smiled and took his small hand in hers. Unbidden, her memories of his infancy surged to the forefront of her mind, and she couldn't help but smile. She was so proud of him, especially how he handled everything involving his medical condition. She wasn't sure she would be as strong and level-headed if their places were reversed.

LATER THAT AFTERNOON, Mina approached the front desk of the hotel. No one was in sight, so she tapped the small bell in front of the sign that read, 'Please ring bell for service.' Moments later, Melody stepped out of the back office.

"Hello again. Is everything with the rooms to your liking?"

Mina nodded. "Oh, yes. Everything is fine on that front. Now that we've settled in a little bit, I was hoping to have a word with Wyatt on a couple matters, but I don't know how to reach him."

"That's easy," Melody answered. "I'll just call over to the admin building and ask Lyssa if she knows where he wandered off to."

Without waiting for Mina to reply, Melody put action to her words, grabbing the nearby phone's handset and dialing a number. Moments later, she said, "Hi, Joey. It's Melody over at the hotel. I need to speak to Lyssa." A few moments of silence passed. "Hi, Lyssa; it's Melody. I have Mina Vickers here at the front desk, and she's looking for Wyatt." More silence. "Ah. Okay. Are you sure about that?" Another interlude of silence. "Okay, then. Thank you. I'm sure Mina will appreciate it, too. Bye!"

Melody returned the handset to its cradle, ending the call, and turned to Mina. "She said Wyatt is out taking a walk around the town, but she's going to call him on his cell. She said you're welcome to wait with her in the admin building, which also serves as the county courthouse, or they could stop by here to collect you once Wyatt appears. How would you like to handle it?"

That was the question, wasn't it. One of her advance team watched Noah, her son, and agreed to do so while Mina discussed her son's situation with Wyatt. But she didn't want to impose if there was going to be a wait before that conversation started. In the end, circumstances settled the matter for her.

"Ah, there he is now," Melody chirped.

Mina looked up and turned toward the direction Melody pointed in time to see Wyatt walk by the hotel's entrance.

"I guess I'll just walk with him, then," Mina replied and rushed to catch up.

THE PASSAGE of a few minutes saw Mina sitting at a table in the admin building's conference room with Wyatt, a stunning woman who introduced herself as Lyssa, a gentleman who looked older and introduced himself as 'Doc,' and another older gentleman who introduced himself as Alistair Cooper.

"All right, then," Wyatt said, in essence calling the meeting to order. "I asked you here to discuss an issue facing us. As she said, Mina has been tasked with creating and overseeing the American consulate to the Shifter Nation of North America. But I'm more concerned with the fact that her son has been diagnosed with Batten disease."

"How old is the boy?" Alistair asked.

"Thirteen," Mina answered.

Alistair winced. "That... makes for a rather dicey proposition. Do you know if he has started puberty yet?"

Mina felt her cheeks heat a little, and she was sure she blushed. "Uhm... well, no. Not really. I don't think so; he hasn't had his first teenage growth spurt yet."

"What say you, Doc? What are your thoughts on this?" Alistair asked, but Mina suspected he was not in favor of the idea.

Doc shrugged. "My thoughts are that I haven't examined the boy yet. I would like to look over his medical records as well. Did you happen to bring them with you, by chance?"

"Yes, I did. The copies I obtained from each of his doctors are in one of my suitcases back at the hotel."

"That's good. If you will, get me those copies as soon as you can. Do you have a cell phone, and does it have signal here in Precious?"

Mina fished her phone out of her pocket and checked it. "Yes, it seems to have full signal."

"Excellent. At this time, I am leaning toward opposing the idea from the simple standpoint that it is an incredible risk to try changing a child into a shifter. Most children's bodies are not robust enough to survive the physical stress of the change. That being said, the disease creates an imperative all its own. I would like to get those records, examine them, and then examine the boy. Based on all that, I will then be in a position to decide whether I recommend proceeding with the attempt."

"Has he shown any special interest in a particular animal?" Alistair interjected. "We should be prepared to offer him his favorite animal if the decision is to proceed."

Mina smiled. "He loves dogs. My youngest sister is coming out with the moving company, and she's bringing our German Shepherd."

"So, he might like the idea of being able to turn into a wolf?" Wyatt asked.

"It's possible. I know he and Duke are almost inseparable if you give them half a chance."

"What does his father have to say about this idea?" Doc asked.

Mina grimaced and sighed. "His father hasn't spoken to either of us since maybe a week after Noah's diagnosis. He filed for divorce and has since remarried. He didn't even try for partial custody or visitation or anything."

The growls Mina heard from every other person at the table shocked her. They sounded far more primal and animalistic than she would've thought human vocal cords could produce.

When Mina's shock became apparent, Lyssa reached over and touched Mina's arm. "Sorry. You'll have to forgive us. Abandoning one's child is a heinous crime in shifter society. The most vile shifter would never abandon a child, even if that was in the child's best interests."

"I want his name," Wyatt said, his voice carrying hints of his displeasure.

"May I know why?" Mina asked.

Wyatt pointed at Lyssa with his thumb. "Because she worked the Shifter Council to name me Consul of the Shifter Nation of North America, and I intend to put his face, his name, and a description of his conduct in this matter into a bulletin to all shifters, blacklisting him from doing any kind of business with us."

Mina's eyes shot wide. "You can do that?"

Wyatt's serious expression dissolved into a lopsided grin and a half-shrug. "Can I publish the bulletin? Absolutely. Does that mean every shifter in North America will abide by it? No idea. But I feel the matter is serious enough to warrant the attempt."

"Is it our place to do it, though?" Lyssa asked. "Do we have the right to expect humans to abide by our values and morals?"

Wyatt shook his head. "I don't expect humans to fall in line with our values. I don't want them to be shorter-lived versions of shifters who can't shift. But I do think we can establish a basic set of values that are non-negotiable and choose to do business with only those humans who meet our standards. Yes, that might not be how modern America does it, but I can't say I've ever been a fan of how hypocritical our society as a whole has become. So, yes... in this instance and in this case, I think it is our place to do that."

Mina watched Lyssa fight a smile that tried to overcome her self-control, but she said nothing further on the matter.

When silence threatened to become awkward, Wyatt looked around the table, asking, "Does anyone have anything else to say?"

No one spoke.

"Very well. We'll consider the matter to be pending until such time as Doc has had a chance to review the medical files and perform his own assessment of Noah. Thank you for coming."

That said, Wyatt stood and led them out of the conference room.

4

I left the admin building deep in thought about the Embassy Row that was now a priority. The problem was that the town planners didn't seem to have considered such a need. Moving deeper into the town away from Main Street, most of the town was residential with lots of open space for us to run around in our fur.

And that wasn't the sole consideration, either. Most of the town's residents had owned their homes in those homes' current locations longer than I'd been alive. I wasn't about to uproot them for a project in which most of us saw little value. After all, there wasn't a person in Precious who didn't consider themselves an American citizen; many of them were veterans of at least one war, if not more than one. In fact, I wasn't aware of any shifter in Godwin County who didn't consider himself or herself to be an American citizen.

So, the government's insistence on treating us like a foreign entity by establishing a consulate was a little... odd. Maybe even a tad backhanded? Especially since shifters were not 'out' to the world. How did the government expect to hide a consulate established inside the country? Maybe call it a State Department field office?

Another side to the problem was that I didn't want to insult anyone—especially not the Magi, when they finally arrived—by putting Embassy Row in a subdivision several streets away from the center of town. That just seemed like a recipe for disaster, no matter how you looked at it.

With the issue on the forefront of my mind, I walked down Main Street to the intersection with First Avenue. Main Street ran North to South, and the town's avenues East to West. With the exception of Main Street, the even-numbered streets and avenues were one way, with the traffic flowing toward the west. The odd-numbered streets and avenues—like First Avenue—were one way, the traffic flowing toward the east. Well, what passed for traffic, anyway. The town wasn't really all that large, and most people walked wherever they needed to go unless their trip involved bulky or freight-grade cargo.

On the north side of East First Avenue, a line of structures looked abandoned or, at least, disused. I counted five or six of them, which was far more than I needed for the two embassies or consulates or whatever the proper term was. I pulled out my cell phone and, opening my app for notes, recorded the number of each building. The structures ran the length of the block from Main Street to First Street, and not one of them looked like they had seen use in the last fifteen years.

It seemed a visit to the town's property office was in order.

THE TOWN'S property office was on the second floor of the admin building, across the hall from the county clerk's office. A mousy fox shifter named Samantha ran the office, and she blushed and gave me a nervous smile when I entered the room.

"Hi, Samantha. How are you today?"

"Oh, I'm fine, Alpha Wyatt. How can I help you?"

I saw a stack of what looked like scrap paper and pointed to it. "Is that scrap?"

Samantha nodded. "Yes, it is."

I pulled a square off the top of the stack and wrote out the building numbers on East First Avenue, then pushed the paper to Samantha. "I would like to know who owns those buildings, please. They looked empty, and I need some real estate."

Samantha read the list, then turned to a large map of the town that hung on a nearby wall. She pointed at the map with her finger as she scanned the buildings in question. "Well, I need to check the property book to be sure, but I think *you* own them... or at least you as in the Alpha of Precious and Godwin County. Give me a minute, please."

She turned and crossed the room to a bookshelf complete with a rolling ladder anchored to the top. She climbed until she could reach the second shelf from the top and scanned the spines, using one foot to push herself along until she found the book she sought. Retrieving it from the shelf, she brought it back to the counter and opened it where both she and I could see it.

The index listed properties by street address, and she went through it until she found the entries for those buildings, making a note of the page number on the paper. Then, she flipped to the page for the first property and scanned it, nodding once. She then flipped the pages to check each of the other properties before returning her focus to Wyatt.

"Yes... the Alpha before Jason McCourtney seized all of those properties in lieu of months and months' worth of unpaid administration fees. I don't know *what* she was going to do with them, and she died before she did it anyway. I don't know that Alpha Jace ever realized the office of Alpha owned them."

Relief washed over me, and I resisted the urge to grin like a fool. "Do we have a plat of those lots? I need to know if the original owners built to fill the space or just built what they needed."

"Hrmmm... we should have a plat I can copy for you. Let me check."

Samantha disappeared into another section of the property office, but my shifter hearing could still pick up the occasional sound of her moving items. After a few minutes, I heard a printer kick off, and it wasn't too long until she returned with a print-out from a plotter printer that showed the half of the block those structures represented.

"Here you go, Alpha Wyatt," she said as she laid the paper on the counter. "Do you mind if I ask you why you needed all this?"

"The federal government wants to establish a consulate to the shifters here in Precious, since Lyssa wrangled the Council into naming me Consul, and the Magi want to do the same as well. That means we have to put them somewhere, and I haven't even considered where they'll live. Buy plots in the new subdivision Evan wants to develop, I suppose."

"But... but... I voted in the last presidential election," Samantha protested. "I have a US passport. How am I not an American citizen?"

"You're not the first person to raise that question," I replied. "I'm not sure the government thought the whole matter through before they leaped on it. The current president in D.C. feels the relationship between the shifters and the government has not been given the attention it's due, especially given the treaty we have... so... we get a consulate. If you figure out how we rate a consulate while still being American citizens, be a pal and tell the rest of us."

Samantha collected the property book from the counter and returned it to the shelf, shaking her head and muttering about the sheer wastefulness of the federal government. I didn't feel like I had anything to add, so I bid her goodbye and left her to her work.

I RETURNED to the main floor of the admin building in search of Lyssa. Once again, her office was empty, and I found her in mine. This time, the rustle and crackle of the paper in my hands alerted her to my arrival before I could surprise her with a hug or kiss.

"And what prize do you bring me, fair prince?" she asked, eyeing the roll of paper I carried.

"A solution to our Embassy Row problem."

Her eyebrows went in search of her hairline. "Oh, really? Do tell."

I motioned for her to join me at the side table and cleared it before unrolling the paper. "These buildings along East First Avenue... the Alpha before Jason seized them for supposedly unpaid administration fees across months and died before she could do anything with them. Jason either didn't know or didn't care that the office of Alpha owned them, and they've sat unused for who knows how long. Well... I suppose we could find out how long with a records search, but I'm not sure it's important."

"No, it isn't," Lyssa remarked, her voice distracted as she looked over the plats. "Yes... I think this solves the issue rather well. I think Mina should get her choice of lots and then decide whether she wants to renovate the existing structure or demo and build new. With your permission, I'll leave a message for Mina with Melody that we'd like to meet with her at her earliest convenience tomorrow morning."

I nodded my agreement as I snaked an arm around her waist. "Yes, waiting until tomorrow morning sounds excellent, especially if Gabrielle and Karleen are still off on their hunting trip. It's been a little bit since you and I played 'Catch the Cat.'"

"Mmm... yes, it has."

THE NEXT MORNING, I met Mina on the sidewalk as she approached the admin building from the hotel. I guessed that Lyssa was already in the office, as I woke up alone and found breakfast waiting for me in the kitchen.

"Morning, Wyatt," Mina said as we met at the entrance. "What did you need to speak with me about? I just delivered Noah's medical records to Doc last evening."

"It's about the embassy or consulate or whatever it's supposed to be called," I answered. "After all, there's no reason we can't multi-task, and there's nothing for us to do until Doc finishes examining the records and then evaluates Noah." I opened the admin building's door and gestured for Mina to enter ahead of me. "After the meeting yesterday, I found a line of buildings on First Avenue that have fallen into disuse. Since I don't want to insult anyone by establishing consulates out in the figurative boonies around town, I don't see why we can't use these lots. It would certainly put you close to the center of town, and as you arrived first, you get first choice. I thought we could show you the lots on a plat first and then go for a walk."

My explanation carried us to my office, and I found Lyssa already there once again. She spent more time in my office than I did, and the thought made me smile.

"Good morning, Mina," Lyssa said in greeting. "How was your night?"

"It was well enough. Noah has always had problems sleeping anywhere new, and he'll probably just be getting used to the hotel when we finally move into a house. But Wyatt was saying you have a location for Embassy Row?"

"Yes, we do," Lyssa replied, gesturing to the paper covering the side table. Mina crossed to it, and Lyssa acted as a figurative tour guide, pointing out the properties' location relative to the admin building and the hotel.

It wasn't even a full minute before Mina nodded her approval. "Yes, I do like the location. The Secretary of State mentioned something about making this a regional field office for such things as passports and travelers' assistance. Personally, I would've thought Seattle or Spokane would be better for that, but mine is not to reason why, as they say."

Lyssa shot me a concerned look behind Mina's back, and I nodded my agreement. "Mina, I'd like to have a conference call with the Secretary of State as soon as possible. We don't want a flood of humans stumbling around Precious or Godwin County. I think it would be best if she abandons those plans."

"Yes... well... what would you have me do then? It isn't like this is an overseas posting. Anything related to the State Department here is essentially make-work."

I resisted the urge to smile as I replied, "You're not the first person to raise those concerns. I'm not all that certain the president's plan is well-conceived. Regardless, the Shifter Nation would very much prefer this consulate *not* be a regional office for anything. Perhaps we should thresh this out before we get too far into the planning stages."

Mina interpreted the subtle hint as I intended, and she wasn't wrong. We didn't *need* a consulate here in Precious, and I was prepared to help her son and tell her to pack up once we were sure the boy was safe.

"Let's head back to the admin building. We can set up for a conference call there. And while we walk, there's something you need to understand about your son."

Mina froze, weaving on her feet just enough to notice. "What is it? Are you not going to help him?"

I shook my head. "That's still to be determined. It's just that you need to understand... he will effectively be immortal if we agree and he survives."

"I... I'm not sure what you mean," Mina said, her voice quavering.

I glanced at Lyssa, and she gave a brief nod before stepping into the conversation. "Mina, honey... shifters don't die of old age. Our accelerated healing prevents it. Yes, if your son becomes a shifter he can still be killed, but he won't grow old and die like a human."

"But... those men... Doc and the other one... Alistair, I think? Doc looks a little older than me, and Alistair looks like my grandfather."

Lyssa turned Mina to face her. "How old do you think I am?"

Mina looked her over, then glanced at me. "I don't... I don't know. Late twenties, maybe? You're certainly nowhere close to my age, and I'm not that old."

"I turned fifty-seven a few weeks ago," Lyssa replied.

Mina gaped, her eyes wide and complexion pale. "No... that's... there's no way."

"And Alistair?" Lyssa pressed. "I'm not sure anyone truly knows how old he is, but I do know for certain that he's over three hundred, possibly even over four hundred. Magi can also enjoy longer lives, if they develop the proper talents; each of Wyatt's grandparents are over eight hundred. Magi do grow old and die, unfortunately; the proper talents and skill can stave it off for quite some time, but unlike us, Father Time always catches them."

"I… I'm going to need a minute," Mina said, almost whimpered. "I'm in no mental condition right now to call my boss."

She staggered to a nearby bench and collapsed heavily onto it. Her head went to her hands as her elbows rested on her knees.

"What do you think?" I whispered far too low for Mina to hear us.

Lyssa shrugged, whispering her reply, "No way to know. We hit her with a lot of information all at once."

After what seemed like ages—but was less than ten minutes in truth—Mina heaved a shuddering breath and forced herself to her feet. Her complexion wasn't yet back to its normal coloration, and I saw slight tremors in her hands and knees.

"You good?" I asked.

Mina shook her head, scoffing at the idea. "Not even close, but I am functional. Let's go have it out with my boss. I'm no longer certain of the wisdom of putting an American consulate here."

"Oh?" Lyssa asked as the three of us resumed walking. "Why is that?"

"Because I find myself wanting to ask about becoming a hawk or falcon shifter. Would that be a problem if you choose to help my son and he becomes a wolf shifter?"

I glanced at Lyssa, who shook her head, and answered, "No. That won't be a problem. We could go ahead and change you now, if you liked."

She shook her head. "No, at least not yet. I need to be there for Noah, regardless of the outcome."

"Fair enough. I can't argue with that at all. While we're still walking, I should probably apologize for my forcefulness when I asked for your ex's name. Yes, it is as Lyssa says; shifters do not abandon children, but it is a much more personal issue for me. I was born to one of the most prominent Magi families in the world, and I was born without a trace of magic. I'm told they were going to abandon me and deny my existence, especially since my twin sister showed indications of incredible Magi talent, but our grandparents wouldn't hear of it. They are now pretty much outcast from the family over their treatment of me."

"That puts the exchange in a whole new light," Mina remarked. "And yes, of course, apology accepted. I wasn't offended at all, and if I'm being honest, I rather like the idea of the shifters blacklisting him. I don't know how much it will affect him, but I like the idea all the same."

The smile that curled Lyssa's lips was downright evil. "Oh, it may hurt him more than you think. Remember what we told you about shifter lifespans? Well, we were here—meaning North America—*first*, even before the Native Americans. More than one shifter family or clan owns a sizable portion of stock in many of the country's oldest and/or largest companies. Not controlling interest, you understand; we don't want that level of scrutiny, but our ownership should be sufficient to make his life *interesting*."

Mina erupted in a fierce laugh. "Oh, my... this day just keeps improving. Wyatt, if I were to resign from the government again and pursue becoming a shifter, would you have any need for a lawyer with experience as a federal judge?"

The idea of creating a fair and impartial justice system for the shifters leaped to the forefront of my mind, and I couldn't help but smile. "Why, yes. I do believe I might have some work for you, and there's nothing saying you couldn't also work as a consultant to help shifters interface with the human legal system and government. There's always work for an energetic and dedicated shifter; you just have to find it… or make it."

"Excellent," Mina almost purred. "In that case, let's call my boss and deliver the bad news."

OVER THE NEXT FEW MINUTES, we claimed the conference room in the admin building, and Lyssa brought out a conference phone with satellite microphones that I didn't even know we had. She then connected the phone to the cameras in the room that would allow us to make the call a video conference if the Secretary of State so chose. Once the technology and we were ready, Mina dialed a number I assumed to be a private line.

On the second ring, the speaker broadcast, "Secretary of State's office, Barbara speaking."

"Barbara, this is Mina Vickers. I need to speak with the Secretary of State regarding my recent appointment."

A few moments of silence interrupted by clicking that I thought was a computer mouse or keyboard passed before Barbara replied, "Oh, I see. Ma'am, I apologize for the delay. I'll put you right through."

The connection went to a double-beep hold notification for a few moments, and then, the speaker broadcast, "This is Lucy Perez."

"Madame Secretary, this is Mina Vickers. You're on a conference speakerphone with myself, Wyatt Magnusson, and Lyssa Westridge. We have video capability if you prefer."

"Hello, Wyatt and Lyssa, and thanks for the offer of video, but it would take too long to set up on my end. What do you need?"

"Ma'am," Mina said, "I do not believe it is in our best interests to establish a consulate with the shifters, and even if we did, they do not want it to be a publicized regional office.

The more I learn about the community, the more I agree that creating an influx of traffic—especially human traffic—into the town would not be even vaguely wise."

Several moments of silence passed before Lucy said, "I'm going to need more than that, if you expect me to convince the president to abandon her idea."

"Ma'am," I said, breaking into the conversation, "it is not in the shifters' best interest for you to drive a surge of human traffic into our territories. From what I understand right now, the existence of shifters is largely unknown to the human world, and we want to keep it that way... for myriad reasons. If you and the president have your hearts set on building a consulate here, I won't fight you on that. But I will fight you—and win—over it being a regional office advertised to handle all sorts of human business."

"That is a very bold statement, Alpha Wyatt," Lucy replied. "What makes you so certain you'll win?"

"The Shifter Treaty. One of the provisions was that we retain full control of our territorial enclaves in exchange for supporting the colonies in the War for Independence. I would much rather there be no fight over it, but I am within my rights to declare all shifter territories in North America non-human territories. I imagine it wouldn't take too much work to get the Shifter Council to agree with me and publish that order within a few days.

"And on top of all that, the idea of a consulate here is a bit insulting, frankly. There isn't a shifter in Godwin County who doesn't already consider him- or herself an American citizen, and what government establishes a consulate to deal with *its own* citizens? Before you bring it up, a Magi consulate is less insulting because there is a history of conflict between us and them. The Shifter Nations and the Magi Assembly actually signed a truce to assist the Allies during both World Wars, but the shifters have always been neutral—if not friendly—toward the governments in North America; from what I understand, one of the ministers in the Canadian government is a shifter. So, you see, ma'am, that there is no need for an American consulate here."

A few seconds of silence passed during which all I heard was Lucy's regular, calm breathing. "Yes, you have a number of excellent points. I shall take this to the president as soon as I can. When I have an answer, I will contact Mina to schedule another conference call. Thank you for sharing this information."

"Thank you for your time, Ma'am," Mina replied.

The line clicked as the call ended.

I turned to Mina, directing a questioning eyebrow quirked upward as I said, "Why didn't you mention your interest in becoming a shifter? Having second thoughts?"

"Oh, no. Not at all. I just didn't want to hit her with too much all at once and risk losing her focus on the most important matter, namely quashing this consulate idea."

I grinned as I stood, which prompted Lyssa and Mina to do likewise. "Fair enough. Be thinking about whether you prefer hawk or falcon. But if you happen to like larger raptors, I do know a Roc shifter."

That said, I left the conference room.

5

Later that day, Karleen and Gabrielle returned from their hunting trip with several prizes. They kept a nice mule deer for the family and delivered three mule deer, three black-tailed deer, and a couple bighorn sheep to Gladys at the diner. Every time someone in town went on a hunting trip and brought back something for the diner, Gladys always sold meals based around whatever the hunters gave her at a lower price because she didn't have any major costs associated with it.

I helped them unload the truck, and as I carried the last prize into the diner's processing room, my cell rang in my hip pocket. I turned toward Lyssa who had kept herself clean and asked, "Mind grabbing that, please?"

"Why, not at all," Lyssa replied and helped herself to a handful of my butt as she retrieved my phone and answered the call. "Wyatt Magnusson's phone, and you're on speaker."

"Lyssa, this is Doc. As soon as Wyatt gets finished with whatever's keeping him from answering his own phone, ask him to stop by the infirmary."

I turned toward the phone and said, "I'll be there just as

soon as I wash up from helping unload the truck from the hunting trip."

"See you soon, then," Doc replied, and the line clicked when he ended the call.

Lyssa replaced the phone in my hip pocket as I asked, "Did you enjoy yourself?"

"Why, yes… I do believe I did." A satisfied smile curled her lips.

I returned the smile and headed over to the wash station, making two passes washing my hands just to be sure, and headed over to the infirmary.

Doc was in his actual office, instead of the treatment ward. The office was tasteful if spartan. Doc's various degrees hung on one wall, and several pictures of Doc with notable people occupied the wall opposite the degrees. Two guest chairs—wooden without padding—faced his desk, which looked to be stained oak that had aged well.

"You wanted to see me?" I asked as I stepped through the doorway.

"Close the door, if you don't mind."

I did so and crossed to one of the guest chairs, retrieving my phone before I sat. "You know, I don't think I've ever seen your office before. It's nice."

Doc shrugged. "My office sees even less use than the treatment ward. I think this is the first time I've spent more than five minutes here in… well… I'm not really sure. But it's been a long time. I called you to discuss my evaluation of Noah Vickers's medical records."

"Oh."

"Yes… oh. Noah is to my knowledge the first case of Batten I've ever encountered, so I contacted a few old friends who have a wider experience with genetic diseases. Based on those conversations, their conclusions are that the estimate of another ten years is rather generous. Whatever doctor told his mother that probably didn't want to break the news that her son had—maybe—five years left. He isn't displaying the common symptoms of Batten yet, but the markers are all there in the latest lab report. Based on this information, I don't feel as though I have a choice but to recommend we attempt to change the boy into a shifter. If we wait too much longer, I can guarantee the physical stress on his body will kill him."

"Have you examined Noah yet?" I asked.

"No. I probably should, just to keep up appearances, but the conversations with my colleagues convinced me this is a matter of some urgency. However, we should discuss the situation with his mother before we bring the boy in. Have you given any thought to who you'll ask to change him?" Doc must have seen my uncertainty in my expression. "And no, don't say Karleen. There are too many unknowns with primogenitors. The boy will already be facing enough risk as it is."

"Okay, then. What about Buddy Carrington?"

Doc remained silent for a few moments, staring at his desk, before he lifted his face to me and nodded. "Buddy has really turned himself around. I'd say he would be good with it. He'll essentially be the boy's shifter father, so it's possible some kind of bond might grow out of it. When we change humans, we generally like to keep them close for a little while to help them acclimate to shifter life."

I lifted my phone and scrolled through the contacts until I found the hotel, tapping the control to dial the number and put the call on speaker.

After the second ring, the speaker broadcast, "Precious Hotel, Melody speaking."

"Hi, Melody. It's Wyatt. Is Mina Vickers in the hotel?"

"No, sir, Alpha Wyatt. She is not. Her whole group—Mina

included—just walked across the street to the diner about five minutes ago."

"Thanks, Melody. I appreciate your time."

"You're quite welcome, Alpha Wyatt. You have a good day now. Buh-bye."

The line clicked as the call ended, and I looked to Doc. "Want me to get a to-go order and slip a note to Gladys to pass to Mina once they've finished eating? I don't want to ruin her meal with nerves if I say something right now."

"That's probably for the best," Doc agreed. He grabbed a prescription pad and wrote out a note. "Here. This will do."

I accepted the note, folded it in half, and slipped it into my pocket. "Do you need anything else from me right now?"

Doc shook his head, then broke into a grin. "Nope. I need to get back to my golf magazine."

I laughed as I stood and left the infirmary. I paused on the sidewalk outside and looked in the direction of the Alpha's house. I figured that Karleen and Gabrielle would be skinning, dressing, and preparing the mule deer right about now, and they might even be planning to use some of it for dinner. Which left me very conflicted. I needed an excuse to visit the diner, but I didn't want to waste my ladies' hard work *or* Gladys's excellent food. It seemed like the best thing to do was call home, and Lyssa might be the best one to contact if Gabrielle and Karleen were still bloody from the work.

After tapping her name, I lifted the phone to my ear. I only heard one ring before Lyssa answered, "Yes, my darling cat?"

"Well, someone's in a playful mood. Do you know what the dinner plans are?"

Lyssa chuckled. "Gabrielle and Karleen are in the shower, and some of the mule deer is in the fridge with the rest in the freezer. I think they're looking forward to anything *but* deer or sheep this evening."

"That's actually perfect. If you don't mind, check with them and call an order into the diner. I'm across the street now, and I'll go over and wait for it."

"Will do," Lyssa replied. "Bye."

The call ended before I had a chance to respond, and I headed over to the diner to wait for the order... and slip Doc's note to Gladys for delivery to Mina.

Our order was ready before Mina and her group finished, so I left the note in Gladys's capable hands after ensuring she knew not to pass it to Mina until they finished.

A PEACEFUL WALK delivered me to the Alpha's house and my waiting ladies. Gabrielle and Karleen dashed straight to me and waited just long enough for me to hand off the food to Lyssa before enfolding me in a hug and peppering me with kisses.

"We missed you," Karleen said, once they both convinced themselves I was still in one piece and unharmed.

Gabrielle nodded as she snuggled into my arm. "It just wasn't the same without you out there. You'll go with us, next time, right?"

I smiled and nodded. "I will if I can. It all depends on when you choose to go and what's happening here at the time. As much as we all might wish otherwise, I can't control the future."

Karleen snuggled into my other side. "We know."

"So, do you want to eat or snuggle?" I asked.

"Both," the ladies said, almost in unison.

I took the initiative and walked us over to the kitchen, where Lyssa laid out our orders. The smell of food that wasn't deer soon worked its way through Gabrielle's and Karleen's senses, and they released me in favor of their food. But I don't think their reluctance could have been more obvious if someone painted it on a billboard the size of Texas.

We ate in a companionable silence, and I had just finished my food when my cell rang. I retrieved it from my pocket and saw it was the infirmary, then accepted the call.

"Yeah, Doc?"

"Would you mind meeting me and Mina in my office, Alpha Wyatt? She just arrived."

I looked up to find three lovely ladies pouting. Talk about brutal...

I didn't feel like I had a choice, though, and answered, "Sure thing, Doc. I'll be right there." I tapped the control to end the call. "I'm sorry, ladies, but Doc asked me to meet him in the office. He wants to discuss Noah's situation with Mina."

"Oh..." Lyssa vocalized. "I should probably be there, too. I'll do a better job of offering moral support than either of you guys."

"Well, let's go if you're going."

Lyssa looked down at her sweatshirt, jeans, and sneakers. "I don't have time to change?"

"Doc and Mina are waiting on us... well, me... as we speak. It wouldn't be polite to keep them waiting."

Lyssa responded with a growl that sounded a bit more leonine than human, but she tossed her to-go container in the trash and met me at the door.

SINCE I HAD USED the 'time is of the essence' card, Lyssa insisted we take her car, and we arrived at the infirmary in short order. I led her to Doc's office—which she also had never seen before—where Doc and Mina waited for us.

Mina looked a little surprised when Lyssa entered with me, but Lyssa went straight to her, offering a warm smile and

ROBERT M. KERNS

speaking in a soothing voice, "You didn't think I'd leave you to fare for yourself in this, did you?"

"Thanks," Mina replied, her voice soft and vulnerable. Then, she turned to Doc. "Okay. They're here. What's the deal with my son?"

Doc relayed what he had told me earlier in the day, and I watched despair take over Mina's expression. When Doc ended his recitation, she sighed as her shoulders slumped, "So, you're not recommending we try to save him, then."

"Did I say that, missy?" Doc asked.

Mina's head shot up, and she glared at him. "Did you just call me 'missy?'"

"It worked to pull you out of your despair, didn't it?" Doc asked, breaking into a grin.

"Yeah, I guess it did, and no, you didn't say what your decision was."

"Excellent. You were even paying attention," Doc remarked. "Contrary to what some people think, I don't just talk to hear my head rattle. The short of it is that I don't see as how we have much choice. If your boy is to have any kind of future, we need to attempt to change him… and soon. From what my colleagues said, the longer we wait, the worse the chances will be."

Mina's struggle with the decision ruled her expression as we all watched weigh the matter. Of course, it wasn't an easy decision; especially with something like this, there was no guarantee. I didn't begrudge her the time to think it through —she was taking her child's life in her hands, after all—but I didn't need to be there while she worked through it, did I?

After several minutes of staring up at the ceiling with all manner of emotions flitting through her expression, Mina brought her focus back to us and asked, "So… is there any reason we can't proceed right now?"

"None whatsoever. Would you mind collecting your son

so we can discuss the situation? And, Alpha Wyatt, would you be so kind as to summon Young Mister Carrington? If Noah likes the idea of becoming a wolf shifter, he'll be handy to have close."

Mina stood and left the infirmary without another word while I scrolled through my contacts and dialed Buddy's number. When we spoke, Buddy said he was about ten minutes away, but he'd be there sooner if possible before ending the call. The way he said that, I wondered if I should alert Sheriff Clyde that Buddy might be coming into town a little hot.

MINA RETURNED WITH NOAH, and Lyssa and I stepped outside the room so that Doc could discuss the issue with them in some measure of privacy. The office door was still closed when Buddy arrived.

"What did you need, Alpha Wyatt?"

"We might need you to shift and bite someone," I replied. "There's a mother with a very sick son in Doc's office, and I gather they're discussing the idea with the son. If he's interested and agreeable, we'll probably proceed."

Before Buddy could answer, the office door opened, and Doc said, "Alpha Wyatt, Young Master Noah would like to see you and Mister Carrington shifted if you don't mind. He's a bit skeptical that shifters exist."

I wasn't keen on shredding more clothes, and it seemed like Buddy wasn't either. He started stripping right there in the infirmary's hallway. I glanced at Lyssa who gave a shrug that implied 'When in Rome...,' so I proceeded to do the same.

Buddy and I both started the shift at the same time, and within seconds, a Smilodon and large wolf stood in the hallway, shoulder to shoulder. Mina brought her son to the door when Doc explained that it would be better for us to shift in the wide hallway, and her eyes shot wide at the sight of us standing there in our fur. Noah's eyes went wide, and he charged straight to Buddy, whose wolf stood at near chest level to the boy.

"You really are a wolf!" he said, throwing his arms around Buddy's neck. "And I love your fur. It feels better than Duke's."

"So how about it?" Doc asked. "Would you like to take a chance on becoming a wolf shifter?"

"Oh, yes," Noah said, still beaming as he slid his hand back Buddy's spine. "This is awesome!"

"And you understand Buddy will have to bite you, which will hurt?" Doc pressed.

Noah nodded as he scratched Buddy behind his ears. "I know. Mom explained how I was really sick and the doctors couldn't help me. I never thought I'd get any better."

"In that case, let's move this party to the treatment ward," Doc replied. "Wyatt, you might as well shift back once we vacate the hall."

I WALKED into the treatment ward on two feet in time to hear Doc ask Noah, "Now, I just want to be clear that there is no going back. Are you sure you want to be a wolf shifter? We have a wide variety of possibilities here in town. Hank—who owns and operates the general store across the street—is a grizzly bear."

"Nope! I wanna be a wolf!"

Doc turned and gestured to the wolf standing a short distance away. "I believe that's your cue."

Buddy trotted over and hopped up on the hospital bed, and Noah dutifully presented his right forearm. Buddy leaned forward and gave him a good, solid bite... making sure he broke the skin and mingled saliva with the wound. While Buddy delivered the bite, Doc stepped over to a nearby surgical tray and retrieved a scalpel.

Mina frowned when he returned to the bedside with it, but before she could say anything, Buddy shifted back to human, crouching on the hospital bed. Doc handed him the scalpel, and he slit his wrist. As soon as a small pool of blood welled in his cupped palm, Buddy extended that hand and slathered his blood all over the fresh bite. By the time he withdrew his hand, the slice from the scalpel was already healed.

"That's as good as we can do," Doc said as Buddy hopped down from the bed.

Lyssa handed him his clothes, and Buddy stepped around the curtain to dress.

"Mom… I don't feel so good," Noah said, almost a whimper.

Mina rushed to his said. "What's wrong, honey?"

"I feel… hot."

Mina laid the back of her hand against her son's forehead and gasped. "He's burning up! Quick… do something!"

Doc shook his head. "Nope. This is normal. It's the first stage. He'll pass out soon, and we won't know anything until he wakes up."

Sure enough, less than five minutes later, Noah laid his head back against the pillow behind him and closed his eyes.

Mina wrung her hands as she looked at her son. "What have I done? If he dies—"

"If he dies," Doc interrupted her, "it'll be more peaceful than he would've faced otherwise. I promise you that."

With nothing else for us to do, Lyssa and I led Buddy out of the infirmary's treatment ward. Only Doc and Mina remained.

6

The next morning, I left the Alpha's house well-rested and eager to face the day. The past few days, I had allowed the issue with the consulate and Mina's son to claim too much of my focus, and it was time I put some attention toward an equally important matter: Eddie Burke.

As far as I knew, she had yet to experience her first shift, which meant we still didn't know for sure that she was a Smilodon shifter. Yes, Smilodon was the odds-on favorite for her animal, but by all rights, I should've been a cougar shifter, too. None of us knew enough about primogenitors to feel comfortable making predictions... but that didn't stop people from making *bets*. Not at all...

The bell over the door jingled as I entered the hotel, and Melody met me at the front desk.

"Good morning, Alpha Wyatt," she said around a beaming smile. "How is your furry self this fine morning?"

I paused, taking a moment to think about my answer, then said, "I'd have to say 'well,' if restricted to one word. It's good having Gabrielle and Karleen home. I wasn't aware how much a part of my routine they were until they weren't there. I slept better with them back."

Melody gave me a conspiratorial wink. "Oh, I'm sure you did, sir. Now, how can I help you?"

"I'm looking for Eddie Burke."

"You're too late," Melody answered. "She and Special Agent Hauser left about fifteen minutes ago, seemed to be headed for the diner."

"Well, I was going to offer to take her to breakfast anyway. I'll see about catching them. Have a good day, Melody."

"You, too, Alpha Wyatt."

I LEFT the hotel and crossed the street to the diner. The bell jingled overhead as I entered, and I returned the several waves of greeting with one of my own while I scanned the tables for the object of my search. It didn't take me long. Winnifred Hauser and Eddie Burke sat at a table near the opposite wall from the general store and a few tables back from the windows. I weaved my way through tables both occupied and not until I arrived at theirs.

"May I join you, ladies?"

Both Hauser and Burke nodded their agreement, so I pulled back a chair that made an isosceles triangle out of our seating arrangement.

"I'm sorry I haven't checked on you before now," I said as I sat. "There's never a dull moment around this town. How are you doing?"

Hauser smirked. "*I'm* doing fine. She's been eating everyone out of house and home like there's no tomorrow."

I chuckled. "Yeah, I was almost ravenous when I woke up after the rogue cougar attacked me. Doc and Gabrielle heard my stomach growl from something like eight feet away. So, have you noticed any other changes?"

"Yeah," Burke answered. "I was a partial vegetarian before this, and now, I can't get enough meat... and the rarer the better. I... I want to be grossed out, but I can't stand the thought of eating plants. Plants are what *food* eats."

"Have you felt any inclination to shift?" I asked.

Burk shook her head. "Not that I know of. The only thing that's different is how I'm eating more than an NFL line-backer without gaining a pound. Part of me wonders where it's all going."

"I know your pain. Wait till you're routinely eating six thousand calories a day and Doc looks at you solemn as a judge and says you're not eating enough."

Burke and Hauser both gaped at me. Burke said, "Seriously? How the hell is six thousand calories a day not enough?"

"Dunno, but I'll give him this much. I started feeling *much* better once I started following his meal plan."

Gladys arrived with a couple plates, one order shifter-sized that she placed in front of Burke and the other a human-sized portion that went to Hauser.

"You want your normal breakfast, Alpha Wyatt?" she asked as she whipped out her order pad better than an Old West gunfighter drawing down on the villain of the week.

I smiled and nodded my thanks. "That sounds perfect, Gladys. Thank you."

Gladys scribbled on her pad and nodded once. "Back in a jiffy."

I pulled my attention from Gladys and back to Burke and noticed something was not right. Burke sat motionless, staring at her plate. She hadn't even reached for her silver-ware yet. What's more, her pupils edged toward vertical slits from their normal round shape.

"Burke?" I asked.

"I... I don't feel right. Something... it's weird. Something's trying to get free."

I stood and circled the table. "Don't try to fight it, Burke, but let's go outside. Okay?"

Burke bobbed a nod and let me help her stand. As I guided her toward the door, I turned my head to the side and said over my shoulder, "Hauser, bring her plate."

We made it not quite three feet from the diner's door when Burke let out a fierce *RAWR* and vanished in an explosion of fabric. When the rain of cloth pieces settled, Hauser and I faced what appeared to be an American lion. I had never seen a picture of myself as a Smilodon, but Burke looked like she stood about half a foot shorter than my Smilodon at the shoulder. Her coat was the tawny color associated with modern African lions, but she easily out-massed her mundane counterparts by an order of magnitude. Her shoulders and ribs were broader, while being their own version of sleek, and her paws looked perhaps an inch smaller in diameter than Gladys's dinner plates.

She sniffed the air and zeroed in on the plate Hauser held, and before either of us could say or do anything, Burke took a half-step and leaned forward to help herself to the breakfast she ordered.

"She's beautiful," Hauser said as she stepped back from placing Burke's plate on the sidewalk for her.

Burke paused her devouring of the food long enough to chuff a thank you and dug right back into her morning venison steak without missing a beat.

Hauser shot me a look as she asked, "Why isn't she a Smilodon like you? I thought that's how these things worked."

"Don't look at me. As far as I know, no one has explained why I'm a Smilodon instead of a cougar. When we answer *that*, we might be in a better position to explain why Burke appears to be an American lion. I wonder if anyone picked this in the betting pool."

Burke stopped eating long enough to give me a flat look and flick me with her tail.

It wasn't long until the steak was gone, and Burke proceeded to lick the plate, pushing it across the sidewalk toward the diner's wall with every swipe of her tongue.

"Would you like more?" I asked.

She nodded mid-lick, and I went back inside to ask Gladys for two more venison steaks. In less than five minutes, I walked back outside carrying a platter with three venison steaks, sized for shifter portions. I didn't even have a chance to set it on the sidewalk in front of her before Burke was already working on the top one.

"As soon as she's had her fill," I said, "we should probably go over to Hank's and see about another set of clothes."

"Is that how your first shift went?" Hauser asked.

I shrugged. "I… don't really remember my first shift as such. I know the story, but the memories are a bit hazy. But Doc said that's normal for turned shifters. Born shifters grow up shifting between their human and animal form, and from what I've seen it's not uncommon for a shifter school to have half the classes filled with animals."

"Do you mind telling me the story?" Hauser asked, still smiling as she watched Burke eat.

Gabrielle and Karleen arrived just in time to hear Hauser's request, and Gabrielle was quick to comply. "Buddy Carrington pushed me into a table inside the diner, and the edge drew a little blood. I had *no idea* Wyatt was that close to shifting, but I guess the smell of my blood did the trick. Faster than you can blink your eyes, there was a growling Smilodon standing inside a rainstorm of clothing remnants, and he took Buddy to the floor in one leap. He then proceeded to make Buddy—and half the diner—piss themselves in submission. I've never seen Buddy so scared in all my life."

Hauser pulled her eyes away from Burke to look at me. "That sounds like something you'd do. You gave off a strong 'protector' vibe even when I first met you."

The sound of ceramic sliding on concrete drew our attention back to Burke, who was licking an empty plate again.

"Still hungry?" I asked.

Burke finished her last few licks of the plate before she shook her head in an obvious 'no' answer.

"Want to get a fresh set of clothes from the store?"

Burke started to shake her head 'no' again, but a huge yawn interrupted her.

I nodded my understanding. "Ah. Want to take a nap in the shade?"

Burke pushed herself to stand and approached me as she nodded.

"Come on, then. If you don't mind a little walk, you can nap in the backyard of the Alpha's House. It has a privacy fence and a massive tree that shades over half the yard any time of the day."

Karleen stepped inside to get mine and Hauser's orders boxed to go and placed to-go orders for herself and Gabrielle while Gabrielle, Hauser, and I walked with Burke to the Alpha's House. The moment we stepped through the privacy fence, Burke trotted over to the base of the giant tree and turned a couple of times in a circle before curling up in the mid-morning shade.

"Come on," I said. "We might as well be comfortable while we wait for her to get her nap out. Karleen will bring our food, plus something for herself and Gabrielle. We can eat here."

It wasn't long until Karleen arrived with a collection of

bags, each labeled for who should receive them, and we wasted no time in breaking our fast while the world's newest feline primogenitor dozed in the backyard.

~

SHE FELT warm and fed as she floated up from the void of sleep. It was a good feeling. She yawned and felt her tongue brush her chin, which jerked her out of her sleepy state to complete wakefulness.

The world looked odd as she opened her eyes, and her body felt... off... somehow. Why was she laying in someone's backyard? She looked down at herself and saw a massive, muscled frame with tawny fur. She flexed what felt like her fingers and watched paws—*her* paws—move.

Her scream came out as a roar.

She leaped to her feet and found herself standing on all fours. Looking behind her, she saw a tail lashing side to side.

What was happening? Was this some kind of dream?

Her ears flicked toward the sound of approaching foot-falls, and she turned to look that way. Hauser and the woman Wyatt had introduced as Lyssa rushed toward her.

"Agent Burke," Lyssa said, her voice calm and soothing, "the first thing you need to do is calm down."

Calm down? That was rich. She wasn't a gigantic cat.

"I know," Lyssa said. "You woke up in an unfamiliar place in an unfamiliar form, but it will be okay. I promise. Concentrate on this morning. Do you remember what happened this morning? Wyatt met you and Hauser at the diner for break-fast? Do you remember that?"

Burke sat on her haunches—it seemed she had haunches now—and wracked her mind. Everything from before was just so fuzzy and distant. It didn't really matter did it? *Now* was all that mattered, and she was full for the first time in recent memory. It felt good.

"Agent Burke, you need to take control," Lyssa said. "Your animal side cares only about the now and needs your human side to put things in perspective. I need you to remember this morning. I need you to remember shifting on the sidewalk outside the diner. Can you do that for me?"

Why was Lyssa being so demanding? It was such a nice day and such good shade. They should all curl up under the tree and nap the day away. Then, tonight, they could hunt together. That would be nice. She'd be hungry by then.

Movement in the distance drew her attention, and she saw Wyatt striding toward them. He stopped when he reached Lyssa and Hauser.

"What's the matter?" Wyatt asked.

"Her animal is too much in control," Lyssa explained. "She's not responding."

Wyatt pursed his lips. "Fine. We'll try Plan B."

He kicked off his shoes and toed off his socks. Then, he became a hybrid cat-man. Half sabertooth, half human. The sight of him sent a host of complicated emotions swirling through Burke's mind, and none of them made sense. None of them had anything to do with enjoying the shade for a lazy afternoon.

Wyatt the cat-man stepped closer and placed his furry hand on her head, his palm right above her eyes and his fingers between her ears. He looked her right in the eye, and when he spoke, she felt his growly voice touch the very core of her being. "*SHIFT!*"

All at once, she felt different, and it made her afraid. But she couldn't stop it. Her legs, body, tail, and muzzle shortened. Her fur seemed to retract into her, except the fur on her head that became wavy hair. Before she realized it, she was human and lying naked on the grass, and in a torrent of memories, feelings, and experiences, her human self re-asserted. She *remembered*.

"Thank you, Wyatt," she said in a small, timid voice. "The cat didn't want to let me go. It was content."

Wyatt shifted back to his human self and smiled. "We should not have let you go to sleep as a cat so soon after your first shift. I didn't know that, but Karleen had some choice words for us when she arrived with food from the diner."

"Is it... will it be like that every time?"

"No... well... maybe. You'll have to integrate the animal side of you with the human side of you. You're no longer the Edwina Burke who went into that underground bunker. And achieving that integration will be an... interesting... experience. My cat always seemed to have a handy supply of snark until we reached full synthesis, which allowed me to achieve the hybrid form. You'll have one, too, someday."

Burke's eyes shot wide. "I will?"

Wyatt just nodded. "Come on. I'm sure you have questions, and I bet you'd rather not ask them with grass tickling your lady bits. Gabrielle will be here soon with some loaner clothes until we visit the store again."

Then, Wyatt walked back to the house, stopping to gather his shoes and socks.

7

I was comfortable in my favorite seat at the dining room table by the time everyone joined me. Gabrielle's clothes didn't fit all that well on Burke, but it was close enough that she wouldn't go around flashing everyone. I noticed my ladies were quick to claim the chairs closest to me, leaving Hauser and Burke to sit across from me. I don't know if Hauser picked up on the subtle demarcation, but Burke did. I saw it in her eyes.

A shifter but not family.

Which was fine, I suppose. It wasn't like I'd choose not to help her because she wasn't one of mine. She was as much my responsibility as any other shifter in North America... well... no. Not really. She was *even more* my responsibility, because she wouldn't be a shifter if it were not for me. The fact that she also would've been dead didn't enter into it.

"So, do you want the good news or bad news?" I asked Burke, meeting her eyes with my own.

She blinked. "Bad news? How can there be bad news? I'd be dead if you hadn't saved me. And no offense, but I'm really digging the whole 'not a Smilodon' thing. You're impressive and all, but the incisors don't really work for me."

I chuckled and shrugged. "Yeah… they can make napping in the afternoon shade challenging. I either have to rest my chin on my stacked paws or angle my head to one side."

"Might as well start with the bad news, then," Burke replied.

"I've never mentored a new shifter, and for that matter, you know how new I am to the shifter world. I'm pretty sure my shifter self wasn't even a week old when we met. Fortunately, I have these lovely, talented, and much more knowledgeable ladies to assist us. They've been invaluable as I've learned what little I know about being a shifter and living in the shifter world."

Burke nodded her understanding and asked, "If that's the bad news, what's the good news?"

"You pretty much get to chart your course, even more so than when you were human, and you'll chart that course across centuries. That's one part of the good news. Another part is that you're not alone. Everyone around town will help you."

Burke leaned back against her chair and sighed. "I've thought about applying to be the legal attaché at the consulate here; that's usually a position held by members of our agency overseas. It's not strictly within the remit of Paranormal Division, but I'm just as much of a Special Agent as the rest of them."

I noticed Hauser working her lower lip between her teeth, and the slight tightness around her eyes and the barely visible furrowing of her brow made it plain to me that she thought through something.

"Come on, Hauser; you might as well say it."

Surprise flickered across her expression for just a moment. "Well, I was wondering if there might be a place for me here, both here as in Precious and here as in becoming a shifter."

Oh, my. I did *not* see that coming, though I suppose I should have. From what I've learned in conversations with Alistair and Gabrielle, more than one human has begged and pleaded to become a shifter once they learned of all the benefits. The rationale for staying separate and hidden from the world at large had never seemed so real... or justified.

Lyssa stepped in and covered for my surprise. "That is certainly possible, yes. We don't have specific rules about changing humans, but I would like to consult our treaty, just to be sure. I doubt it ever came up during negotiations, but I feel it best to make sure we're not risking anything."

Hauser nodded. "Yes, that makes sense, and I probably shouldn't have mentioned it."

"Don't go there," Karleen interjected. "It's just not worth it. More people should speak their minds. There'd be far less strife and fewer misunderstandings."

Lyssa stood, saying, "Excuse me," and disappeared down the hallway. A few moments later, she returned with a folio. She resumed her seat and opened the folio on the table, revealing a modern reproduction of the treaty between the Shifter Nation of North America and the United States.

"Let's see here," Lyssa said as she scanned the document. She turned pages as she finished each until she ran out of pages. "There's nothing in here about limiting how often or how many people shifters can change. I see no reason we couldn't proceed, especially since you don't have the risk factors associated with Mina's son. Have you thought about which animal you'd like?"

Talk about another surprise...

I don't think anyone at the table expected Lyssa to go that route, especially as quickly as she did.

Gabrielle recovered first. "You should be one-hundred-percent certain it's what you want. Once you make the change, you can't go back."

"I don't see as how there's much of a downside," Hauser replied, then blushed as she gave Gabrielle a demure side-eye. "Uhm, I don't know how to ask this, but what are your thoughts about changing me, Gabrielle? And if you agreed, would I be a melanistic jaguar, too?"

I fought to hide a grin. Gabrielle was a beautiful cat, and I loved it when she lounged around in her fur.

"It's certainly possible," Gabrielle replied, "but I don't know the odds of that versus a regular jaguar."

Hauser pursed her lips and sat silent for several moments, then said, "Well, if you're willing to take the chance, so am I."

"Let me think about it," Gabrielle countered. "I'm not inherently opposed, but we normally don't run about changing humans willy-nilly. And there's a certain amount of responsibility associated with it, too. You would essentially be my shifter child and my responsibility to educate in the ways of shifters and all that, just as Burke is for Wyatt."

"I understand," Hauser replied, adding a nod for emphasis. "I didn't mean to put you on the spot."

"Oh, you didn't, but it's a lot to consider."

A thought occurred to me during the ensuing silence, and I looked to Burke. "Have you called your supervisor yet?"

"I checked in with him to let him know I survived, but I also requested to go on medical leave until I get things sorted out. It's not like I don't have leave saved up, either. I could almost take an entire year off and still have time left over. He also put Hauser on leave, too. She's on three weeks' medical leave and then has to go in for a psych eval, but that's standard procedure after what happened."

I turned to Hauser. "Do you think your interest in becoming a shifter is part of your reaction to what happened?"

"No, at least I don't think so," she was quick to answer. "Ever since my initiation into Paranormal Division, I've always been fascinated with shifters. It just wasn't until that abduction case right after you were turned that I had much opportunity to interact with shifters. And I've always loved the big cats."

At that, Gabrielle nodded. "Okay, then. I personally think you should wait until you've sat down with the psychologist, but after that, I'll change you if that's what you want."

Hauser frowned. "What made up your mind? Saying that I've always loved the big cats?"

"That and your enthusiasm for us. We could tell that you have been honest and genuine in all you've said, and it settled my mind that you've thought about it for a while."

Hauser started to say something else when my phone rang. I didn't recognize the number but still felt I should answer it.

"Excuse me, please," I said, thumbing the control to accept the call, then lifted the phone to my ear. "Wyatt Magnusson."

"Wyatt, this is Mina Vickers. I've heard back from the Secretary of State. How soon can you do another conference call?"

"Hang on, Mina. I'm going to put you on speaker." I took the phone away from my head and thumbed the control to switch the call to speaker. "Mina, are you still with me?"

"Yes, I can hear you okay."

"Good. Would you please repeat that so Lyssa can hear it?"

"I've just heard back from the Secretary of State, and she would like to do another conference call. When can you be available?"

I looked at my professional keeper, and Lyssa smiled and shook her head, answering, "We're at the Alpha's House right now, Mina, but we can be at the admin building in five minutes or so."

"That's fine. I'll call her back and get things arranged. I'll meet you in the reception area of the admin building."

"Sounds good. See you soon," I replied and thumbed the 'end call' control. "Well, from the sounds of it, duty calls. If you four will excuse me and Lyssa, we need to head out."

Burke stood as well. "Do you mind if I walk along with you? I'd like to visit the general store, so I can return Gabrielle's clothing."

I shrugged. "Why would I mind? Anyone else wanna go for a walk?"

Gabrielle, Karleen, and Hauser stood, each saying they would go with Burke, and we left.

TRUE TO HER WORD, Mina stood in the reception area of the admin building when we walked through the doorway, and she held a note out to us with a phone number. I nodded and motioned for her to follow us to the conference room. It took little time to set up the conference phone and satellite microphones again, and once everyone had their seat, I accepted the note from Mina and dialed the number.

We heard three rings before someone said, "White House operator, how may I direct your call?"

I hoped my expression didn't mirror the stunned feeling that took over me, but Mina came to the rescue.

"Hello, I'm Mina Vickers, and the Secretary of State gave me this number for a conference call."

"Yes, Ms. Vickers, they are expecting your call. One moment, please."

The line switched to a *beep-beep* in a lower pitched tone, and we heard five sequences before a click, then Lucy Perez said, "This is Lucy Perez, Secretary of State, and I have President Williams here as well."

"Hello, Madam President and Madam Secretary. This is

Mina Vickers. I have Wyatt Magnusson and Lyssa Westridge with me."

"Hello, Wyatt," President Williams said, apparently taking over the meeting. "So, what's this I hear about you not wanting a consulate?"

Her conversational tone, edging toward banter, pulled me out of my surprise. "Well, Madam President... I never said we didn't *want* the consulate. I did say that I don't think it's a great idea to make it a regional office and publicize its existence, especially given that the existence of shifters is not common knowledge and publicizing the consulate could attract a great deal of human attention to what is a shifter territory.

"Now, if I'm being completely honest here, I also did say that we don't understand the reasoning behind the plan, because it just sounds ludicrous for a government to establish and maintain a consulate with its own people. Yes, I realize the Shifter Nation has a treaty with the United States, but if you went door to door polling the shifters in my county, I would be amazed if you found even one respondent who thought he or she wasn't an American citizen. We register for selective service. We pay taxes. We vote in elections. There are active-duty shifters in the American military as we speak. I'd have to ask around, but I know I have a social security number. Lyssa, do you?"

Lyssa rolled her eyes at me but answered, "Yes, Wyatt, I do."

"So, there you have it." I paused for a breath to order my thoughts. "Madam President, I understand that you feel the shifters represent an untapped relationship, but I'm unsure how you expect the relationship to develop further than it is right now."

"I see what you're saying, Wyatt, and you make excellent points. What would you suggest then?"

I can't say I was all that surprised that she kicked the can back to my side of the playground. I turned the idea over in my mind, looking at it from a couple different angles before I nodded. "Well... maybe what you're looking for isn't so much a closer relationship but a more easily accessed line of communication. So, why not leave Mina here as the official liaison between the Shifter Nation and the United States, which would make her well placed to facilitate communications either from the government to us or from us to the government?"

"Hmmm... it has possibilities," President Williams remarked, her tone thoughtful. "Mina, what are your thoughts?"

"That sounds fine with me, ma'am," Mina replied. "I am happy serve in whatever capacity you need."

Silence ensued for several moments before President Williams responded, "Very well, Wyatt. That works for us. Lucy will publish a memo to all persons with need to know that Ms. Vickers is the official contact should members of the government need or want contact with the Shifter Nation of North America."

"Thank you for understanding, Madam President," I replied. "I'll ask Lyssa to publish Mina's contact information to the Council and all Alphas for any of us who need to contact the United States government."

"Mina, as long as we have you, how is your son?" President Williams asked.

Mina blushed, but her voice did not betray her slight embarrassment. "We are awaiting the outcome of an attempt to change him to a shifter, Madam President, and thank you for asking. The local doctor advised us that Noah's case showed signs of accelerating, based on consultations with professional contacts with experience in Batten disease, and he argued that we shouldn't wait. Noah agreed, and we're all waiting to see if he comes through it."

"Well, I know Lucy and I will be sending warm regards and hopeful thoughts his way and yours. Lucy will be in touch about the staff you'll need. I honestly doubt there will be much business right away, but that might very well change once people are aware of an actual conduit for contact and information flow."

"Yes, Madam President, and thank you."

"Thank you, everyone," President Williams said, and the line clicked as the call ended.

Mina gave me a half-scolding expression as she asked, "So, do you feel better? It's not a consulate, but I'll still end up with a staff, so we should probably continue our talk about a building on First Avenue."

"That's fine," I replied. "Let me know what Lucy thinks you'll need in terms of staff, and we'll go from there. I'll locate an engineer to perform structural assessments of the buildings, so we know whether to renovate or demo and re-build."

Lyssa lifted her hand. "I'll take care of that. You have a new shifter to mentor and a host of other matters vying for your attention."

I wasn't sure what *other matters* she referenced, unless there was something she hadn't handed me yet, but she wasn't one to hold things back. So... maybe it was some kind of territory thing, like this was her bailiwick? I didn't see how that would play out, though, unless she was limiting Mina's access to me... which frankly didn't make a lot of sense. But who knows? Now that she had staked her claim to it, I wasn't about to embarrass her.

"Fine by me. Just let me know if you need me somewhere for something. Is there anything else?"

Neither answered, so I took that as a 'no.' "Right, then. On to other matters…"

I pushed up from my seat and made my way out of the conference room. It seemed like a good time to check on the ladies at the general store.

8

Lyssa watched Wyatt leave the conference room and, not for the first time, felt a swell of pride. She had despaired of ever finding someone who met her exacting standards, and yet, she did... in a man less than half her age. Sure, in a couple hundred years, a thirty-year age difference would be laughable at best, but that was just a fact of life as a shifter. What humans viewed as 'traditional' norms often simply did not apply.

"Do you think I should have told them I'm considering becoming a shifter?" Mina asked, pulling Lyssa out of her thoughts.

Lyssa blinked and re-focused on her. "I'm sorry. You caught me wrapped up in other thoughts. Do I think you should have told them you're considering becoming a shifter?"

"Yes."

She leaned back against her seat and considered the matter. After a few moments' thought, she said, "Truth be told, it could go both ways. On the one side, it's your personal decision and, as long as you have the available time off, it shouldn't be anyone's business but your own. The opposite side of that coin is that you're a federal employee, and the federal government takes a broad view of what is its business. As much as I would like to say 'do what you want,' it's probably polite to have a quiet one-on-one conversation with Secretary Perez. I don't think you're approaching an issue where you'd have to register as a foreign agent, especially since the shifters in the United States are American citizens, but it would keep her in the loop and prevent her from being blindsided. And she could back-channel the news up the chain to President Williams, so *she* is never blindsided by it, either."

Mina sighed and nodded. "You're right. I should be polite and upfront with this, absolutely. I agree that it should not be something that requires foreign agent status or anything like that, but no one likes to be blindsided. They'll probably be a little jealous, more than anything else."

"You sound like it's a done deal in your mind," Lyssa remarked.

"In a way, it is, as long as everyone is agreeable to it. I don't want anyone to feel like I'm violating oaths or loyalties or anything like that, and I don't want any of you to feel like you have to. I just know how hard it will be for Noah growing up with the knowledge that he'll outlive everyone he's ever known; I don't want him to feel alone like that."

Lyssa gave her a soft smile. "That's why family is so important to shifters. I don't think any of us could survive it all on our own, and you're right that becoming a shifter yourself is probably part of what's best for Noah, too. He shouldn't have to face that alone, at his age."

Mina answered with a smile of her own. "I really appreciate how welcoming and helpful everyone has been. I know it didn't have to be this way."

"Oh, there you're wrong," Lyssa countered without

missing a beat. "You should've seen how the news of your son's condition affected Wyatt. He has a soft spot for children. As far as he was concerned, it was never a question of *if* we'd try to help your son."

"You three are very lucky ladies; there's no doubt of that."

Lyssa nodded her acceptance of Mina's statement and pushed to her feet. "Come on. Let's go check in with Doc and make sure your son is still doing well."

MOIRA LOUNGED in the window seat of her room and reflected on how relaxing Precious was. It was so genuine. So uncomplicated. She rather liked the sleepy little shifter town. She still had not confessed *why* she had been a prisoner in that bunker, but she thought it was only a matter of time until Wyatt asked.

Wyatt. A feline primogenitor who had achieved full synthesis. If the clans back home knew about him, they would be on the war path... and terrified. A resurgence in the primogenitors was *not* in their best interests at all. Oh, no... not even close.

Unlike most of her people, she spent time reading the ancient chronicles. The collected works that told of the battle for control of this wonderful world and all its resources... especially its raw and powerful magic. Had the primogenitors never interfered, Earth—as the simpleminded and totally unaware humans called it—would not have been the first world the Fae drained to empower their own.

She found it laughable that even the shifters had lost so much knowledge, awareness, or perhaps understanding that they didn't recognize the primogenitors for what they were. In the ancient chronicles, there were no 'primogenitors.'

There were merely *shifters*. Somewhere along the way, they diluted themselves until the true shifters of old became fearsome creatures, far outstripping even the greatest of the modern 'shifters' in power. If she looked at Wyatt with her ethereal sense alone, he would blind her. He *thrummed* with power. A lute string on the cusp of being too tight.

She knew she should slip away and report his existence to her clan. It was the right thing to do. It was what any good Fae would do. But if that were so, why did she linger in this sleepy little town? Why was she content to while away the hours watching its people go about their lives, uncaring of how she shirked her duty?

If she was being honest—and she didn't want to be—she didn't want to go home. The realm of her birth held nothing for her, not anymore. But if her people had even the slightest whisper that she might abandon her mission, they would dispatch dozens of hunters to see her dead. And not just *dead*... oh, no. A gruesome example of what awaited any Fae who dared betray their people.

Movement caught her eye, and she watched Wyatt cross the street; he seemed intent on the general store. She loved watching him move, seeing him in unguarded moments. That was when one could see the true Wyatt, not that the personality he showed the world was all that different from his true self... at least from what she had observed thus far. No... his unguarded moments revealed his full character. His uncertainty that everything *might not* be 'all right.' She very much liked that side of him and hoped the primogenitors—now much smaller in number, all of one as far as she knew, or maybe two if that woman he bit carried the blood—could once again stand against her people and prevent their plunder of this world.

A deep sigh heaved her chest as her eyes roved over what she could see of the town from her perch. In that moment, she realized she was already a traitor to her people. She didn't want them to win and claim this world.

Wyatt's left foot crossed the double yellow line painted down the center of the street when an older man appeared out of nowhere. Moira focused on the new arrival, and her superior vision found his face without delay. Icy claws of terror clutched at her heart.

What was *he* doing here? Emrys, known the world over as Merlin. The most powerful and knowledgeable Magi to have ever lived. Everyone back home assured her... *promised* her... *swore on their very power and essence...* that the Bane of the Fae Courts was no longer active in the world. They had wanted to say dead, but no one had ever been able to prove that. And now, Moira knew why. What interest did *he* have in Wyatt? Had he told the primogenitor about the Fae yet?

Oh, no...

Had he seen her? She rolled out of her window perch to land on all fours on the floor of her room, out of sight and fighting with all her will to keep from fleeing the town at a full, screaming sprint until she collapsed.

She needed to calm herself. Yes. Calm above all. If she let herself slip into one of those panic attacks it seemed the humans always spoke of, her power would flare to the point that Merlin *couldn't miss* it. The last thing she wanted was to attract the attention of the one human capable of wiping out a Fae regiment all by himself.

IT SEEMED like a thousand and one thoughts swirled through my mind as I stepped off the sidewalk to cross the street. I still doubted my ability to mentor Burke in her new status as a primogenitor, but that was natural. I was so new in my status as both a primogenitor and a shifter that it seemed I still learned things two or three months into it that most people took for granted. Perhaps, I best served as a kind of living example that she could indeed survive the changes and the new world she faced.

Yes. Teach her what I have learned thus far. Show her that it's okay to feel a little overwhelmed. Then, Karleen and Gabrielle and Alistair could help us with the rest of it, like they had already been helping me.

Thoughts of Burke and her new status as a primogenitor seemed to snowball into thoughts of Moira. I needed to visit her soon and make sure she was still doing well. One of these days, I needed to sit down for a discussion with her, especially about why she was locked in one of the bunker's anti-magic cells. She didn't *seem* to be a creature of magic—unless you count the magic that all attractive women have—so what made those black ops people think she was?

I was of two minds on her. Something whispered in the back of my mind to be wary of her. To guard myself well whenever she was near. But she didn't give off a dangerous vibe, and reconciling the two reactions was... difficult.

Maybe it would be best to leave the matter of Moira until we knew whether Noah survived the transition to shifter. I had enough distractions as it was, and the extra matter of whatever Moira represented... well... I did not want it to be one straw too many.

An odd feeling pulled me out of my thoughts. It was strange. Almost like being close to high-voltage electrical equipment. All of my hair felt like it wanted to stand on end, and I could feel the same thing from my Smilodon's fur. I couldn't ever remember feeling *anything* like this, and whatever it was grew closer or stronger or...

The sensation vanished like a bubble popping when an old friend appeared a few yards in front of me. He stood at the edge of the far sidewalk, and he focused on me the moment he was there.

"Lad, we need to talk," Miles said.

I smiled. "You know, from what Vicki tells me, I need to be a bit jealous. She tells me that she had the opportunity to see you in all your glory, but I didn't."

The old man's eyes narrowed just a bit, and he pursed his lips. "Aye, she did at that. I would tell ye that life isn't a competition with yer sister, but no sibling ever born would buy that one. I can tell ye this much. The day will come when ye see everything yer sis witnessed and still yet more. Now, come. As I said, we need to talk."

THE WORLD BLINKED, and we stood *somewhere else*. Worn stone walls surrounded us. Empty, rusted sconces dotted the walls but didn't light the room. A slight musty smell wafted across my nose.

"*Where* are we?" I asked.

Miles chuckled. "I suppose the honest answer is nowhere and everywhere. Certain people who believe certain stories would call this place Avalon." Miles shrugged and turned toward a wooden door banded in iron, saying over his shoulder, "I call it home."

He worked the latch on the door, and it swung open on silent hinges. All at once, I made the connection, and I looked up to see Miles turn right after he stepped through the door. I hurried to catch him.

"Avalon... like the tales of King Arthur Avalon?"

Miles nodded. "Aye, lad, but not everything ye read in tales is true. Yes, we brought Arthur here, but no, he will never return. He died of his wounds. Could I have interfered and saved him? Yes, but I had very firm instructions that it was not my place."

ROBERT M. KERNS

I noticed Miles's accent was stronger here than I had ever heard it.

We walked through an arched hallway with windows overlooking a small lake or perhaps a very large moat, passing several doors that Miles paid no mind. The place smelled *old*, like musty basements with cobwebbed corners old. It carried the weight of countless years, far more than any one human could ever see, and fought the ravages of time with all its might.

Miles led me to a room that felt very much like my grandparents' sitting room for guests. A few chairs and a few couches dotted the room. A large area rug covered the stone floor that seemed as ancient—though well-cared-for—as what I'd seen so far of the rest of the structure. Tapestries hung on the walls, depicting various scenes. Everything from a line of knights in shining armor charging toward a line of black-armored knights to what looked like a man throwing lightning or power or *something* into a charging horde of... *winged elves?*

"Uhm, Miles? That tapestry over there... the one with the lightning or something?"

Miles didn't even spare the tapestry a look as he eased himself into an armchair. "Aye, lad. That is some poor artist's depiction of me standing against a charge during the Fae War. Not exactly proud of me conduct, there, but it had to be done. And that's that."

His words jerked my focus away from the artful weaving. "Wait... did you say the Fae War?"

"Aye, lad, I did. Have yerself a seat. What I have to tell ye might take a while."

9

F ae War? What was all this about? Having a sit-down with Moira suddenly didn't seem so bad. I left the tapestry and sat in an armchair across from Miles... and couldn't believe how good the chair felt. It straddled the line between enveloping softness and firm support like a professional tight-rope walker, and I wasn't too sure I'd want to leave. I couldn't remember any other chair in my life ever being so comfortable.

Miles smiled as if he could read my thoughts. Maybe he could. The man was *Merlin*, after all. Who knew what all he was capable of?

"This is a very comfortable chair. I might not leave."

"I'm afraid ye'll have no choice, lad. The world at large needs ye and yer kind... far more than it knows."

Well, *that* didn't sound reassuring. "Okay, Miles... lay it on me."

"I suppose I could start with all the whys and wherefores and the 'before times,' but none of that rot really matters so much. It's good history to understand how we came to be at the point we are, but this is one case where I dearly hope history does not repeat itself." He paused and pursed his lips once more, maybe trying to decide the best place to start. After a few seconds, he nodded once and leaned forward, resting his elbows on his knees. "Right, then. Let's start with shifters. As of today, there are five *true* shifters known to exist in the world. You. Yer lady Karleen. Her counterpart over here in Europe. That fine *èan* ye found, Sloane. And the lady ye saved with yer bite in that bunker; I'm afraid I don't know her name."

Five *true* shifters? What was this *true shifter* business? When we stood on the street in Precious, shifters *surrounded* us. Godwin County has something like twenty thousand people living in it, and over ninety-nine percent of them are shifters. Wait... he just listed the five known *primogenitors*. How could we be 'true' shifters when the regular shifters were not? Then, it clicked. The hybrid form. Synthesis, my growly voice called it.

"So, most shifters alive today don't have the hybrid form?" I asked.

Miles beamed. "Och, I'm proud of ye, lad. Ye connected the dots on that one well. Aye. Thousands of years ago, the shifter world as ye know it did not exist. Hundreds of millions of them walked the earth, and they were all primo-genitors... every single one. Lad, I tell ye... it were such a sight to behold. Great Rocs like the lass Sloane filled the sky. Smilodons by the score—"

"Wait... you were alive back then?" I gasped, interrupting him. "Just how old are you?"

"I was born in 543 in a small village of what is Wales these days. In my youth, I developed a penchant for... biting off a bit more than I should probably chew, as ye might say... and, through total fault of my own, spent a decade or so in prehistorical times. Which was how I came to fight in the Fae War. Ye see, lad, faeries and Fae creatures come from a different dimension than we do. They are not native to Earth, and they are a race of abusers and plunderers. They go from world to world draining each of its resources—and I don't just mean inanimate resources—plus any power the world might have, using all of it to enrich their own. I have not the slightest idea how they came to discover Earth, but they did. And they came for it. It seems our world is something of a smorgasbord to them. With me so far?"

I nodded. "I think so. It's kinda hitting me a little fast, but I suppose my experience becoming a shifter will help with that."

"Aye, lad... it should, at that," Miles remarked, beaming a huge grin. Then, continued. "The shifters back then—what ye and yer friends would call primogenitors today—won the Fae War... were the only reason we won it, in fact. But... so many of them died in the conflict that they started having children with humans instead of each other, which led to the shifters ye know today, like Gabrielle and Lyssa and Alistair and so on. By the time the 'true' shifters realized their children or grandchildren were not—quite—as powerful or capable as they were, the deed were done, so to speak, and there was no turning back.

"Now, why I sought ye out? Do ye remember the ward that ye tripped outside the bunker? Yer sister may have told ye what I said—or maybe not—but it was Mab's work. I recognized it the moment yer sis described it to yer grandparents. No mistaking it, really. If the Fae are once again meddling in the world, they're working up to having another go at us, and if that's the case... well... five shifters ain't enough. Not by a long chalk. I'm not saying the lesser children—such as your other fine lasses—are worthless, but I

79

swear to ye, boy, they canna' survive an equivalent amount of injury or punishment that ye and yer kind can. They simply can't. Ye saw it yerself in the duel with that Carlyle lad; he could nae harm ye to any great extent at all, could he?

"And the little tiffs yer kind has been havin' with the Magi over the years? All that pointless shite needs to stop and stop *now*. We cannot afford to be divided like that when the Fae finally rip open rifts between worlds. Plus, it'll make for a lot of difference having more Magi on-hand than just meself. *That* made for rather invigorating challenge, last time 'round."

I leaned back against my seat and tried to consider the full scope of what Miles told me. On the surface, it seemed too outlandish to believe. But it was *Merlin* telling me. Vicki had been *very* descriptive in the sense of sheer power that radiated from him when he shattered the ward on the bunker's entrance.

"Any idea how long we have?"

"Och, no, lad. I wish I did, but that ward was the first indication I've had that there be something amiss. *If* we could find a Fae and *if* that one had operational knowledge, it might help, or it might not. They're capricious devils, the lot of 'em. During the war, I saw 'em change whole campaigns on what appeared to be little more than whims…" he snorted a laugh "…or developing inter-family feuds. They're bad about that, too. Makes our feuds seem rather tame in comparison."

"Okay. What about the survivors of the first war? From everything I've heard, we're immortal, so they should still be around somewhere, right?"

"I canna' say what happened to 'em. When I returned to me own time, the world had lost all awareness of 'em. Shifters the world over were the lesser children, and no one even realized matters had ever been different. If any of 'em still live yet, they're being quiet about it. The emergence of yer lass Karleen rocked the shifter world like ye wouldn't believe, and less than a decade later, another dire wolf appeared over here in Europe. But the survivors? I have searched the world these long years and not found even a whisper of 'em."

I leaned my head back and rested it against the chair's high back for several moments before resuming my focus on Miles. "The way you're talking, it makes me feel like we need a war council."

"Such a thing might be wise. I've spent the intervening days investigatin' on me own, and I've not found anything conclusive yet. Now that I'm looking for them, I *have* located traces of dimensional rifts, but those traces be so old, I canna' tell ye anymore. Could've been a Fae animal or a full regiment for all I know. One of 'em was fairly close to that bunker ye raided. I think me time be best spent giving that a thorough going-over. Do ye have any other questions of an immediate nature?"

I laughed. "Oh, I have *all kinds* of questions, but none of an immediate nature, as you put it. I'd love to sit with you and spend an afternoon talking. I can't imagine all the things you've seen in your life."

Sorrow flitted across the old man's visage before he banished it with a smile. "Lad, there are days even I have problems believing everything I've seen and survived. Like the song says, it's been a long road."

Miles stood, and I did as well. Once again, I noticed no gestures or words or anything. The world... just blinked... and we stood on the street in Precious once more.

"I'll be in touch, lad. Start yer preparations. They could come fer us next week, next year, or next century... but we need to be ready."

That said, Miles vanished once again, and I felt the weight

of my new knowledge and responsibilities settle around my shoulders.

~

MOIRA CRAWLED to the window seat that overlooked Main Street. It had been almost an hour since she saw the Bane of the Fae Courts talking with Wyatt. She couldn't imagine they'd still be standing in the middle of the street. She prowled up the window seat and edged close enough to peek through the curtains. No... whew! The street was empty. Wherever they were, they were no longer in front of the Precious Hotel.

Then, in no more time than the snap of a finger, both Wyatt *and* the Bane re-appeared, and Moira bit her tongue to forestall a terrified shriek. She watched the pair exchange a few words, and then, the Bane of the Fae Courts vanished once more.

She didn't know what to do. Wyatt had helped her once before, so in her mind, that made him pre-disposed to help her again. But he seemed friendly with the Bane. If—no, *when* —the Bane found her, would Wyatt choose her over him? Would he stop the Bane from eradicating her long enough to hear her story?

The urge to flee threatened to overwhelm her. It was the sole option that made complete sense. If she ran—and ran far, far away—maybe she'd live a little longer.

Unbidden and without warning, a memory forced its way to the forefront of her mind. A young man leaned close against a backdrop of a horrendous alarm and spoke directly into her ear, "Hi, I'm Wyatt, and I guess I'm here to rescue you."

No one had ever helped her before, at least not without motive for very near-term personal gain. And Wyatt hadn't pursued any of the most immediate personal gains with her. Of course, with those beauties who clung to him, it wasn't difficult to understand why, but Moira would've thought she merited at least a second glance.

No. She needed to stop allowing herself to be distracted. The important part was that Merlin was alive and *close*, and when he found her, Moira's remaining life would measure in seconds… if that long.

As much as her people would shout betrayal and send the hunters, Moira knew what she had to do. Throw herself on the mercy of the Smilodon. Maybe, if she went to Wyatt now and told him everything, he would save her again when Merlin came for her.

She glanced at the street once more to make sure Wyatt was still there. He was. She only paused in front of her room's full-length mirror long enough to make sure she was (mostly) presentable before resuming her head-long rush to speak with Wyatt. She wasn't quite as fast as a cheetah shifter or even a mundane cheetah, but she gave it her best effort.

Not even three minutes after making the decision, Moira skidded to a stop no more than a couple yards from Wyatt. As he turned around to face the commotion at his back, she dropped to one knee and bowed her head.

"Wyatt Magnusson, I am Moira MacCallan ab Tuatha, ninth in my line of the Court of Unseelie Fae, and I beg your mercy and protection in exchange for my unreserved and undying service."

Silence reigned. Then extended. The only sounds she heard were her heavy breathing from her sprint and car engines that drove around them. After Wyatt's lack of response extended well past even an intentional breach of protocol, Moira shamed her family yet again by looking up to see his expression.

She was not prepared in the least for the sheer incomprehension Wyatt's expression betrayed. Moments after she looked up, Wyatt blinked, shook himself like a wet dog divesting itself of excess moisture, and reinforced his reputation for eloquence, saying, "Uhh... what?"

10

I stared down at Moira's blank expression as she looked up at me, and for the life of me, I had no idea what she said. Don't get me wrong; I understood the *words*, but that doesn't mean I understood the *meaning*. And the one person who could help me understand just vanished off to parts unknown.

We remained unmoving for long enough that I realized a crowd gathered around us, and I wasn't sure we wanted that. I glanced around without moving as best I could and noticed more people meandering our way in the distance.

"I don't understand what you're asking," I said, breaking the silence. "Can we sit somewhere and discuss it? I don't want to answer without understanding *what* I'm answering."

Moira stared up at me in silence from her kneeling pose. Whatever her feelings on my words, she betrayed none of them. After more moments still, she dropped her head and stood, glancing around and taking in the crowd for the first time.

"Where should we go?"

Talk about a good question…

I fought to keep my sudden relief from showing in my expression as the perfect answer erupted in my mind. Lyssa! She would understand this and explain it to me.

"This way. We'll go to my office in the admin building. We'll have privacy and all the time we need to discuss whatever it is you asked."

Moira nodded, and I turned. The crowd parted as I started walking, and by the time we reached the doors to the admin building, most of the crowd had disbursed. I tossed a wave to the reception desk as I half-jogged through the vestibule and went straight to my office. For once, Lyssa wasn't there.

I gestured for Moira to pick a chair of her liking as I said, "I just need a minute. I'll be right back."

She jerked an uncertain nod and eased into a chair, as I pivoted on my heel and went in search of my lioness. I found her in her office, and she smiled as I opened her door and poked my head inside, then fully entered once I saw her and closed the door behind me.

"Do you mind coming back to my office with me? Moira came up to me in the street, knelt in front of me, bowed her head, and said something about Unseelie Fae and mercy and protection. I don't understand what's going on, and I'd appreciate it if you were there when I get her to explain it."

Lyssa stood without comment, setting aside the papers she held.

I smiled. "Thanks. I really appreciate you."

MOIRA'S MIND swirled in turmoil and confusion. First, Wyatt just stared at her when she made the traditional offering of her life in exchange for protection, and then, he dumped her in this office while he disappeared. Oh… if her family knew the depths of her shame, they'd kill her, erase any record of her being born, and strike her name from the rolls.

Her offer wasn't outside the bounds of propriety in Fae culture, but it carried all kinds of obligations—going both ways—that caused most Fae to avoid it at all costs. Her mother certainly inspired all kinds of reticence—if not fear— of the oath when she instructed Little Moira in all of its myriad meanings, interpretations, and obligations. Moira never once believed she would ever *think* the words—let alone utter them—and yet, she had. And shame upon shame, Wyatt didn't even understand what she asked.

Perhaps it would just be best to surrender to the Bane and let come what may. The damage to her family as matters stood now was nigh incalculable. The more she thought about it, she was not all that certain she wanted to continue living.

Before she could examine her feelings on the situation any further, the door flew open and Wyatt returned, a stunningly beautiful woman on his heels. No... oh, no. He thought to parade her demeaning request for his closest to see? Did he not care how much he shamed her? It took all Moira's willpower to keep from bursting into tears.

LYSSA FOLLOWED Wyatt as he dashed back to his office. Sure enough, the woman he had found in the bunker waited in a chair. She turned as they entered, and Lyssa watched her freeze as soon as she laid eyes on the lioness. The sudden tightness around her eyes and lips. A sudden sheen of wet glistening in her eyes.

"Wyatt, would you give us a minute please?" Lyssa asked.

He turned, and if he noticed Moira's state, he made no reaction to it. "Okay. You sure?"

Lyssa gave him one of her reassuring smiles and nodded. "Yes, of course I am. Go for a walk or something, and I'll call you when we're ready."

"Okay." Wyatt turned and trooped out of the office, closing the door behind him.

As soon as the door latched, Lyssa pulled a chair over to sit with Moira. "Hi, there. I'm Lyssa Westridge. I'm one of Wyatt's mates and the one he calls when there's something political or deeply interpersonal to understand. I can see you're right on the edge, and I'd like to help if I can. Can we discuss whatever it is that has you so keyed up?"

Moira sat in silence for quite the while, which she ended with a deep breath. "I... I should've realized that he wouldn't understand. Especially an ancient protocol that we rarely invoke among ourselves, let alone to an outsider. When I saw him today, just standing there in the street and looking so much like the accounts from the war, I... I guess I panicked." She dropped her head to her hands. "Oh... I have made such a mess of things."

"It's okay," Lyssa said, adopting what she hoped was a soothing tone. "You haven't messed up anything we can't fix, but it would help me if I understood. Who did you see today? I'm sure you don't mean Wyatt. As far as I know, he hasn't been in any wars."

Moira chuckled. "No, not Wyatt. I would never have ran to him, if I recognized him from my people's accounts of the war. I mean the Bane of the Fae Courts; the people of this world call him Merlin."

"What? *Merlin* was here today? I thought he was just a myth."

"Oh no, child. Merlin is *not* a myth. Not at all. He is the most feared person in this world... well... after shifters like Wyatt."

Lyssa felt lost. She *thought* she understood what Moira

said, but it sounded more like snippets and not the whole story. "I still feel a little confused. Do you mind starting from the beginning?"

Moira heaved another sigh. "Okay. Thousands of your years ago, the Fae attempted to invade this world… claim its resources and power for our own. The shifters of the time—plus one very fearsome Magi—defeated us. I have read multiple accounts that the single inciting incident for our withdrawal was Merlin's single-handed destruction of a regiment of our finest warriors." She snapped her fingers. "They were gone almost as soon as they took the field. Many of them were the heirs of their clans. We spent years recovering from it, and I mean Fae years… not Earth years. Whole centuries fly by for you when we take an afternoon nap. Well… that might be a tiny exaggeration, but not by much."

"So, I gather that you are one of Fae also?" Lyssa asked.

Moira bobbed a nod. "Yes. My family gave me to service as an advance scout, but the intellectual giants responsible for cross-dimensional rifts put me right outside that bunker where Wyatt found me. The people there put me in that cell, but Wyatt came before they could do anything nasty."

Now Lyssa felt like she was making progress. "Okay. So, what happened in the street today? You said you panicked. Help me understand all that."

Moira's shoulders slumped as she leaned back against her seat. "So, I kinda panicked when I saw Merlin appear with Wyatt an hour or so after I saw him the first time, and as soon as Merlin vanished, I ran to Wyatt to throw myself on his mercy for protection. When a Fae child misbehaves, our parents say, 'Be good, child, or Merlin will get you.' The only thing I could think about was Merlin finding me in the hotel, so I ran to Wyatt, hoping he could protect me from him."

Something didn't add up. If that's truly what happened,

Wyatt would have understood. Yes, he was a tad slow on some things as most guys can be, but if she truly feared for her life and asked for his help, Wyatt would never have turned her away, let alone make her wait this long for an answer.

"I feel like we're really close to understanding things," Lyssa replied. "Do you mind taking me through exactly what you said? Wyatt didn't understand the full meaning of what you said, and I've never known him to refuse anyone asking for help or protection."

Lyssa fought the urge to show her surprise when Moira's shoulders slumped even more. "I… I kind of invoked an ancient Fae rite. If he accepts, I will give Wyatt my life in exchange for his mercy and protection. It's… it's a very powerful oath, and even discussing it carries a certain amount of shame, let alone invoking it. If my family learned I'd used it—and with an outsider like Wyatt, especially someone like Wyatt—they'd devote their full resources and effort to killing me and making sure no trace of my existence remained. And now that I've invoked it, nothing moves forward until Wyatt responds."

"And if Wyatt declines?

"Then, I'm an outcast now. I suppose I could try to hide that I have invoked the rite and been denied, but they'll find out eventually. And their response will be worse than if Wyatt accepted."

Lyssa sat back in her seat as she worked to process what she now knew. For Moira to do *that*, the thought of Merlin finding her must terrify her. At first glance, the obvious answer was for Wyatt to accept, but there was still too much she didn't know.

"And what if Wyatt accepts? What happens to you then?"

Moira pursed her lips. "Well, at a minimum, Wyatt protects me from Merlin when he finally learns I exist, but on a grand scale, I become the property of Wyatt and his family line. I will serve him or his descendants without hesitation or reservation for as long as I live, devoting my full training and knowledge to whatever task he sets before me."

Well, now. Talk about the proverbial sticky wicket...

She knew Wyatt well enough to know he would want no part of Moira being his property. She had heard a few stories of his reaction to the group buying children for trafficking, and his response to Buddy Carrington's casual striking of Gabrielle was almost legendary by this point.

"And his behavior since you first asked him intensified your anxiety further?" Lyssa asked and, when Moira just nodded, continued. "Okay. I think I understand the situation well enough. I'm going to ask Wyatt to come back."

She withdrew her cell phone and texted Wyatt to return. She hoped he kept his cool long enough to understand the full extent of Moira's situation now. The poor soul didn't need him flying off the handle and stomping about the room in a rage.

I BLINKED at the utter incomprehensible thought. "Hang on. Let me be sure I understand. You are offering your life to me and my service in exchange for protection from Miles?"

Moira blinked. "I do not know a Miles. I speak of Merlin. The one who stood with you in the street earlier."

"Yeah... Miles. At least, that's how *I* know him. He was a groundskeeper at my grandparents' place my whole childhood. You could've knocked me over with a feather when I figured out who he really was."

I almost blurted out that I was his direct descendant, but I realized that I didn't know if that would be good or bad in the current situation and held my tongue.

"So…" Moira said, drawing out the word like a teenage champion, "Lyssa has helped me explain the full situation, complete with outcomes for me if you accept or decline. All that remains is for you to answer."

"What if I don't like those options?" I asked and hurried on when I saw her face start to fall. "Hey, hey… it's okay. I'm fine with protecting you. I personally don't think you're in as much danger as you do, but I'm not going to argue that. My sticking point is that I don't own *people*. I own things, items without sapience. You are a thinking, feeling, self-aware being. No one can own you. No one should even try. But I am not a fan at all of what happens if I say 'no,' so I have to hand it to you, Moira. You have created a masterful Catch-22."

Moira frowned and angled her head to one side. "I do not understand the term 'Catch-22.'"

"I think it came from sports, but I might be wrong," I replied. "How about this? Damned if you do or damned if you don't… that better?"

"Ah, yes. That, at least, makes perfect sense. And for a Fae to be in such a state that the oath I offered is preferable, it is most appropriate. But we get nowhere with all this prevarication. Please, state your response. If you decline, I need time to run as far and as fast as I can before Merlin finds me."

No matter how much I doubted that Merlin would hunt her and end her, I knew I would always regret leaving her to face her fate all alone. That much was no question. Beyond that, it would be stupid to throw away such a handy resource on our imminent invaders. I took a deep breath and released it as a slow sigh. Once again, I found myself in a situation I didn't want and never dreamed was possible. There had to be a better way to go about Life.

"I accept your oath."

By the time I started to speak the word 'oath,' I had two

arms' full of Moira as she leaped to wrap her arms and legs around me, clutching me like a castaway with a life preserver as she whispered relieved thanks over and over in my ear.

I shot a concerned look to Lyssa, trying to ask her what I should do without saying anything that might hurt Moira.

If she understood my distress, she didn't comment, regardless of whether she shared it. Instead, a small, happy smile dominated her expression, the same happy smile Gabrielle or Karleen had when I made them proud.

All Lyssa said as she watched Moira cling to me was, "You're a good man, Wyatt Magnusson."

11

It took a little while for Moira to wind down and stop hanging off me like a sloth on a tree branch. When she did at last return to standing on her feet, she still looked like she was afraid to be too far from me. If that's what it took for her to feel safe, though, I would find a way to bear up under the strain. The first thing the three of us needed to do was update Gabrielle and Karleen on everything, especially my chat with Miles at Avalon.

Or should that be *in* Avalon? I assumed Avalon was somewhere in the British Isles, but the way Miles talked about it being everywhere and nowhere kinda made me wonder. Maybe I'd ask Vicki about it. If anyone knew, she would.

People stared as Lyssa and I walked with Moira from the admin building to the Alpha's House. I figured I needed to make some kind of announcement about Moira and her status before the situation with the Fae erupted. If she was going to be under my protection for the rest of her life, people needed to know that. I didn't *think* anyone would do something stupid, but it was always wise to head off that kind of thing as quickly as possible.

Gabrielle and Karleen were both sunning in the backyard when Lyssa and I brought Moira home. They looked up from their lounges, Karleen lifting her sunglasses for a better look.

"Hey, you two," Gabrielle said. "Who's the new face?"

Before Lyssa or I could utter even a syllable, Moira stepped forward and dropped to her knees, bowing her head before my other ladies. "I am Moira MacCallan ab Tuatha. I have sworn an oath to serve Wyatt and his family in exchange for mercy and protection."

Karleen frowned her confusion, looking from the kneeling Moira to me to Lyssa and back. Gabrielle just scrunched up her face in that pretty way she had when something didn't add up.

"Okay... so, that probably wasn't the best way to go about introducing yourself or why you're here," I remarked, then looked to my confused ladies, "but she's not wrong. There's a huge kerfuffle headed our way, and I think Moira is a part of it. Miles—or Merlin, if you prefer—definitely is, and he wants me to institute a war council, involving at least the shifters and the Magi. To be fair, since this affects Earth as a whole, we should probably invite the US Government at a minimum. Once we have a better idea of the particulars, we can expand it out as needed, but I'd rather as few governments get involved as possible, because they're all political animals and will most likely only contribute complications to our lives."

Now, I had Gabrielle's and Karleen's respective confusion focused solely on me.

"Do what now?" Karleen asked, her sunglasses falling to the ground forgotten.

"Let's deal with introducing Moira first, and then, I'll call Vicki and find out if she's available for a conference. I started to say 'quick,' but who knows how quick it'll be? That way, I only have to go through the whole story surrounding the Fae once... at least I hope so."

"I can also provide what information I have, Master," Moira said from her kneeling position.

I felt my hackles try to rise at that, and I didn't even *have* hackles in this form. "Nope. There will be *none* of that. You can call me Wyatt. You can call me 'Hey you.' You can even call me, 'Smilodon,' but I will never answer to 'Master.' And get off your knees already. You're a capable, sapient person. Stand tall. Stand strong."

By the time I finished speaking, Moira stood facing me, her expression betraying uncertainty. "But, Ma—Wyatt, I am your property. I merely seek to act—"

I fought to keep my voice even and relaxed. That was *not* easy. "Moira, I don't *care* what that oath means in Fae culture. You are not—nor will you ever be—my property. If we're ever surrounded by Fae, we *might* re-visit this, simply because I have no desire to embarrass or belittle you in front of your people. But otherwise? None of that bowing and scraping or genuflecting or whatever you want to call it. Okay? We good?"

Moira looked like she fought to keep from smiling. "Yes, Wyatt, we're good."

"Right, then," I remarked and re-focused on Karleen and Gabrielle. "Okay, so, long story short, Moira saw Miles talking with me and freaked out a little bit. Apparently, Miles is something of the boogeyman to the Fae... to the point that they have an almost culturally ingrained terror of him. She is certain beyond words he will proceed to torture her or just kill her the moment he lays eyes on her and pretty much swore her existence to my service in exchange for my protection. I want to be upfront that I don't think she needs my protection, but she believes she does. And just the act of invoking her oath apparently makes her an outcast in Fae society if I refuse, so here we are. If you have any questions, ask Lyssa, as she was there while we worked this out. I'm going to call Vicki, and I'll let you know what we decide in time to change if you wish."

I withdrew my phone from the hip pocket of my pants and stepped inside the Alpha's House as I thumbed through my contacts and tapped my sister's phone number.

KARLEEN WATCHED Wyatt step into the Alpha's House and tried to process the mental and emotional whiplash he had just delivered. She brought her eyes back to Lyssa and Moira. Lyssa appeared serene and in control, as she usually did, but Moira? Not so much. Anxiety—and maybe hope?—leaked through her self-control.

Karleen suspected she had a better appreciation than most for what Moira felt. There wasn't a week that went by when she didn't think of the small town where she grew up and the circumstances that led to her abandoning shifter society for almost sixty years. And if she was being honest with herself, she still missed Buttercup, but... those were thoughts for another time.

She pushed herself to her feet, recovering her sunglasses in the process, and approached Moira. She placed her hands on the woman's shoulders and made her best attempt at a warm and pleasant smile as she said, "Welcome to the family, Moira. I'm not sure what all Wyatt said, and he can gloss over details sometimes if he feels rushed. I'm Karleen Vesper, and this is Gabrielle Hassan. I am the North American dire wolf, and Gabrielle is a melanistic jaguar. Wyatt hinted that you're Fae, so I'm not sure how much you know about modern society and, specifically, shifter society."

By that point, Gabrielle joined them and filled Karleen's

pause. "Yes, Moira, welcome. This will be a learning experience for all of us, I think, but I'm confident we're up to the challenge. Please, be patient with us, because as new as shifter society and culture is to you, I promise that Fae society and culture is just as new to us."

Moira's growing smile eradicated any hints of anxiety in her demeanor. "Thank you. I... well, I was very rash when I offered Wyatt my oath, and I never once stopped to consider how it would affect anyone else in his life, or even if he had people in his life."

Karleen smiled and shook her head. "Don't worry about that at all. More than one of us has leaped before we looked, probably far more times than any sensible person would claim. We'll get through this and define our new 'normal' as we go along."

"So, the first thing we need to do is move your stuff into the house," Gabrielle opined, "and make sure you have the proper accessories like a bikini for such fine days as this."

Moira blushed. "Oh, no... I couldn't. Not without Wyatt's permission."

Gabrielle made a point of running her eyes down and up Moira's form before adopting a confident smirk. "Trust me, Moira. The first time he sees you in a bikini sunning with us, I promise he'll never even think about anything like forgiveness or permission."

"Yeah," Karleen added, speaking around a huge grin, "and if we're all laid out in a row, chatting and laughing and enjoying ourselves, he might not even think at all."

Lyssa rolled her eyes outside of Moira's view. They were such shameless flirts sometimes, and they enjoyed teasing Wyatt and getting him all worked up far too much sometimes. She didn't mind playing, herself, but there were times for it… and facing an impending extra-dimensional invasion *was not* the time.

She stepped forward and drew Moira's attention to her. "While I might not share their choice of timing for teasing Wyatt, Gabrielle brings up an excellent point. The Alpha's House, here, has plenty of space, and you have been staying at the hotel in town. Is that correct?"

Moira bobbed a nod. "Yes, I'm staying at the hotel. Wyatt said something to the nice lady at the counter—Melody, I think she is—about being a guest of the Alpha. What does that mean?"

"It means he will cover the cost of your room," Lyssa answered. "He probably also had a quiet word with Gladys at the diner, too."

Moira frowned. "I didn't witness that, but she never lets me have a bill. Always says my meals are covered."

"Yeah, that's our Wyatt," Gabrielle remarked, grinning.

Lyssa considered the situation a little more, then nodded once as she reached her decision. "Yes, let's go to the hotel and get any things you have there. While we're out, we'll stop by the general store and make sure you have all the necessities."

"Give us a minute to pull on shirts and shorts, and we'll come with you," Karleen said, already moving toward the door.

"Would one of you please tell Wyatt where we're going?" Lyssa asked.

Gabrielle replied with a thumbs-up over her shoulder as she followed Karleen into the house.

~

I CLOSED the door behind me as I listened to my phone ring. One of these years, I needed to pick up a set of earbuds or something, so I wasn't walking around holding a phone up to my head. Given the length of the phone calls I had these days, not even shifter endurance saved my arms from getting tired.

Soon enough I heard, "Well, hello there, brother mine. How's the furry side of my family today?"

"Hi, Vicki. We're doing well enough over here, but I've come into some information I think the Magi side of the family needs to know. Do you have some time soon-ish for a conference?"

"How soon-ish are we talking, Wyatt? Grandpa and I are at this quarter's convocation of the Magi Assembly this week."

Well, damn… That put a bit of a damper on things.

"Uhm, as far as I know, it'll keep a week. I'll write up notes on everything, so nothing slips my mind."

Vicki was silent for far longer than I felt she should have been, but when she did speak, no trace of the playful prankster remained, "Grandpa can keep everyone in line without me. This sounds a tad more important than glad-handing old-power families. Let me pull Grandpa aside for a word, and I'll be right there. See you soon!"

Before I could say anything else, the line clicked, and I pulled my phone away from my head to see that she ended the call. About that time, the door behind me opened to admit Karleen and Gabrielle, and I took a moment to appreciate them and their choice of attire… or lack thereof.

"Aren't you supposed to be talking to your sister, instead of ogling us?" Karleen asked.

"She hung up on me," I replied, then explained. "She and Grandpa are at a quarterly meeting of the Magi Assembly, but something in my voice when I said it could wait until they returned home must have clued her into the idea that I really didn't think this should wait a week. She's going to have a quick word with Grandpa and pop over here."

"Oh, good, so we have a little bit of time," Gabrielle said. "We're taking Moira to the hotel to gather her things and then stopping by the general store to make sure she has everything she needs."

It took me less than ten seconds to connect the dots. "Ladies, Moira should not come home with a bikini unless she *wants* to come home with a bikini."

Karleen and Gabrielle both smirked, then chorused, "Oh, yes, she should!"

I shook my head as they disappeared down the hall toward our master suite. Those two were incorrigible. They sashayed back and out the back door not even three minutes later in deck shoes, short shorts, and oversized t-shirts tied into knots at their waists. Damn… I hated to see them go, but I loved to watch them leave.

Lyssa waved to me as they collected Moira, and I waved back before she disappeared out of sight. I didn't imagine it would take Vicki all that long to have a quick word with Grandpa, so I started expecting her to pop in at any second. Part of me felt like calling the ladies back, if she did arrive in the next heartbeat or three, but we really hadn't had a chance to catch up since the bunker. The aftermath was a little too chaotic for anything other than promising her that I was alive and Burke was healing, so I figured we could chat until the ladies returned. It was a coin-toss whether Vicki would like that, but I didn't want to tell the story more than once. I really hoped the ladies hurried.

12

The ladies were out of sight for at most five minutes before my sister appeared in the backyard of the Alpha's house. I saw her stockinged legs ending in heels peeking out from beneath a stylized velvet robe that bore all manner of sigils or runes or glyphs or... I'll go with symbols. They were certainly symbols, and I wouldn't offend my sister with my lack of knowledge. The robe covered her from shoulders to just above her ankles, and I could not imagine anyone ever thinking such attire would be comfortable.

Vicki trooped inside without a word, striding straight to one of the barstools at the bar that separated the kitchen from the great room. She slipped a hand inside the robe, and after a few moments, the sides came free and revealed interior buttons and loops. She shrugged out of it with something approaching unseemly haste—at least if I were a stodgy old grump who believed such attire appropriate—and draped it across the barstool, abandoning it without a second thought.

"Hello, brother mine," she said, taking the few steps necessary to approach me. She pulled me into a tight hug for several heartbeats, then released me and took a step back. "You look well. How is Consul life agreeing with you?"

I knew she was just poking at the title, and I fought the urge to give her a flat look. I really did. But I failed.

"Oh, that fun? Yeah... sounds like having to deal with the Assembly. I swear... if I have to hear the phrase, 'but that's how we've always done it,' one more time to justify some idiocy that wasn't even smart in the 1700s, I'm going to scream. I mean, look at me! Have you *ever* seen me in a *gown*? This shit is intolerable. I'm working my way through the daughter heirs, though. One day, we'll rise up and force some common sense and intelligence on the Assembly meetings."

I waited to make sure my sister was finished speaking, not just taking a pause for effect. That was a hard lesson learned many years ago. When she seemed wound down for the most part, I smiled my reply, "I have seen you in a gown, sis... right now."

Yes. It's never wise to poke the bear, but it had been a while—too long—since Vicki and I had a good go of it. The sudden change of her expression implied dire circumstances in my future.

"You should thank your lucky stars I'm in this stupid gown right now, brother mine, or you'd be defending yourself in a tickle fight fit for the ages. Now, what was so important you didn't want to wait a week to tell me?"

"Yeah... so, about that... do you mind hanging out and just catching up until the ladies get back? They went over to the hotel and the store, and I'd rather not have to repeat myself. The story is *that* involved."

Vicki gave me a flat look with narrowed eyes, and I'm surprised I didn't see smoke coming out of her ears. After several seconds, she puffed out a breath, fluffing her bangs into the air. She stomped into the great room and claimed the sole loveseat, flopping into it before crossing her arms in an apparent huff, yet daintily crossing her ankles.

"Fine. We'll wait." A few more seconds passed, and her expression softened, and she then uncrossed her arms. "If I'm going to be honest, I should probably thank you. I hate convocations with a passion, and it always annoys me when Grandpa or Grams drags me to one. Yes, I know. I'm the heir or heiress, whichever you prefer. I'll have *both* of their seats on the Assembly one day. But that doesn't mean I have to like it. And I wasn't joking about making alliances behind the scenes. As soon as enough of us inherit to wield real power, we're changing some of that draconian shit."

I gave it another healthy pause to be sure she was finished. "For what it's worth, I'm on your side. I don't have the foggiest what 'draconian shit' you're talking about, but if you and the others think it should change, have at it."

"Sorry. Sorry. I shouldn't bring my problems into your house. That was unkind of me."

I chuckled at that. I couldn't help myself. "Vicki, you're my sister. Your problems are my problems. They always have been, and they always will be. One day, I'll look at my niece or nephew or both and tell them the same thing."

"So, does it ever freak you out? The idea that you might very well outlive everyone alive today? Even newborn Magi? With my talents, odds favor I'll live a good, long time... much like Grandpa and Grams... but we've talked, and you would not believe the number of friends they've outlived."

I shrugged. "I don't really think about it, and there's no telling what will happen. I mean... sure... shifters supposedly are immortal, but if that's the case, why aren't there more of us who lived back in Roman times walking around? Something tells me that we don't have all the information, but I might be wrong. There may be some little Italian guy in New York City slinging pizza and pasta and whatever else is in

Italian cuisine who saw the conquest of Gaul firsthand. If they don't talk about it, how are we supposed to know?"

"You make a good point. I don't know. It's been tough getting Merlin out of my mind. I doubt anyone likes to sit around contemplating their own mortality, but just how old is Merlin? What all has he seen or lived through? I'm sure none of us will ever know."

Without thinking, I blurted out, "He's a little under fifteen hundred."

Vicki blinked. "Excuse you? What makes you say that? Did you just pull a number out of your furry butt?"

"He told me he was born in 543, somewhere in modern-day Wales. So... fourteen-eighty or thereabouts."

Her expression hardened again, and she gave me her patented Stink Eye. "And just *when* did our revered ancestor share this with you?"

Me and my big mouth...

"Earlier today. It's part of everything I have to tell you."

"Which you're making me wait to hear until Karleen and everyone else return... why exactly?"

The front door flying open heralded the return of my ladies and Moira, saving me from my sister's wrath. At least for the moment. There was always the chance she'd enlist one or more of them to her side of the discussion, and I'd find myself besieged on all fronts. Wouldn't be the first time, but the make-up tended to be epic...

"So, what do we have here?" Gabrielle asked, her tone almost playful. "I don't believe we've ever seen you in a *dress* before, Vicki."

My sister swiveled to Gabrielle like a SAM launcher acquiring its target. "Get a good look. Maybe take a picture. Because the days when I and my peers in the Assembly will submit to this tomfoolery are numbered... and... it's a *gown*, not a dress."

Gabrielle just beamed in the face of my sister's wrath. "You say gown. I say dress. Potayto, potahto. So, how late were we?"

"Oh, you're right on time," I replied. "She hadn't worked up to the truly gruesome threats to my health and wellbeing yet."

"That's good," Karleen remarked. "We always hate to miss the good stuff."

Lyssa chuckled and shook her head as she moved past us, leading Moira through the great room to the stairs that went up to the second floor. "I'm going to put Moira in the first upstairs room, unless anyone has a better idea."

Before either Gabrielle or Karleen could speak up, I opined, "That sounds perfect, Lyssa. Thank you."

Both ladies in question gave me speculative looks but kept their peace. Talk about small mercies...

Vicki, Karleen, and Gabrielle chatted among themselves while we meandered toward the dining room table. Sure, we could have had the discussion in the great room, but serious planning always requires a table in my mind. Unless we all wanted to troop down the street to the admin building conference room, the formal dining room was our only option.

By the time Lyssa returned with Moira, we already claimed seats. Through some method known only to them, Gabrielle and Karleen decided it was Lyssa's turn to sit at my right hand and gave the seat on my immediate left to Vicki. While Lyssa accepted their silent instruction with grace and a smile, Moira stood off to one side, looking a tad anxious.

"Moira, sit anywhere you like," I said. "Don't worry. We don't bite."

"Unless you ask nicely," Karleen added.

I shot a glance toward my dire wolf, and she merely returned my look with an unrepentant grin of her own.

Moira eased into a seat further down the table from Vicki, still acting and looking very much like she was somewhere she didn't belong.

"So, earlier today, Miles appeared right in front of me as I crossed Main Street and told me we 'needed to talk.' The next thing I know, we're in some musty old stone structure that he claimed was Avalon... but all the King Arthur myths aren't quite correct."

I proceeded to relay the entire tale from that point all the way through Moira joining our little family. Early on, Vicki lost all trace of mischievous sister and adopted a more serious mien. It was easy to understand why.

"Wait a minute," Lyssa said, holding up her hand in a 'Stop' gesture. "The shifters today are the primogenitors' *lesser children*? I don't know if we can sell that, hon. In case you haven't noticed, the default stance for most of us is arrogant bravado."

I chuckled. "Yeah. I learned that the hard way with Thomas Carlyle." I glanced toward Gabrielle. "Say... how is he getting along?"

Gabrielle shrugged. "Just like the rest of us. He has his good days and bad. The good days are slowly outnumbering the bad, though, which is always nice."

"It makes perfect sense, though," Karleen interjected. "The lesser children thing, I mean. I certainly know I haven't encountered a shifter yet who was a serious challenge. It wasn't until Wyatt and I started sparring that anyone really made me work for the win."

Lyssa shook her head. "I wasn't saying it wasn't true, just that I doubted we could sell it. The average shifter on the street doesn't know you or Wyatt or Sloane or the European dire wolf. Burke is—for all intents and purposes—still a child, so I'm not including her."

"We need more primogenitors," Gabrielle spoke into the

sudden lull. "Yes, the Magi are a force multiplier, but from what Miles said, only the primogenitors—or true shifters— stand a chance against the Fae. When should we tell Mina and, in turn, the government?"

Vicki grimaced. "I don't think we have enough information to take to them yet. Yeah... it's all well and good to say, 'look, there's an ancient enemy coming for us,' but without proof—without a tangible timeline—that's worse than useless. They are simply not used to thinking long term... not like we are. Hell. It makes national news when one of them lives over a hundred years. Maybe just the eleven o'clock news, but still..."

"I agree with Vicki." I added emphasis with a couple nods. "I think our best bet is to start planning and preparing between us. Get the Assembly onboard. Get the shifters onboard. In our case, I think we should relax the heavy bar on adding humans to our ranks, and I think we should research special cases to become primogenitors. Yes, Merlin was adamant that modern shifters could not stand up to the Fae when they come, but unless a bunch of primogenitors have been hiding all these centuries, all we have right now are the four of us... well, five, if we can get Karleen's counterpart in Europe onboard."

No one seemed to have anything they wanted to add, so I looked to the sole person at the table who hadn't said a word. "Moira, what can you tell us about the Fae preparations?"

The red-haired vixen lowered her eyes to the table for a moment before lifting her head to look at me. "I am over two hundred of your years old, but compared to humans or even Magi, we age at an almost geologic pace. The eldest of my family... *former* family... watched the humans here develop writing. The Fae Courts are even older. The more power we bring back to our realm, the slower we age.

"This would've been the third campaign to claim a realm

I have participated in, and they are moving cautiously. They told us we once tried for this world and its bounty in ancient times but were driven back, beaten almost to the point of famine and ruin. The humans of this world have the saying, 'pride goeth before a fall,' and the Fae have always been a prideful people. Some might say too prideful. This world is our first—our only—defeat, and my people will not stand for a repeat. When they come for you, it will be at a time most advantageous for them, and they will bring—what is to them—overwhelming force. According to all the ancient chronicles, our leaders of the time were woefully unprepared for the level of resistance the shifters could deliver. Most paid for their lack of scouting and planning with their lives... if they survived the retreat to our realm."

"So, based on past campaigns, how much time do we have?" Vicki asked. "Do you have any idea when this overwhelming force will arrive?"

Moira shook her head. "I do not... at least not for certain. I am—well, *was*—one of the advance scouts. It is our job to travel the world and amass as much information about your capabilities as we can, before we take our reports back to our realm."

"How many scouts have your people sent?" I asked.

"I have no way of knowing, not for certain. My cohort was thirty-two strong, and I have not seen or heard from them since the people in the bunker captured me."

Lyssa frowned. "Thirty-two is a strange number, at least to us."

Moira smiled. "After significant negotiation spanning weeks, the eight families supplying my cohort agreed to four scouts per family, and I'm quite sure they would still be arguing over the matter, but the Queens forced the issue."

My ladies, Vicki, and I shared a look. From the sounds of

it, the Fae were less than united. That could be useful down the road.

"Queens?" Vicki asked. "I know in our folklore there are Seelie and Unseelie Fae, sometimes called the Summer and Winter Courts respectively, and they each have their own queen. How close is that?"

Moira refused to meet my sister's eyes as she answered, "There are the Seelie and Unseelie Courts, each with their own queen. That much, at least, you have correct. But I do not understand what you mean by Summer and Winter Courts."

"In our folklore, the Seelie Fae are lighter Fae and closer to benevolent, while the Unseelie Fae are darker and often nowhere close to benevolent," my sister explained.

"Ah," Moira remarked. "That is both correct and incorrect. Much like humans, Fae have equal capacity for goodness or evil, but it is one of our foundational beliefs that all beings who are not Fae are lesser creatures. And there has never been a Fae who did not ensure his or her own success before any other considerations, even such that might benefit the Fae as a whole."

The ladies and I shared another look, and Karleen spoke. "So, where's your success in this? How are you coming out ahead?"

Now, embarrassment—or at least what I *thought* to be embarrassment—colored Moira's features. "As I intimated, I am... young. I have not experienced much of life as yet, and when I saw a man who matched the Bane of the Courts in the ancient chronicles, I... well... I panicked. Seeing *him* here of all places made me certain beyond any doubt—at least in my panic—that my death was nigh, and I don't want to die. So, I threw myself on the hopes of Wyatt's kindness, and he accepted my oath, even knowing what it entailed."

"And just what, pray tell, does it entail?" Vicki asked. "And before you answer, it might be best if you knew that my brother and I are his great-great-grandchildren... in a direct line. Our grandmother is his granddaughter."

In the blink of an eye, Moira's demeanor went from embarrassment and slight discomfort to looking like she was two heartbeats from stroking out. Full-blown panic attack. Her eyes—wider than I'd ever seen them before—ping-ponged between me and Vicki as she hyperventilated. Her jaw slackened enough that her lips developed a tiny 'O' through which I caught glimpses of her white teeth.

When she started weaving in her seat, I shot out of mine, rounding the table. I pulled her into my arms and turned us so she couldn't see Vicki while I whispered in her ear, "Hey, calm down. You're safe. Remember my oath. Remember my promise. You're safe with me. You're safe with us."

I continued whispering what I hoped were calming words as I rubbed her back. Over a short span of time, her panic eased. A shorter time after that, she pulled away from me, giving reassuring nods that she was past her panic. I helped her back to her seat and returned to mine.

As I eased into the chair, Moira said, "In exchange for his mercy and protection, I am your brother's property to do with as he wills for the rest of my life."

That sat Vicki back, which was good to see. Sometimes, when she went all 'big sister' to protect me, she could take the bit between her teeth and run roughshod over everyone.

"You were so afraid of our ancestor that you *chose* to become my brother's property as long as he protected you?"

Moira replied with a silent nod.

Silence settled around us for several moments. At last, Vicki spoke. "I am sorry I scared you. I won't tell you that it wasn't my intent, but I wouldn't have done it if I had known the full extent of how much Merlin terrifies you."

"Thank you." Moira's voice wasn't a whisper, but there was zero challenge or strength in it.

Vicki turned back to us. "I think the best option is for me to talk with our grandparents. If Miles pops in again, do what you can to corral him until we can get back here. We need to hear more about this, and I'm not sure there's anyone better to tell us than him."

Lyssa lifted her hand from the table, and we all turned to her. "I will start working on just how to tell the Shifter Council both that we're the descendants of the lesser children and that we have an invasion coming. I fear they will be a more difficult sell than the Magi Assembly."

"Miles might have to visit both groups and establish himself before we make any progress," Vicki cautioned.

"Agreed. I still remember the frightened disbelief when he etched his sigil into the tabletop during Sloane's inquest. I *never* thought I'd see that anywhere in my lifetime other than in books."

When silence reigned for several minutes, I decided no one else had anything to share, so I stood, saying, "I think we've done all we can for right now. Let's work on our respective pieces and talk in... what... a week?"

Heads bobbed in agreement around the table, and everyone stood. Vicki retrieved her robe from the barstool before she blinked out, and Lyssa helped Moira upstairs, whispering something about a nap being good for her.

13

The question I felt around my shoulders was one of next steps. Where do we go from where we were? I had no military experience to speak of, so I didn't have that to fall back on. But... a lot of my favorite authors *were* veterans and often wrote military-themed novels. Yes, fiction should not be my sole guide with the fate of the world hanging over us, but I had to start somewhere, right? Besides, one of my top favorite authors once wrote in a novel: amateurs study tactics; professionals study logistics.

That made excellent sense to me. It doesn't matter what fancy moves or formations or plans you have. If your people don't have food, proper equipment, or even clean clothes, they will not be the best fighting force they can be.

It seemed to me that the Magi would be indispensable for logistics. Set up a supply corps around a group of Magi that were Grandmaster-certified in long-range teleportation, and we could have most of what we needed anywhere in the world. Not to mention the ease of transporting troops...

No, the major problem was that we didn't *know* anything

beyond the Fae were coming and that they already had scouts on the planet.

That they were an internally fractious lot seemed rather fortuitous to me, but I'd have to remember not to let us dwell on that. Plan for it, yes. Utilize it if we could, absolutely. Get complacent because we relied on our invaders to spend as much time fighting or disagreeing with each other as they did us? Not wise. Not wise at all.

I found myself standing at the edge of the backyard at the Alpha's house as I considered all this and more surrounding Miles's revelation. The sun hung low in the western sky, creating reddish-orange rays of light around the taller hills and mountain peaks.

And all at once, understanding hit me. Most shifters responded to strength from what Gabrielle kept telling me... and Lyssa, too, since she joined us. I was hands-down the strongest shifter in North America, with the possible—or maybe probable—exception of Karleen. If my duel with Thomas Carlyle was any indication, even experienced and veteran shifters would not be able to stand up to me.

Burke, too, once she progressed past the early 'growing pains' stage. It was all still so new for her, though, that she had to re-learn everything about Life. A lot was still the same for her, now that she was a shifter, but the list of topics at least subtly different would probably wallpaper the Rockies. We needed to get her up to speed as fast as possible... and we needed to get her away from the Feds. If she took their money, they had a claim on her. Her time. Her knowledge. Her talents. Since she was the fifth primogenitor—that we *knew*—we needed her more. And as much as I might prefer otherwise, I needed to discuss becoming a primogenitor with Hauser, assuming she was still intent on becoming a shifter.

I stopped my random walk around the backyard. I felt the urge to sigh. It didn't seem like I'd be getting out of that

'Consul' business now. Too much rode on there being someone who could *lead* the shifters. Heh… there were times I missed being a lowly tech support geek.

As I turned toward the house, I caught a glimpse of Lyssa and smiled, thinking of my ladies. Yeah… maybe I didn't miss being a tech support geek so much after all.

~

BURKE'S STOMACH was a monster all its own now. She sat at one of the tables in Precious's diner, awaiting the arrival of her order with eagerness and faux patience against the backdrop of a growling stomach that sounded louder than a kitchen garbage disposal. She wasn't all that certain her spine and the other organs in her torso were safe unless her food arrived *damn soon*.

"Have you visited Doc again since you woke up?" Hauser asked.

Burke shook her head, fighting the urge to watch the door leading to the kitchen. "I know he wants me to, and I know I probably should… just to learn more about the health and dietary implications of my new life if nothing else. But I haven't managed it yet. You still thinking about becoming a shifter?"

Hauser nodded. "There's a lot to recommend it. Part of me wants you to be the one who changes me, even. You're a beautiful cat."

"Thank you," Burke replied, adding a smile. "That's something you should discuss with someone who's been a shifter a while, I'd imagine. I don't know if I'm capable of changing someone, since I'm so new, and I wouldn't be surprised if my body is still changing. I know these huge platters of food I keep putting away are going somewhere, and precious little of it seems to be going to my hips or thighs."

"Yeah… the ease of maintaining a certain level of fitness is *very* appealing. I have always struggled with my weight, and it would be nice to eat whatever I want and not have to worry as much."

Burke chuckled and shook her head. "I'm learning it does have its drawbacks. If I don't eat a certain amount each day, I wake up in the middle of the night with the worst case of munchies I've ever had. The other night, it was so bad that I went hunting. Helped myself to a nice mule deer after I checked to be sure it wasn't a shifter. That was the only morning since I woke up here in the infirmary that I haven't felt like my stomach wanted to eat me."

"Wow. Yeah, I can see a case of the midnight munchies being a whole other thing for you now. Did you see anyone else while you were out?"

"I won't swear to it, but Sloane might've been doing some night flying. I kept hearing something big glide by overhead, and once, I think I maybe heard a sheep bleating like there was no tomorrow. I don't see how these people eat sheep on the hoof. I'm all for fresh mutton, but getting through all that wool is a major turn-off for me. I'll get mine from the butcher, thank you very much."

Hauser erupted in laughter. "I never thought of that. You're right. That does seem like a problem. I wonder how they handle it."

Right around then, Gladys arrived with a ginormous platter balanced on one arm and a dainty little plate in the opposite hand. She placed the platter in front of Burke and delivered the plate to Hauser.

"It's not as bad as you might think," she said, once she delivered the food. "I won't go into it right now, since you're eating and all, but letting your animal take over lets you ignore quite a bit."

That said, Gladys disappeared back into the crowd, checking her tables to be sure no one needed anything.

Burke blinked, and she stared after her. "You know, I never considered that, either. I'll have to try it."

Hauser held up a hand in a 'stop' gesture. "Okay. No talking about shifter eating habits with food on the table."

Burke chuckled at her friend's antics and focused on the platter of food that might as well have been ambrosia in front of her. Yes, being able to eat what she wanted and as much as she wanted was certainly a perk.

I ENTERED the diner and scanned the crowd. It was outside the normal times I visited the place, and a hush soon seemed to settle on the room as everyone waited to see who I sought. It didn't take me long to find Burke and Hauser, and I watched Burke push away an empty platter as she leaned back against her seat with her eyes closed, a satisfied smile dominating her expression. By the time I was halfway to their table, the ambient chatter in the diner had returned to a 'normal' level.

"May I join you?" I asked as I arrived at their table.

Burke opened her eyes but didn't lose the smile. Hauser shrugged, and Burke gestured for me to sit with a lazy wave.

"So, how is life treating you?" I asked as I assumed my seat.

"I'm a little jealous of how much Burke has to eat now," Hauser remarked, a teasing grin soon curling her lips.

Well... *that* was a perfect opening if there ever was one. "Yeah... about that... are you still thinking about becoming a shifter?"

"Burke just asked me the same thing before our food arrived. Yes, I am. Why?"

I didn't answer right away, choosing instead to scan the diner around us. I didn't like how many ears might be listening.

"Just wondering. Burke, have you given any more thought to what comes next? You have a whole wealth of options now that you didn't before."

Burke shook her head. "I still need to call my supervisor and go through all the post-incident crap, and how do I talk to someone for the required psych eval about becoming a shifter? I don't think any of the agency shrinks are cleared for Paranormal Division operations."

"Well... you don't have to continue with your agency. I have a number of jobs I feel would be perfect for you both... assuming Hauser continues her plan to become a shifter."

Burke shot Hauser a look. I didn't try to interpret it. After a moment, Hauser said, "What's going on, Wyatt? You're acting a little weird."

"Nah, not really. I just wanted you to know you have shifter-specific options available if you didn't mind leaving federal work. I'd better get back to it. I'm afraid if I leave Lyssa alone too long, I'll come back find three more jobs she gave me. You two have a good afternoon."

I stood and left the diner. It was a fine line. I needed to give them enough to tempt them without tipping my hand or coming right out and saying I wanted to discuss things with them but not as long as they remained on Uncle Sam's payroll.

Without a better idea of where I needed to be, I headed for the admin building. Sure... Hauser and Burke *knew* something was going on, but by watching me go in the admin building—if they chose to do so—they would see me following through on what I said about Lyssa, at least as far as they knew.

Considering it as I walked, I supposed that it might seem

like I was trying to deceive or manipulate Hauser and Burke, and that wasn't the case... well... not completely. We needed primogenitors and *lots* of them. When the time came, I'd speak with Sloane about changing Mina, instead of one of the eagles, hawks, or falcons; I'd speak with Mina and be (mostly) upfront with her about the situation, but one roc does not an air corps make. Yes, the other avian shifters could help with recon, but I wanted as many primogenitors as we could have to act as front-line combatants.

A sigh escaped me as I opened the door to the admin building. I also needed to sit down with Moira and get a comprehensive understanding of the make-up of the Fae army. I really hoped their invasion forces didn't have winged Fae, but that didn't seem realistic, especially after the tapestry I saw at Avalon.

I gave the young guy at the reception desk a smile and wave as I walked by, intent on Lyssa's office. Miracle of miracles, she was there. I entered her office and closed the door and turned back to see her already walking around the desk, a happy smile brightening her features.

"Hi," I said as she melted into my arms.

"Hi yourself," she replied, her voice muffled somewhat by my arms and shirt.

Yes, it had just been a few hours since I'd seen her, but I wanted my ladies to have an almost-instinctual awareness that I valued them, missed them when we were apart, and yes... loved them. Even though Lyssa was the newest to the family, I didn't want to go back to the life before her.

"So, what brings you to my office?" she asked once she stepped back from the hug.

"A couple things. First, I'm thinking we should get Moira started on a comprehensive break-down of the Fae military... or at least as much as she knows. Will their invasion force have winged Fae, mounted Fae, or unit types or structures we haven't encountered or imagined? So on and so forth. I'd like to have as much information as possible.

"Second, what do you think about creating a quiet recruitment drive? We need primogenitors, and there are people out there with incurable diseases or life-altering conditions. We could approach them, offer a solution to their situation, and in exchange, they help with the Fae invasion. Once the invasion's over, they do what they want."

I stopped and thought about that last idea. The more I considered it, the less I liked it. If we weren't careful, we'd give unscrupulous people the power of not just a shifter but a primogenitor. I didn't like that. Not at all.

"Okay," I said, interrupting the silence. "Scratch the second idea. I don't like risking unscrupulous people getting the power of a primogenitor. I know Hauser wants to be a melanistic jaguar like Gabrielle, but if she comes to us wanting to become a shifter, I'm going to see if I can sway her over to the idea of me turning her instead of Gabrielle. We still don't know why Burke is an American lion instead of a Smilodon, and who knows? Hauser might be something different from both of us." I fell silent as I considered the situation. "Damn... I really need to study Pleistocene-era animals, specifically predators."

Lyssa smiled and moved close, pulling me into another hug right before she gave me a brief kiss. "See? You know what you need to do... and what you *don't* need to do. You don't need me."

I tightened my arms around her and shook my head. "Oh, yes, I do. I need you and Karleen and Gabrielle very much. I wouldn't be the man I am without you."

"I think you're wrong about that," Lyssa countered, "but out of sheer self-interest, I'm willing to concede the point. Now... don't you have a Fae to visit to discuss a couple tasks?"

She was right. I nodded and pulled her back in for another tight hug and kissed the top of her head. "Yeah, but I love the feel of you in my arms. I don't want to leave yet."

Lyssa lowered a hand to swat my butt. "Go on, mister. Get out of here... before we use the office for something not safe for work."

I released her with a laugh and left the office. As far as I knew, Moira was at the Alpha's house, so that would be the first place I checked.

I FOUND Moira right where I expected to find her and set her to the task of writing up what she knew about the Fae military and what we might face in the invasion force... whenever it arrived. I had no idea how long that would take her, either, especially since I asked her to be thorough.

14

The first couple days, I kept expecting Moira to walk up with a piece of paper or two to present her write-up. By the third day, I figured either she knew a lot and worked to organize it all for the best presentation or she didn't know squat and was afraid to tell me. If I hadn't heard from her in a week, I'd ask Lyssa to check on her.

I couldn't shake the feeling that she feared me more than she used to... what with Vicki's revelation of our familial connection to Merlin. I didn't like that at all, but I didn't know how to overcome it. Especially if the terror was something ingrained from a very young age and was as much cultural as personal. I wasn't sure how she'd take having Lyssa as the primary liaison, but I just could not handle how she flinched every time she saw me or heard my voice now. The longer this went on, the more I wished my sister had just kept her mouth shut.

IT WAS five days or so after I gave Moira her task, and it definitely seemed like she was avoiding me now. Aside from knocking on her door and asking her for the write-up, I hadn't seen her at all since. She no longer shared meals with us. Didn't come to movie night or lounge around the deck in the backyard or the house's pool.

"Lyssa," I began once I was one glass of tea into my morning, "do you mind checking on Moira? I haven't seen her since I spoke with her about starting the write-up, and she doesn't come to family things anymore. It seems like her behavior changed after Vicki blurted out that we're related to Merlin."

Lyssa nodded as she carved up her pancakes. "I'll do that before I head to the admin building this morning, and I'll also see what I can do about her change in behavior. It's probably a bit unsettling to think you've found a safe harbor and then learn the harbor's connected to the storm you wanted to avoid in the first place."

"Thanks." I focused my attention on the bagels. After all, that chive-and-onion cream cheese wouldn't spread itself.

A short time later, I sat alone at the bar separating the great room from the kitchen, skimming headlines from the major news services around world. I saw no reason to subscribe to physical publications, but I—or rather the Shifter Council—maintained several subscriptions for me and themselves to stay current on human international news.

It just made sense. We were dependent on human society —at least to a certain extent—and I couldn't imagine anyone not thinking that ignoring the largest sapient population on the planet was a *good* idea.

The more I read, the more I wondered if the shifters or Magi had their own intelligence sources. It wasn't all that neighborly, but I also wondered if we could work out some kind of arrangement where any shifters in the world's intelligence agencies copied *us* on what crossed their desks. In my mind, it wasn't like they'd be a double agent. They were shifters *first*, and I could see the need to be just as aware of what was happening in the world as the world governments.

Hrmm… something to discuss with Lyssa first and possibly the Shifter Council as a whole. After all, if they were going to insist that I was the Consul for North America, I might as well take it out for a spin and see what it could do.

I WASN'T sure how much time passed with me sitting at the bar, skimming the news, but the back door opening pulled me from my focus. I smiled when I turned, seeing Miles standing just inside the doorframe.

"Hello, Miles," I said. "Be welcome in this house and wherever I call 'home.' I can offer you coffee or tea here, or if you'd like something more substantial, we can visit the diner or I can call them for a to-go order."

Miles smiled and crossed the space to claim a barstool. "Thank ye for the welcome and offer, lad. Maybe later. Have ye had a chance to consider what we discussed?"

"Yes. I've updated Vicki and my ladies on the matter, and while I have a representative for the American government here in town, I haven't told her yet. Until we have something more concrete, I'm not sure what value there is in getting the humans—even a small number of them—wound up."

Miles leaned back against his seat and crossed his arms. I recognized his thinking posture, having seen it many times when I thought he was just a simple groundskeeper at my grandparents' estate. After a few moments, he shrugged.

"I can see both sides of the idea, lad. Besides, the humans will be worse than fodder when the invasion arrives… unless we can mass produce charms or tokens that will protect 'em from the Fae's ability to influence—or outright dominate—their minds. Magi and shifters be immune fer some reason, which is odd since Magi can use their magic to influence each other. Not even I can influence shifters... not for very long anyway. The last time I tried, the shifter shook it off in seconds, and I doubt one such as yerself would take that long, if it even took hold at all."

I'm sure I wasn't hiding my surprise well. "Fae can influence peoples' minds?"

"Oh, aye, lad. It's almost second nature to 'em. The ones really proficient at it can turn people into what are essentially meat puppets that exist solely as extensions of the controlling Fae's will. And there be no guarantee the person they were will re-assert if the control is broken. I watched it go both ways during the last invasion, but humans have come a long way since then. I suppose we'd need to test it, but I don't know how to do that without risking the test subject."

My mind reeled at the idea we might face dominated or influenced humans once the invasion began. And that led to another thought.

"There's no way we'll be able to stay under the radar like we've been, is there?"

Miles shook his head. "Nae, lad. Shifters will be the first line of defense when the Fae come for the world, with the Magi acting as fire support. I do nae see how the lot of ye could do what ye need to do without the world at large learning ye exist."

"Well, shit. This is going to be a colossal mess, no matter how we look at it."

"War always is, lad. There be nothing clean or pretty or neat about 'em."

I leaned back against my seat and let that settle into my mind. I wasn't sure the world was ready for the knowledge that we existed, but I'm sure children would love us. I could see visiting local group homes and pediatric wings of hospitals as a Smilodon and giving rides for those who were well enough. I'd just have to be careful not to turn any of them.

"So… how do we start preparing the world for the Great Reveal?"

Miles snorted. "Not me problem, lad. I'll stand off to one side and give ye moral support or be prepared to step in, but this is for ye and yer sister to accomplish. The two of ye are well-suited to yer tasks, and I have faith in ye."

It was so tempting to give in to the old feelings that used to dominate my life. *I'm not that guy. I'm not a leader. I'm not capable.* And a whole host of others, but the simple fact was that I *was* a leader, and I became more capable each day. After all, my ladies would not have given the old Wyatt—the computer geek Wyatt—a second glance, unless they needed me to fix something. I needed to remember I wasn't that guy anymore. I was Wyatt Magnusson, feline primogenitor. Alpha of Precious and Godwin County. Consul of the Shifter Nation of North America.

I felt a swell of approval from my cat and fought the urge to grin. I didn't hear or interact with the growly voice much anymore, not since I achieved synthesis. But I did get the occasional flash of primal emotion, usually around mealtimes or when I wanted to go for a run as my Smilodon or when one of my ladies wore something particularly attractive.

Of course, considering my ladies, any one of them would make a burlap sack look damn good, so it wasn't like they ever *didn't* look attractive.

"I think we need to establish a war council," I said at last.

Miles nodded his agreement. "Aye, lad, ye do."

"And I want you on it. Not just as Miles, my grandparents' friendly groundskeeper, but Merlin, Bane of the Fae Courts."

"Lad, I gave up bein' adviser to world powers centuries

ago," Miles said as he grimaced. "I do nae *want* to be known around the world as Merlin. Not anymore."

I sighed. "As much as I'd like to say you're welcome to hide in the shadows and be mine and Vicki's unseen counsel, we need the leaders of the world and the war effort—who might not always be the same people—aware of who you really are and accepting of your knowledge and authority in these matters. There may come a time when you need to commandeer a unit, and if we haven't established who you are from the outset, that will not be easy."

Miles's expression suggested he chewed on something rather sour. "There be many reasons I stepped away from advisin' kings and sages, lad, and damned good ones, at that. Besides, I've seen what the world has become. Do ye honestly think *any* of these people are prepared to accept a man who's approaching his fifteen-hundredth birthday? I will nae be *anyone*'s lab rat, and I will nae be all that kind in me refusal."

I nodded. "I would not blame you at all. In fact, that's part of my consideration. I wouldn't put it past the governments of the world to try to capture a few shifters and Magi for study when we come out of the shadows, and if you were there in all your glory, they might give the matter a second thought."

Miles sat with that for a few moments before he gave a decisive nod. "Aye, they might at that. While I would step in for any Magi or shifter some government tried to claim for study, I would take it as a personal affront should any of 'em be daft enough to come after yer sister or yerself or any others I name kin. And trust me, lad; they should go to great lengths to avoid offending me."

"Alistair hinted something about that when Vicki was kidnapped a few months ago," I remarked.

All semblance of the kindly old man vanished in less time

than it takes to snap one's fingers. "What did ye just say, lad? Someone dared lay hands on me granddaughter's girl?"

Well, shit... me and my big mouth.

"It was right after the dust-up at the fake orphanage down near the Oregon border. Once everything was handled in the aftermath of that, she went to Seattle to visit some of her favorite shops... boutiques, nail spas, and such from what she told me later. Well, someone grabbed her on the sidewalk and injected her with a sedative, and the next she knew, she was in some kind of mechanical room with piping and such.

"To make a long story short, she was able to contact Grams, who in turn contacted me, and a Magi capable of assault rifts dropped me and five hundred volunteers about two miles from Vicki's location. I don't know who did the actual snatch-and-grab, but we slaughtered everyone there who wasn't a child or Vicki. We think more of the organization is still out there, but we're having problems locating them."

Miles sat silent atop the barstool, with his jaw clenched to the point that I expected him to start spitting diamonds onto the counter.

"I want everything ye know about these foul excuses for humanity," he said at last. "That they continue to breathe the same air as people who *care* about this world is an affront to all I hold dear. If I must take the place I once endured and be known to the world at large, I shall start by eradicating this filth wherever it hides."

"Uhm, I didn't lead the shifter war party for that, but Vicki commanded the 7th Magi Expeditionary Unit. Still might, come to think of it. I'm not sure the Assembly ever shut it down."

"I care not who has the information I seek, lad... just that I have it."

Right, then.

"Excuse me a second," I said and retrieved my phone. I first texted my sister:

Miles is in my kitchen and would like a word. Bring everything you have on the org that kidnapped you.

Then, before Vicki had a chance to respond—assuming she would rather than simply teleporting here—I called Gabrielle.

"Hey, Wyatt," she said, answering on the first ring.

"Hi. Do you mind running by the admin building and bringing all the records we have about the organization that was doing the kidnappings a few months back?"

A couple heartbeats of silence. Then, she said, "Why do you want that? It's a dead end right now, anyway. They've gone to ground so hard that I doubt dwarves could find them."

"Wait... dwarves are a thing?"

All I heard for a few seconds was Gabrielle's laughter. "Not outside of fiction that I've ever heard, but who knows? Now, are you going to tell me what's going on?"

"Nope. You'll find out when you bring me the info." I thumbed the control to end the call before she could press me further, then turned back to Miles. "I have it in the works."

Miles nodded once. "Thank ye, lad. I appreciate that."

About ten minutes passed before Gabrielle walked into the house with Karleen and Lyssa in tow. Each pulled a pair of large, rolling totes. Each of my ladies blinked at seeing Miles perched atop one of our barstools, but before they could answer, Vicki arrived in the backyard with several totes of her own floating on a pocket of condensed air and entered without knocking.

I didn't *quite* sigh at the thought of re-hashing all of that again, but I certainly wasn't looking forward to it. "Come on.

If we're doing this, the dining room has more space to spread everything out."

"Ye do nae need to worry about that, lad," Miles said as he stood. "I'll take possession of it and handle the matter to my satisfaction. Build yer war council and develop allies. The next time we meet, we shall start working toward announcing ourselves to the world."

Not even a full five seconds after he finished speaking, Miles vanished... along with Vicki's collection of documents and the contents of the ladies' totes.

"What just happened, Wyatt?" Vicki asked, surprising me with my name. She rarely used it.

I returned to my perch atop a barstool and sighed. "I didn't watch what I said and let slip that you were kidnapped a couple months back. Miles... did not take it well. I'm pretty sure he plans to take steps."

"You think? I just hope he brings all the documents back. The Assembly entrusted them to me, and I can't afford for them to be lost on my watch."

I couldn't keep from scoffing. "I feel very safe in saying those documents will no longer matter when—or even if— you see them again, and if the Assembly wants to get surly about it, refer them to Miles."

Vicki stood silent for several heartbeats before she shook her head. "No, I'm not sure I will. I don't think that would be good for the Assembly's leadership."

Lyssa approached the bar and claimed a seat of her own, gesturing for everyone who wasn't seated to do likewise. "What was that he said about coming out to the world?"

Oh, yeah... that. I wasn't sure I wanted to get into it right then, but I never lied to my ladies. Or Vicki for that matter.

"So, to fight this war, we're going to have to announce ourselves," I said. "There's no way we can fight off the Fae's invasion while still being unknown to the people of the world. I don't know where that will lead, but we don't really have much choice in the matter."

Lyssa worked her lower lip between her teeth for several moments. "Well… most of the world's governments already know about us. Shifters, anyway. I don't know about the Magi."

Vicki nodded. "Yeah, we have some contacts here and there. Nowhere close to what we have with the American government, though. Whoever negotiated that treaty was a genius."

We discussed the matter for a few more minutes, along with trading family updates. In the end, though, we all had other items requiring our attention, so after a half-hour or so of chatting, Vicki vanished much like Miles had, while my ladies and I returned to our respective days.

15

B urke and Hauser walked into the building that served as their office. They spent most of their career at their desks or in interview rooms... until Hauser's supervisor handed her a case involving abductions a few months before. Hauser hadn't realized it at the time, but that case was a crux point in her life, where her life wasn't the same afterward as it was before.

Just the day before, Doc gave Burke a clean bill of health with formal, written instructions for her new dietary guidelines. He also provided his formal assessment of Burke's ability to return to duty with the Paranormal Division of their agency. Except... Burke was no longer certain she *wanted* to return. Still, though, they owed their supervisor a sit-down chat, which led them to return to Washington's main field office.

Like most federal buildings, the interior resembled every bland office building ever made. Neutral tones everywhere. Now that they had spent so much time around the shifters and how they decorated their lives, the place seemed more than a little depressing.

. . .

BURKE NODDED for Hauser to knock on their supervisor's door. On the whole, she was acclimated to her new strength, but every now and then, she slipped up, and the last thing either of them wanted was for Burke to break down the door by accident.

"Enter," a voice called from within the office.

Hauser opened the door and led Burke inside. Kent Fergusson sat behind his desk, an array of family pictures on the credenza along the wall where he could see them at a moment's thought as well as show them off to guests. Kent was on the upper end of middle age. He was a former Recon Marine whose silent intensity had always intimidated Burke a little bit, but now? She didn't understand how she could have ever felt that way. While Kent might hold the edge in training, there was no doubt in Burke's mind who the office's most dangerous occupant was... and it *wasn't* Kent.

"Burke... Hauser," Kent said as he stood, extending his hand to shake, "welcome back. It's good to see you both."

Hauser gave him a perfunctory handshake, because of his tendency to crush grips, even with women, but Burke felt no such compulsion. She watched Kent's eyes tighten as she matched him grip for grip and bit back a predatory smile when he released the handshake first and surreptitiously massaged the affected hand as he returned to his seat. Kent wasn't a bad guy, just a tad old school at times; he liked his dominance games, which had led Burke to wonder what insecurities lived at his core more than once.

"Thank you, sir," Hauser said as Burke eased into the seat beside her.

"Have you scheduled appointments for your psych evaluations yet?" Kent asked. "Yes, I know they're a pain, but I'm afraid they're required."

Burke pursed her lips. "How should I handle my new... uhm, well... status?"

Kent didn't *quite* wince. "Yes. I read Hauser's after-action report, and it made for an interesting recounting. We also need to hold an inquiry into the matter, since there were deaths involved, but given the nature of the situation, that's just a formality. I can't imagine any review board ruling any of those deaths as unjustified.

"But regarding your psych evaluation, don't mention that you're now a shifter; none of the psychologists available at the moment have been cleared for that information. We've provided sanitized reports to those who will handle your evaluations, and you should read over them, just so you know what they've seen."

Kent pulled a manila folder out of a stack and extended it across the table. Hauser accepted it.

While that was a relief of sorts, Burke wasn't sure it was such a good idea to lie to psychologists. But... if that was the game they had to play, so be it.

"Sir, I've given the matter some thought," Burke said, "and as soon as all of my responsibilities stemming from our last case are complete, I will resign. A wealth of unforeseen opportunities now stands in front of me, and I would be a fool not to grab them with both hands."

Kent nodded. "I understand, and if we're being honest, I suspected such a decision would not be long in coming. What of you, Hauser?"

Hauser smiled. "I, too, am looking for other challenges in life, and I will turn in my resignation at a similar time. Probably the exact, same moment..."

"I saw that one coming, too," Kent replied, adding a rueful chuckle. "I will be sorry to see both of you go. You've been commendable assets to this office and the agency, and I can't help but feel you will be missed. Please use me as a reference if you ever need such."

Both Burke and Hauser thanked him for the offer of a reference, but no one in the room expected they'd ever use it. Burke wondered if Hauser should have mentioned she had decided to pursue becoming a shifter, but decided it wasn't his business… or hers for that matter.

"Well, I'll see about expediting the review boards, and the psychologists are waiting on you," Kent said after a few moments of silence. "Stop by when you finish the reviews, but otherwise, consider yourselves on terminal leave. The past few days barely touched the time you've accumulated."

Burke thanked him first, with Hauser right on her heels. Then, they stood and left his office.

"Let's stop by our desks and read through these," Hauser said, indicating the manila folder with the sanitized reports. "Then, we might as well get those psych evals out of the way. I have to admit I'm eager to get back to Precious."

Burke grinned. "You and me both. I want to go hunting again."

"I thought Godwin County was one of those weird prohibited-hunting zones," a passing agent remarked.

Thinking fast, Burke gave him her best salacious expression. "That depends on what one is hunting, Skyler."

The poor soul swallowed hard and backed away, before turning and hustling on his way.

They waited for him to get out of earshot, then erupted in laughter as they settled at their desks.

TWENTY MINUTES LATER, they leaned back in their seats after reading through the reports. It seemed Kent 'sanitized' them by removing any mention of Burke's gunshot wound and Wyatt saving her life with a bite. On the one side, it was effective, but it struck Burke as trying to use a cleaver for delicate surgery. Then again, considering what she knew of Kent, it kinda made sense.

"You finished?" Hauser asked.

Burke nodded. "The sanitizing seemed a bit heavy-handed."

Hauser snorted. "It almost had to be. Did you want to try to explain why you're up and walking around when you otherwise would've been in an ICU somewhere if not a grave?"

"You have a point, I suppose," Burke admitted, adding a grimace. "I don't know. I guess I just prefer to handle things with more finesse, but simple stories are easier to remember and use. Let's go do this. Who are you seeing?"

Hauser consulted the card that was waiting on her desktop. "I have Wacky Wilbur, it seems. You?"

Burke turned her card so Hauser could see. "Snoring Cora. One… two… three… break!"

They both jumped up from their seats and strode at a fast walk toward their respective appointments. The evaluations should only last an hour at the most, but with these two psychologists, there was no telling. It could be anywhere from thirty minutes to three hours.

FOUR DAYS LATER, Hauser and Burke returned to Precious, each driving a rented moving truck pulling an occupied car trailer. They eased their small convoy to a stop across from the hotel and climbed down from the driver's seats.

"My, oh my," Burke said as she stretched. "Smell that clean and *free* air."

Hauser laughed and shook her head. "It's not like they

were holding us against our will, you know. You could've resigned at any point."

Burke snorted. "And do what? At least now, we have interesting options to compete with everything we did and saw as special agents. Come on. Let's go find Wyatt and tell him the good news."

"Sure we should just leave the trucks here like this?" Hauser asked, scanning the street. "I think we're mostly off the street and in the parking lane, but maybe we should ask someone what we should do with them first."

"Wyatt can tell us what to do with them," Burke replied, adding a shrug. "Besides, if we're going to live here, we'll need houses. I like the hotel, but I'd rather not *live* there. I wonder if there is any property for sale in town."

Sheriff Clyde rolled to a stop beside them and tipped his hat. "Mornin', ladies. How goes it?"

"Morning, Sheriff Clyde," Burke chirped. "We quit our jobs and hope to move to Precious. What should we do with these rigs until we find somewhere to put down some roots?"

Clyde scratched his chin for a second before answering, "Well, they'll be okay there for a while, but if you'd like to get them off Main Street, the easiest would probably be putting them in the park's car lot. Everyone around town tends to walk, anyway, so it's hardly ever used... let alone full. You serious about resigning from your federal agency?"

Hauser nodded. "Yes. Wyatt offered for me to become a shifter, too, and... well... we spend so much time here anyway that it seemed like the best idea."

Clyde nodded. "Well, if either of you find yourself missing law enforcement, run me down. I'm always looking for good deputies, and once you get past the change, you two would be excellent."

"Thanks," Burke said, "but Wyatt was hinting around

about something if we weren't Feds, so we should probably have a word with him first… just so we don't make him mad."

"You ain't wrong there," Clyde agreed. "No reason to have his dander up over poaching the two of you from whatever he wanted." He lifted his hand in a friendly wave. "Well, I'll be gettin' on. Welcome to town."

He eased off the brake of his pickup truck and headed on down the street.

Burke turned to Hauser. "You said you wanted to get the convoy off the street. Want to move these to the park's lot before we find Wyatt?"

"That sounds good to me." Hauser said as she returned to her truck. "We need a place to unload everything before we return the trucks and trailers, too. But I figure a few days won't be too bad."

They ascended to their respective driver's seats and fired up the engines. A few minutes later, they were back on Main Street, headed to the hotel. Melody seemed to know what happened around town, so maybe she could direct them to a realtor or something. They hadn't seen any signs for one during all their explorations, so it was a bit of a puzzle where they should go to see about places to live.

A SHORT TIME LATER, they stood in Lyssa's office and watched while she consulted a large map of the town hanging on one wall. Most houses or lots had a red dot on them, but several didn't. Lyssa made a list of available houses and a second list of available lots where they each could build a house to suit them.

"Here you go. Let me know if you see any you like," she said after making a copy of the lists so both of them could have one of each.

Burke frowned. "But how will we pay for them? We don't have a job yet."

Lyssa smiled. "Don't worry about that just yet. See if you find a place you like, and we'll go from there."

They left the office and scanned the lists. Each stretched onto a second page, and there were a few available houses that were either side by side or across the street from one another. Most of the available lots were part of what seemed to be a burgeoning housing development on the town map Lyssa had.

"How do we want to do this?" Burke asked. "Each of us take a list and combine notes at lunch or dinner? Or do we work through them together?"

Hauser shrugged. "We don't really have anything important that requires our attention, so it's not like we're pressed for time. Why don't we work through the lists together?"

Burke nodded, and they set off to the first house on the list.

16

Lyssa wanted to rend something with her claws. But… she wasn't sure that would help. Yes, making her feel better was 'help' in a general sense, but she wasn't sure it would assist in achieving her goal. The Shifter Council was being… difficult. The councilors resisted her efforts to alert them to the threat posed by the Fae. Enough of those councilors said the same things that she suspected they worked as a bloc, either following the same councilor or the same idea.

No matter how she approached the matter, she hit a wall. Her friends and allies on the Council agreed with her that they needed to prepare, but those were just *her* friends and allies. And as much as she disliked the idea, she saw no alternative but to 'bring in the big guns.'

Guns? Ha! Try nukes. When Wyatt saw some of the emails she wanted to show him, a handful of councilors would be lucky to escape alive.

She collected her laptop and secured it as she reflected on how happy she was for finding someone who valued her for her. Not because she was a lioness. Not because she came from one of the more prestigious lion families. Not because she was a councilor. Not even because she was an attractive woman. Wyatt loved her for the person she was, and *that* was a very special feeling.

Lyssa left the admin building with a bright smile accessorizing her professional attire.

SHE FOUND him in the diner, lingering over a glass of tea with his tablet. His expression suggested he was working through the human news, as he liked to do.

"Hello, there," she almost purred as she arrived at his table. "Have room for a lioness in need of attention?"

Wyatt looked up and smiled. "I always have room for you."

Lyssa moved to the chair closest to him, and Wyatt stood and pulled it back from the table before she could grasp it. She smiled her thanks as he helped her with it before returning to his own seat.

"I wasn't expecting to see you until this evening," Wyatt remarked, glass of tea in hand once more.

"I know, but there's something you need to know. The Council—well, members of it—are resisting my efforts to get all of us pulling together. That's not such a surprise, but I had hoped it wouldn't be so bad. It would really help if Miles were still around to show himself, but there's no telling when we'll see him again."

Wyatt eyed her with a thoughtful, considering expression. "That's part but not all. I've learned many of your tells, Sweetheart; what are you *not* telling me?"

Lyssa scanned the diner, all of a sudden feeling uncertain that this was really the place to show him the emails. They were *not kind*. But as much as she might like to divert Wyatt's attention until she could relocate him, that ship had sailed.

She recognized the intense undertone of his expression. He knew *something* had unsettled her.

Fine. So be it.

She turned to her satchel and retrieved her laptop. Raising the lid and signing back into it, she brought up the specific emails in their own windows... six in all. Then, she slid the laptop over to him.

His calm happiness flowed out of his demeanor, the more emails he read, and she knew when he read the last one. His white-knuckle grip on the tabletop *cracked* it.

"Are the councilors in Chicago right now?" he asked, his voice deceptively calm.

Lyssa nodded. "Except for me, the entire Council is."

"No one leaves until we get there. I'll hunt anyone who runs like the prey they are."

I DROPPED a fifty-dollar bill on the table and left the diner. The emails Lyssa just showed me had me seething, and I could feel my nails trying to shift into claws and my incisors trying to lengthen. How *dare* they use that kind of language with anyone, let alone Lyssa?

I pulled my phone out of my hip pocket and dialed Karleen.

She answered on the first ring, "Hello, sweetie. What do you need?"

"Do you have anything planned for the next... say... five days or so?"

"Not really. Why?"

I fought to maintain a calm, even tone in my voice... no matter the actual truth of my feelings. "I'm taking Lyssa to Chicago to educate some councilors, and I'd like you and Burke to attend. I don't want Gabrielle to feel slighted, so she's invited, too. Besides, if any of the cowards run, I'll need the Huntress."

Silence ensued and spanned several seconds before she responded, "So, they've finally crossed a line even you won't forgive?"

"Have Lyssa show you the emails on the plane. I'd rather you find Gabrielle and pack a suitcase or three. I want to be in the air soonest."

It was horribly rude, but I ended the call without saying goodbye or waiting for her answer. But I couldn't afford the thought-space. It was a miracle I hadn't crushed my phone already, given the incandescent rage that coursed through me.

I went back to my contacts and sought Burke's number. I paused, realizing I didn't know if the number was a government phone or not, and saw the nail of my index finger looked far more like a claw than a fingernail. I needed to relax. Save the destructive rage for the councilors who crossed the line.

I tapped the number and listened to the phone ring.

Burke answered, "Hello?"

"Hi. It's Wyatt. I need you to come with me and the ladies to Chicago. I have learned that the Shifter Council requires *education*, and you're going to help me prove a point."

"Uhm... okay... I don't really understand, but whatever. I'll grab Hauser—"

"No," I interrupted her. "This is shifter business. If or when she makes the change, then she'll be welcome, but until then, she cannot follow. Frankly, it would be dangerous to take her into this. Humans are far too fragile. Pack for a week and meet us at the Alpha's house."

Once again, I ended the call without proper phone courtesy. I didn't like that, and I made a mental note to apologize later. As soon as I didn't feel like I was teetering on the edge of the abyss...

I needed to get some anger out, but I didn't want anyone in that line of fire who wasn't one of six very specific councilors. Instead, I went home. I needed to pack too, and as I walked the sidewalk, I noticed other citizens of the town crossing the street before they met me.

It was *that* more than anything that drove home what kind of mood I projected. I didn't like it, but my sole thought —my *only* thought—was rending six councilors limb from limb. The speed at which I did so was negotiable. Number Six... well, it might take me a day or two finish with *him*.

I ARRIVED at the Alpha's house at the same time Gabrielle and Karleen did. They took one look at me and shook their heads.

"So, who screwed up?" Karleen asked.

I shook my head as I turned toward our bedroom. "I don't remember their names. Get Lyssa to show you the emails on the plane. I'm going to have Burke kick one of their asses, just to prove the point that they're not the hot shit they think they are. I'll deal with the other five myself."

By that point, I had a suitcase on one of the luggage stands, and I was reaching for my clothes to start stuffing them inside. Gabrielle stepped in front of me.

"No, Wyatt. You're too keyed up right now to do something delicate like this. Go pace in the backyard. Karleen and I will take care of it."

As much as I hated the idea of anyone doing something as menial as packing a suitcase for me, she was right. In my current state of mind, I'd shred my clothes before they reached the luggage.

"Thank you," I said and did as she asked. Well... mostly.

At the bedroom door, I stopped and turned, saying, "Be sure to pack the knife Grandpa gave me, too."

The moment I stood on the patio of our backyard, I stripped and shifted to full Smilodon. That blunted the edge of my rage a bit. As a cat, I understood that I couldn't act *right now*; I needed to stalk my prey. But its time would come.

I padded across the backyard and curled up under the shade of the tree, closing my eyes for a nap and trusting one of my ladies to wake me up when everyone was ready.

KARLEEN AND GABRIELLE almost pounced on her when Lyssa walked through the door of the Alpha's house. She saw the Smilodon dozing in the shade of the massive tree in the backyard, and she felt like thanking someone—she wasn't sure quite who—that Wyatt had the presence of mind to retire to the shade and let them handle the preparations.

If she were being honest... she expected a certain level of anger over the content of the emails she showed him, but she never expected they would enrage him to the degree that they did. Certainly not enough to storm the Council chambers in Chicago. And that's what it felt like Wyatt was doing.

Part of her was afraid of where it would lead. The Shifter Nation was *stable*. Everyone worked with the Council. Everyone respected the Council. For the first time, she saw the danger of having a Consul of the Shifter Nation, but at the same time, she also knew that no army led by a committee ever won. There needed to be someone out front waving a sword or flag or gun or *something* while shouting, 'This is a righteous fight! Follow me!'

But what would it mean for shifter society in general if Wyatt succeeded in bringing back the primogenitors? She didn't see how he could do it in the time he had, even though they didn't *know* how much time they had, but what would that mean for shifters like her? The 'lesser children' Merlin had called them. Would a resurgence mean that they became second-class citizens in their own society? After all, it was a society based on strength, and no modern shifter could ever hope to stand up to a primogenitor, especially one on one.

All this and more swirled through her mind as she led the other ladies back to their master suite in the house. As she herself packed and helped Gabrielle and Karleen pack for Wyatt, she gave them an overview of the emails that set Wyatt off and promised to show them once they were in the air. After all, she didn't want to repeat the story for Burke.

All too soon it seemed, they had their luggage packed. Burke stood with them, a suitcase at her feet as well. All three of them gazed out the back windows to the dozing Smilodon. He was so calm and relaxed just then that no one wanted to disturb him, but Lyssa remembered his expression as he walked out of the diner. She *knew* where his mind was, and if he had to work out some anger, she wanted it to be on the offending councilors and not some innocent tree or animal.

She left the house and trudged across the backyard, stopping when she reached the gigantic cat. He didn't react to her arrival, so she leaned over and ruffled the fur on his head. He... well, meowed but a baritone meow... and pressed against her hand.

"Oh, you like that, do you?" she asked as she moved to rub his ears.

If Smilodons could smile, Wyatt surely was at that point.

"We're all packed, and Burke is here with a suitcase too."

Wyatt huffed a sigh and opened his eyes as he pushed himself to his feet. He padded across the backyard and shifted back to human, because he didn't want to wait for them to locate a truck that could transport a thousand-pound cat without endangering the suspension. His clothes were right where he left them, and he dressed. He didn't rush, but he didn't waste any time.

He slipped his phone into his hip pocket and slipped his arm around Lyssa's waist, pulling her close to him. He kissed her forehead and held her for another moment or three. Then, he released her and went inside.

It was time to go to Chicago.

17

I spent the flight from Spokane to Chicago re-reading the language of the document that invested me as Consul of the Shifters of North America. We were still about an hour from landing when I leaned back and considered what I held. Lyssa and her people gave the office some teeth and claws, and that wasn't just a shifter pun. If I chose to use the authority the document entrusted to me, I was the de facto ruler of all shifters from Mexico's southern border to the geographic north pole.

That's right. The *ruler*.

As Consul, I had the authority to override the Shifter Council, and I couldn't believe they agreed to that. I couldn't believe they agreed to limit themselves to an advisory and executive body if I so chose.

Lyssa sat diagonally to my left, those two seats facing mine and the empty one to my immediate left. She seemed engrossed in a paperback that had a shirtless guy with a hottie wrapped around him on the cover. But when I drew breath to ask her if she had a minute, she slipped a bookmark into her place and focused on me.

"Yes, Wyatt?"

"Did the rest of the Council realize the full extent of the authority you gave me?"

I watched as she fought the urge to smile as she said, "Well... maybe not precisely, no. My friends and I talked for so long and refused to move on to other business that they pretty much threw up their hands and told us to do what we wanted, and they'd sign it, too."

Lyssa should've been a cheetah. She pulled *that* many fast ones. Either that or a fox.

"So, when I was planning to hit them like gangbusters, they would've been caught totally unawares and probably not realized they were impinging upon authority that they themselves granted me?"

She shrugged. Her expression of faux innocence reminded me of a street hustler getting interrogated by the police. "Maybe."

"Just how many of the councilors am I going to have to kill, Lyssa? You know I don't like to do that, but I don't mean the six in the emails. They're already dead. I'm talking about the rest of them."

"Well, I hope not too many. I know my friends and allies are behind you, but it depends on whether the rest dig in their heels 'on principle' or not."

Yeah... there was no way this wasn't coming home to roost eventually. But now wasn't the time. I needed to keep my head right and focused on the six who chose to call Lyssa the kind of names one wouldn't even use for street-based sex workers.

Damn. I still needed to track down someone to teach me unarmed fighting. Maybe a shifter somewhere had developed a fighting style... no, probably not. Since modern shifters only had two forms without partial shifting or the hybrid form, it was unlikely anyone had developed a fighting style that utilized claws while humanoid.

"Remind me to find and change a top-shelf martial artist to a primogenitor. Preferably one who has already developed his or her own style," I said in that distracted tone that communicated the thought didn't have my full focus.

Lyssa frowned, then asked, "Why?"

At a mere thought and flex of will, my left forearm became a furry arm capable of extending claws from my fingers and thumb. "Because we need a fighting style to take advantage of the abilities only we have."

She stared at my partially shifted arm with wide eyes. "Oh."

I absently nodded and delved back into my thoughts. The fact that the councilors might not understand they worked for me now changed the entire dynamic of the situation. Yes, six councilors would not leave Chicago alive; that much was a given. I had half a mind to print out their emails and stake them to the corpses, but that might be a bit much. I'd have to ask Gabrielle. She tended to help me understand what was appropriate in shifter society. So much of it still seemed alien even three or so months in.

The flight attendant walked through the cabin asking us to fasten our seatbelts as we were about to start our descent into Chicago. We complied, and as I nodded my thanks, she gave me a wink in return.

It wasn't long until we taxied into a hangar, and I had to hand it to the pilots. Even with my enhanced senses, I never felt the wheels kiss the runway. Must've been former Air Force; they never needed to hook the arrester cable on a carrier.

As we gathered our belongings and deplaned, I asked Lyssa, "So, the Council doesn't know we're on the way, right? This will be a surprise?"

Lyssa nodded. "I promise you it will be a surprise, Wyatt. I was supposed to attend this time via video conference from Precious. They have no idea we're in town."

"No spies at the airport or anything like that?"

She just shook her head.

I glanced around as we walked to our waiting transportation. From our location, I couldn't see much of the fabled Windy City's skyline, but perhaps that would change. This was my first visit... in fact, my first time east of the Mississippi River... and I almost wanted to take an extra day or two and explore the city. I wasn't certain we'd have the chance, to be honest, but it's always nice to dream... right?

We all piled into an SUV with three rows of seats. Lyssa took shotgun, and I found myself sandwiched between Gabrielle and Karleen in the second row, with Moira and Burke in the back row. My ladies seemed intent on keeping me safe—from what, I wasn't sure—and as much as I would've liked to rubberneck near a window, it cost me nothing to let them do their thing. I supposed we could always come back to Chicago to do the tourist thing when corrective education wasn't on the docket.

THE SUV ENTERED an underground parking area beneath a stately structure that looked old enough to have survived the last time Chicago as a whole burned. A massive edifice of cut stone with gargoyles on every corner of the roof and aged-bronze door fixtures, it looked rather impressive and damned old. Waxed and polished stone flooring. Marble columns everywhere. I was almost afraid to enter the place for fear I'd get it dirty and devalue the priceless work of art.

Lyssa's heels echoed down the otherwise-vacant hall as she led us to the elevator. All of us managed to fit inside, and my lioness tapped the button for the third floor.

"I thought I saw four floors of windows," I commented as the elevator started to rise.

Lyssa smiled. "You did. We remodeled the top two floors to become the Council's meeting chambers when we took possession of the building."

"And how long ago was that? Were sections of Chicago still smoldering at the time?"

A faint smirk curled one side of Lyssa's perfect lips as the elevator dinged and opened its doors. She stepped into the hallway as she said over her shoulder, "Maybe."

She led us to a set of massive wooden doors with exquisite carvings of a multitude of animals, all rampant. Before she opened the door, I held up my hand and leaned close to examine the artwork. Each animal had textured fur or feathers, and they looked ready to leap out of the wood and into reality. Impressive work.

"This... is remarkable," I said. "Gorgeous, even."

Lyssa beamed. "Thank you. Poppa did them."

She had yet to mention *why* her father wasn't around anymore, and I wasn't sure if he was just elsewhere in the world or dead. I didn't want to poke an old wound, so I just let it be and stepped back, nodding for her to proceed.

She squeezed the latches and threw the doors wide, and I entered an indoor amphitheater with massive hemispherical seating that was full, except for two seats. I suspected the individual who should occupy one of them was the frowning fellow standing behind a lectern to my right.

"How dare you interrupt the proceedings of the Shifter Council!" he growled, then blinked when Lyssa stepped out from behind me. My other ladies and Burke fanned out as well, Burke acting very much like she was on a protective detail as she watched everything and nothing.

Lyssa approached the lectern and slipped the gavel right

out of the man's startled hands, striking the block three times in quick succession. My shifter hearing did not appreciate the *crack!* each time it struck.

"Hear ye, hear ye," Lyssa intoned in a hall-filling voice. "All rise for the Consul of the Shifters of North America, Wyatt Magnusson."

Only a handful moved to stand at first—Lyssa's friends, I figured—but the motion was enough to start a cascade of people standing until the entire Council stood to receive me. I felt my Smilodon want to preen at the grandiose respect, and I fought the urge to snort a laugh. What was next? Beads in his fur? A silver-studded collar?

I crossed the distance to the lectern as Lyssa led the still-frowning fellow to stand in front of their respective seats. When I arrived, I produced a folded piece of paper from my hip pocket and unfolded it on the lectern's document stand.

"Thank you, one and all. Please, be seated." I waited as everyone returned to their seats, my ladies and Burke finding their own seating close to me. "I am primarily here to have a not-so-quiet word with six of your number, but once I've accomplished that and someone has cleaned the blood off the floor, there is some other business we can discuss."

I paused in my remarks, which led some brave soul to shout a question, "And just what makes you think your blood won't be what's cleaned off the floor?"

I lifted my eyes from the paper in front of me and gave that worthy fellow a smile that suggested he'd taste rather nice slathered in barbecue sauce with a side of steak fries. "Thomas Carlyle. Despite his full effort, he never broke my skin. Now then... let's see."

I scanned the paper in front of me for a few moments, then read off the six people whose life expectancies measured in minutes. "Step forward please."

When Lyssa showed me the emails back in Precious, it shocked me a little bit that two of the offenders were women, and aside from perusing my investiture as Consul during the flight, I considered whether they should face the same fate as the men for what they said in writing. At the end of it, I couldn't shake the anger that they would attack one of my ladies like they did.

The six impressed me by stepping forward and standing in a line. I left the lectern and walked over to stand about ten feet away from them.

"We're here because of the abuse you levied upon Lyssa in emails this morning," I said to them, pitching my voice for the room at large to hear. "Now, Lyssa is more than capable of fighting her battles, but each of you used rather offensive language against a lady I hold rather dear. So, I shall give you the choice." I reached behind my back and drew the shifter-bane blade that bore the Magnusson Glyph and held it up for them to see. "You can do the deed yourself, thereby admitting your guilt to one and all, or I shall challenge you and kill you... eventually." I pointed to the woman standing at the end of the line to my left. "You first."

Her eyes flicked back and forth between my face and the naked blade in my hand. Her expression betrayed a barely controlled terror. She took several deep breaths, and then, I watched her eyes harden into a glare. Her hand shot out, and she grasped the hilt, pulling it free of my hands and looking triumphant.

But not for long.

The runes engraved into the blade soon glowed an angry red, and her eyes shot wide as the sound of sizzling flesh reached our ears moments before she screamed and dropped the knife.

"Yeah... about that," I said, reaching out to catch the falling knife by its hilt. "Grandpa always embeds a protection in any blade he imbues. Only direct blood members of the Magnusson family may wield them and must give intentional permission to anyone else to touch them." I turned to one of my ladies. "Gabrielle, please hold this for me."

The woman known throughout the western half of the continent as the Huntress crossed to my side and allowed me to place the blade into her hands, then wrapping her hand around the hilt. The runes in the blade glowed silver in the presence of a shifter—well, several shifters—but otherwise, nothing happened.

The woman who helped herself to my own blade and probably thought to stab me with it held up her hand, revealing the Magnusson Glyph burned into her palm, her face a mask of agony enshrouded in rage. "You bastard... you *knew* this would happen."

I snorted. "Damn, I wish I was that lucky, but no. My parents are very well acquainted with each other. But yes, you're correct; I did know. And... you tried to kill me. Thanks for the excuse."

I moved so fast I probably looked like a blur to everyone else in the room. When I stopped moving, I stood at my starting point, except my left forearm was partially shifted and ended in five bloody claws. The woman collapsed—first to her knees, then her side—clutching the shredded remains of her throat, an injury delivered by a shifter's natural weapons and exempt from our incredible healing.

I watched her bleed out, and soon, the light faded from her eyes. I turned to the remaining five just in time for the scent of their sheer, unmitigated terror to reach me. Yes, they pissed themselves, one and all... and more than a few of the audience, too. The air handlers circulated the scents around the room. All five of them stared at my bloody claws, like the Grim Reaper himself—or herself, who am I to judge?—stood before them. Almost as one, they fell to their knees, and garbled groveling ensued.

"Lyssa, darling," I said as blood still dripped from my claws to the floor below, "they appear to be rather interested in maintaining their lives. What penance do you feel is worth their disrespect?"

The lady in question kept her seat but spoke loud enough for the entire hall to hear. "I've heard whispers around town of something you did to Karleen's brother. I'd say that's fitting."

"Are you sure?"

"I think so, yes."

I partially shifted my right arm, because despite being ambidextrous for most things since becoming a shifter, my left-handed penmanship still looked like drunken scrawl. I approached the sole remaining woman and extended the claw from my right index finger.

And carved 'PRECIOUS' into her forehead to the accompaniment of her pained screams. Then, I went right down the line repeating it for each of those remaining.

When I finished, Karleen was at my side with wet wipes to clean the blood from my—paw-hands?—before I shifted them back to human. As she helped me, I considered the matter and didn't feel Lyssa's solution was enough.

"On further consideration, that is insufficient penance for your transgressions," I said, piquing their terror once more. "Those who hold seats on the Shifter Council should represent the best of us. The most honorable. The most self-sacrificing. The most compassionate. Councilors should be role models for shifters everywhere. You will vacate your seats immediately and publish the unvarnished truth of what prompted it. I will review your publications and find you if you lie in any way. Do you understand?"

The remaining five bobbed nods that sent drops of blood flying.

"Good. Now, leave. The Shifter Council has serious business to discuss." They pushed themselves to stand and headed toward the door. "Oh, one more thing…" They froze. "I trust it goes without saying that you will not enjoy the outcome if we cross paths again."

Without another word, they fled the chamber.

18

The Shifter Council sat in their seats, lining the hemispherical meeting hall, and I had their full, undivided attention. They were now down six members. One bled out on the floor near my feet, and the rest fled. I considered myself an easygoing guy, by and large, but I could not countenance people abusing one of my ladies. And the language used in the emails those six sent to Lyssa was indeed abusive.

But we had bigger fish to fry, as the saying goes.

I scanned the area around me and found a stack of chairs that looked mostly comfortable. I gestured to them, saying, "Ladies, help yourselves. I'm not sure how long this will take."

Truth be told, *I* wanted to sit, too. But I remembered something someone told me once, and I wasn't even sure who said it at that point in my life. Stand when you lead. I probably butchered the quote, but the gist was there.

I walked back to the lectern and had to force myself not to lean on it as I surveyed my audience.

"Hello. Like Lyssa said, I'm Wyatt Magnusson, and I'm

afraid I have a few things to discuss that will unsettle you. Probably many of you. But maybe only a few. I can't read minds, so I have no way to know."

I paused for a breath that took all my willpower not to come out as a sigh. This was not how I wanted to spend today, but it needed to be done. We needed to start preparations.

"So, the first topic that might unsettle you. You work for me now." Yep. Unhappy frowns. Some anger. A few mutters. "And you have since you invested me as Consul of the Shifters of North America. Don't believe me? Read the document all of you approved. I have. My favorite part was the sentence buried deep in the bottom third of it that said the office can only change hands or be revoked through a dominance challenge, according to our laws and traditions." Oh, boy. That woke more than a few of them up. They did *not* like that at all. "Now, for the most part, I don't care what you do. From what little I've learned of shifter society, you seem to do your jobs rather well for the most part. But I will not countenance people who act like Thomas Carlyle before our challenge—or the five I just sent packing—to stain this group with their dishonor. Take the time to absorb and understand that. It is the bedrock principle of this Council now; treat others with respect and honor... from the lowest of the low to the highest of the high. If you have a problem with that, I live in Precious, and you're welcome to drop by anytime and lose the fight over it."

More than one person chuckled at my phrasing, but I saw no indications that anyone *doubted* it. Good.

"Okay. I'm not one to percuss a deceased equine. I hope I've made myself clear, but if I haven't, I live in Precious, like I said. Moving on."

I turned and walked over to Moira where she sat,

gesturing for her to meet me, and I led her back to the lectern.

"The next unsettling topic—and I'm here to tell you it has certainly unsettled me—is that we have a war coming. What many of you might not realize is that I am the great-great-grandson of Merlin, the Magi of legend. I knew him for years as a kindly old groundskeeper at my grandparents' estate, but that's another matter. We had a chat not too long ago about certain signs he has uncovered recently that point to a coming invasion by the Fae. They've attempted it before, but your ancestors—the primogenitors—fought them off... along with his help. They are inter-dimensional scavengers, it seems, invading worlds to harvest power and resources to enrich their own. We need to start preparing, because they're coming back."

I gestured to Moira.

"I rescued her from the bunker serving as the base for the group hunting Sloane Martinez. She is a Fae scout. She now works for me and has prepared a report on everything she knows about their military, strategies, and tactics. I will be releasing that information to our war council in the days and weeks ahead, but first... we should probably form said war council."

Chuckles at that. Good. I was dumping a lot of information on them in a short amount of time, and I didn't want them overwhelmed.

"But here's one more truth I know most of you won't like. We can't fight this war alone, folks. We simply cannot. I'm sure most—if not all—of you have heard eye-witness accounts of the challenge between me and Thomas Carlyle, and I hope those accounts included the fact that he never drew blood. Neither his claws nor his teeth penetrated my Smilodon's hide. That alone should attest to the power disparity between shifters and primogenitors, but there's something else, too."

I shifted into my hybrid—or synthesis—form. I felt my clothes tighten around me, so I knew not to try any acrobatics, but If I moved slow and careful, I should be able to pull off my demonstration.

"We can also do this." My spoken voice now sounded like the growly voice that had shared my head for those first several weeks of my shifter life. I lifted my hands and extended claws from every finger and thumb. "And this."

I stood in that pose for several seconds. Arms raised just enough to show my furry paw-like hands that now sported five claws each. I wanted everyone to get a good look. When I heard what I thought was a seam starting to rip, I shifted back to human.

"I want you to think about this. The Fae *killed* primogenitors, folks. All of you together are probably a danger to me, but one on one? Not a chance. Probably not even five on one. And there is an enemy coming who can kill me. So, take a second and think about what that means for you... what it means for the modern shifters. That's why we're going to build closer ties with the Magi. During the first Fae war, we only had *one* Magi, and he walked away with the title Bane of the Fae Courts. We still have him, but there's no reason to rely *solely* on him."

I paused and scanned the faces looking back at me. I saw more than one person start to realize the full extent of my message.

"And the last thing you're not going to like is that we can't fight the war in the shadows. The shifters—and the Magi—will have to announce themselves to the world. I know this goes against everything you believe. Everything you've lived your whole lives. I know it won't be easy, and there will be conflict and unease on all sides. But the fact remains that we don't have a choice, no viable choices anyway."

Once more, I roamed over the audience with my eyes. *None* of them liked the idea of revealing ourselves to the humans. I expected that.

"The thing is, I wanted you to know first. I wanted you to be aware of what was coming and help us make the best plan possible to achieve our goals. The plan will fail; expect that. No plan survives long. Lyssa can be the liaison between me and the Council for day-to-day matters. For major matters, like our discussion today, I'll come here. But next time, I'm not taking a plane, folks. That's too damn slow. Next time, I will arrive via a Magi portal, and that's something you also need to understand and accept. We need them now, just like they need us. Just like the humans need both of us. So, the petty sniping and feuds and discontent stop now. As with the other points, I live in Precious, and you're welcome to come disagree with me as violently as you like... just don't be surprised when I hand you your ass once the violence passes a certain threshold. We all have better things to do now."

I started to turn toward the door but had a thought.

"Oh... and I'm sure you'll have more than a few irate alphas once you communicate all of this. That's fine. Be sure to tell them where I live along with everything else, and be sure they have my invitation to conduct a personal conversation if they so choose. Just be sure to warn them what they're in for if they come with claws instead of words. Lyssa or I will share more information as we have it. Good day to you."

That time, I did turn and lead Moira and my ladies out of the meeting chamber. I probably should've waited to see if Lyssa followed, but it was too good of a moment to let pass.

When we reached the elevator in the hall, I pressed the button and casually looked behind me, smiling when I saw Lyssa hustling to catch us. Yeah... there would be fallout from everything I just dropped in their laps, but I figured they'd need time to bluster and posture about it before they settled down into a working mindset. I didn't want to be there for the blustering and posturing. They were already down six councilors, and they didn't need any more vacancies.

The elevator bell dinged right before the doors opened, and we all piled inside. As the doors closed and the car started to descend, I realized I didn't even know the breeds of the six councilors I had dispatched.

LYSSA FELT like reeling as she rode the elevator back to the underground parking with everyone. In all the annals of the Shifter Council she had read, *no one* had ever been as abrupt, dismissive, or straightforward with even one councilor as Wyatt had just been with the *entire Council*. It shouldn't have surprised her. Wyatt had never seemed to care for the more involved social niceties, and she shouldn't have expected him to start now.

But he certainly left her a mess to clean up.

Because at the end of the day, the Council wouldn't hound *him* with their questions and their complaints and their excuses. Oh, no. They'd come for *her*. Her, they knew. She was just like them. They could relate to her. Possibly defeat her, if it came down to a fight.

Unlike Wyatt… in all respects.

When they made it home and he had a chance to sleep off the trip—maybe go for a run in his fur—she would sit him down and explain the situation he just created. Make sure he understood it from all angles.

She fought the urge to snort a laugh. It wasn't difficult in the crowded confines of the elevator. A part of her just wondered if this was his revenge for how she had shoe-horned him into the office in the first place. That part of her wouldn't put it past him, but at the same, he wasn't the petty or vindictive sort. She *knew* those types of people. Knew them well. Avoided them when she could, and documented *everything* when she couldn't.

Unbidden, memories floated to the surface of a smarmy TV repairman in the next town over from where she grew up. He was a little guy, far too impressed with himself, and seemed to think he was God's gift to women, the way he strutted around like a banty rooster. He played the game well enough, but there was no mistaking the unsettling vibe he carried with him.

As the elevator eased to a stop, she realized he had to be in his eighties at least now, and he was human. So, there was that small blessing. Not that there weren't men like him among shifters, just that they tended to be fewer... and smarter, unfortunately. More than one father had won a duel against a young punk when the punk had mistreated a daughter.

She allowed herself a small smile as she followed everyone to the SUVs. That was one of the advantages of being a literal lion among the shifters. Outside of the primo-genitors, lions were one of the strongest shifters. The only breed that really gave them any competition were the tiger shifters. It was the rare punk who had the nerve to try anything with her or her sisters. They themselves were supremely capable of removing the offending appendage without any interference from dear ol' dad.

Her train of thought extended to the idea of she and Wyatt having one or more daughters, and that time, she didn't catch herself fast enough. She *did* snort a laugh. She almost felt sorry for any boyfriends they had the nerve to bring home. Wyatt would terrify them.

She realized more than one person sent questioning glances her way, but she waved them off as she resumed her seat in the SUV. With everything he already had on his plate, she didn't want to add the additional stress of thinking about children to Wyatt's shoulders.

No. When they were home and slept off the trip, she'd conspire with Gabrielle and Karleen to take Wyatt on a run in their fur.

The SUVs began the trip back to the airport, and the more she considered the idea of a run in their fur, the more she liked it. They needed the uncomplicated, stress-free existence their animals provided, and it had been far too long since they had partaken of it.

19

Moira looked out the window of her room that overlooked the backyard. It was so surreal, watching four predators lounge around in the shade or romp among themselves. A Smilodon. A melanistic jaguar. A lioness. A dire wolf. The Smilodon and dire wolf were familiar to her from the sketches and accounts in the ancient chronicles. The melanistic jaguar and lioness were new to her.

Before they went outside, Lyssa invited her down to join them, even though Moira couldn't shift. She liked Lyssa. Gabrielle and Karleen were nice, too. She still battled an existential terror every time she laid eyes on Wyatt. Ever since his sister revealed their ancestry, the familial resemblance was glaring to her... especially after having seen them together.

On the one side, she *knew* she didn't need to fear Wyatt. Every time they encountered one another, he was still the pleasant, patient, kind man who had saved her from that bunker. He did not treat her any differently than he had when she first followed him back to Precious.

And yet... she treated him oh so differently.

She still had problems believing she held it together well enough to stand beside him in front of the Shifter Council. She hoped the gibbering panic she felt at being so close to one of Merlin's line never touched her face, but there was no denying it had come entirely too close to taking control of her.

She avoided him as much as she could now. She knew everyone noticed it... at least those who lived in the Alpha's house. She never ate with them. Never joined in any of the family events. Every time she was near him now, she wanted nothing more than to be as far away from him as possible.

He didn't deserve that from her, especially not after accepting her oath.

Did anyone realize the depth of terror her people had for Merlin? How could they? They had no way to understand the full meaning of his name among the Fae. The Bane of the Fae Courts. On the surface, so simple. But in the Fae language, it carried emotional experience beyond the capacity of human speech to deliver.

She cast an idle glance through the window and couldn't keep from smiling at the sight of Gabrielle the jaguar and Lyssa the lioness leaping on the Smilodon. She watched them, her smile growing as she saw the care Wyatt took not to harm them with his massive incisors or accidentally unsheathe his claws. In this form or the hybrid, he didn't terrify her, and that felt good. It felt... relaxing.

Perhaps, it wouldn't be so bad to spend an afternoon sunning on a chaise lounge.

At Moira's first cautious step outside, the four animals looked her way. When Moira stepped fully onto the patio and closed the door behind her, Karleen hopped to her feet, wagging her tail and charged across the backyard. They met at the chaise lounge closest to the house, and Karleen stopped in front of her, her tail wagging and her tongue lolling out one side of her muzzle in a canine grin. Moira smiled at the welcome and extended her hand to scratch between and behind Karleen's ears. The tail wagging kicked into high gear.

Moira sat on the chaise lounge, which put her just below eye level with Karleen. She half-expected the dire wolf to lick her, but Karleen didn't. She hung close until Moira relaxed onto the lounge, then dashed back to resume playing with Wyatt, Gabrielle, and Lyssa.

THE NEXT MORNING, I realized it had been a little bit since I checked in with Mina about her son Noah. Doc should have called me if there was bad news, but I still felt bad that so much time had passed.

On the walk to the infirmary, my mind wandered back over the day before. It was nice that Moira had joined us in the backyard for our relaxing afternoon and evening. I especially liked how she didn't seem to be afraid or uneasy around Smilodon me. So, maybe it was just human me reminding her of Merlin. I made a mental note to discuss that with Lyssa before we delved deeply into the war council. I wanted both Miles *and* Moira to attend, but Moira wouldn't be much help if she sat in the corner gibbering in terror at the sight of Miles.

I didn't expect that would be a particularly quick fix, either. That kind of pervasive, culturally ingrained fear… well… it was sometimes easier to convince the person the world was flat. But nothing worth doing is ever a quick, easy win, and I figured Lyssa would have a good idea on where to start with that. Me? No clue. I was a recovering IT geek who could turn into a pre-historic predator, not a psychologist.

And that brought up another thought. Would human psychology even be the place to start? After all, Moira *wasn't* human. Sure, she looked human, but I suspected that might be magic of some type. Something else for Lyssa to ask her.

Lyssa told me at breakfast that she had seen the draft of Moira's report on Fae military, and it was good. Comprehensive from what she could tell, and very detailed. Which was to the good. We needed as much information as we could get.

My thoughts carried me through the main entrance to the infirmary, and I turned left, intent on visiting the treatment ward first. Doc spent most of his time there.

The doors swooshed open at my approach, and Doc looked up from the publication in his hands. The cover I saw carried the name of a prominent medical association, but I would not be surprised to find a golf magazine inside it. Not for the first time, I wondered if Doc had chosen a career in medicine to have a cushy life and plenty of time for golf. Shifters didn't get sick, and it was rare that one of us actually needed emergency treatment. So, the 'city' of Precious pretty much paid him to sit at his desk and hide golf magazines inside whatever medical publication took his fancy.

I suppose I should've been a bit miffed at that, but honestly, I considered it to be a retainer. It wasn't uncommon for someone to need his medical expertise or his contacts, and having a good doctor in town was a lot like having a home defense plan. I'd rather have it and not need it, than need it and not have it.

The thought of a home defense plan made me chuckle. It seemed I hadn't completely rid myself of human views. A human had far more need for a home defense plan than a shifter, especially a primogenitor who lived with another primogenitor and two shifters. Like the man said, I pitied the fool who invaded our house; that poor dumbass was in for a bad night.

"Hey, Doc," I said as I crossed the ward to him, noticing the treatment bed where I'd last seen Noah was now empty.

Doc stood and extended his hand, giving me a respectful handshake. "Good day to you, Alpha Wyatt. What brings you to my side of the neighborhood?"

"I just wanted to check in with you about Noah Vickers. I hadn't heard anything, which I assumed meant good news. Or at least neutral news."

"Ah, yes," Doc said, nodding a few times. "Yes, I released young Noah to his mother's care as soon as he woke up and I made sure he was stable. As far as I know, he hasn't shifted yet, but it's only a matter of time. I believe Mina purchased a house in the new development over on Eighth Avenue. Buddy should know for certain; he's been visiting the young man for a few hours each day since I sent him home."

"Thanks, Doc. I appreciate it."

When I was over halfway back to the door, Doc asked, "Should I have contacted you when I released him?"

I shook my head. "Nope. Not unless there was a reason you should have. Thanks, Doc!"

SINCE I DIDN'T KNOW of anything pressing for my attention and since I had my cell phone, I decided to walk over to the housing development Doc mentioned. I didn't know of any property changing hands for Mina to create an office for her liaison duties, so as far as I knew, she was either working on that or operating out of her house for the moment. It didn't make much difference to me one way or the other; I was just glad we talked the government out of establishing a consulate in town.

When I arrived on Eighth Avenue, I saw Mina's place at

once. It was the only house in sight with two blacked-out SUVs sporting US Government plates. It was a charming ranch-style house on a decent-sized lot, and a couple of her protection detail stood at the end of the driveway having what appeared to be a heated discussion with someone.

As I entered into earshot, I fought to keep my expression impassive.

"No, ma'am," the agent said in that tone of forced patience trained into agents and officers the world over. "Miss Vickers does not need a plate of cookies right now. We appreciate the gesture and thank you."

The object of their denial turned enough that I recognized her. Nina Carstairs. She was the town's busiest busybody. She'd been all over us as we moved into the Alpha's house, and it took Karleen growling at her before she got the point she was being a bit too nosy for her own good. Part of me wondered if she was aiming to start a community newsletter, but I didn't see how she'd have enough material.

The agents saw me before Nina did, and they stiffened into a posture that wasn't *quite* an attention stance. That drew Nina's curiosity, and her smile was downright predatory when she saw me. Well, if she was going to make this difficult, I might as well have fun with her.

"Morning, folks," I said as I arrived on the scene. "I see you've met the local representative of the Shifter Intelligence Service." I fought the urge to grin when the agents stiffened even further. "You haven't let her in Mina's house yet, have you? This one's an expert at hiding listening devices in full view of three or four people. If you're not careful, she'll have Mina's house wired for 8-channel sound."

One of the agents stepped away and lifted her wrist to her mouth. She waited until she was a good distance away and spoke low, so I couldn't hear what she said, but the expression on Nina's face was priceless.

"Now, Alpha Wyatt, I have no idea what you mean. I'm just trying to welcome the new family to the community. There's nothing wrong with that, is there?"

She said all that around a shit-eating grin that would put a smarmy used-car salesman to shame, and that fact wasn't lost on the remaining agent.

"Ma'am," the agent intoned, "I'm going to have to ask you to move along. This is private property, and the owner isn't entertaining guests at this time. Alpha Wyatt, Ms. Vickers is waiting for you."

That wound up Nina's dander worse than a Category 5 hurricane. "Are you telling me that you're discriminating against me? What? Is it because I brought cookies? Everyone *loves* my cookies, I tell you. Everyone!"

The agent didn't bat an eye or change his expression in the slightest. "Ma'am, Alpha Wyatt is here on business. Should we decide a social hour is needed, we shall be sure to invite you. If you persist in refusing our request to leave, we shall be forced to contact local authorities."

I remembered the last time Nina pushed herself into someone else's business around town and the threats Sheriff Clyde made when she did, and I couldn't hide my smile. "Oh, please do, Agent. I'm sure Sheriff Clyde would love to have another word or four with Nina. Their last encounter was only a month ago, and I'm sure he's feeling withdrawal."

The agent snorted a laugh at that, but Nina didn't see the humor.

"Are you siding against one of your own, Alpha Wyatt? Well, I never!"

The agent who stepped away chose that moment to return. I adopted a thoughtful, considering pose as I said, "You know, that might be the problem. Maybe you should."

I half-expected to see smoke escape her ears any second,

but she remained strong. "Fine! I know when I'm not wanted. Good day, Alpha Wyatt!"

She pivoted on her heel and strode up the street, tossing the cookies into one of the city-sponsored trashcans that dotted the sidewalks around town. I watched her leave, and when she turned the corner and stomped out of sight, I turned back to the agents.

"Well, it is a good day now. You said Mina's expecting me?"

The agent's struggle to maintain a professional expression was obvious as he said, "Yes, Alpha Wyatt. Please, proceed inside."

I APPROACHED THE HOUSE AND, despite the agent's instruction to proceed inside, knocked. The door opened to reveal Mina, who smiled. "Please, come in, Alpha Wyatt."

"Thank you."

I stepped inside and saw they seemed to be still in a state of unpacking.

"Please forgive the moving boxes," Mina said as she led me to the dining room table. "My sister just arrived with the moving truck yesterday. We unloaded it, so she could return it, but we're still deciding where everything goes."

I waved her concerns away. "Don't worry about it at all. I just stopped by to see how Noah is doing."

Mina smiled. "Oh, he's doing just fine. He and Rex are playing in the backyard right now."

"Rex?"

"Rex is the German Shepherd I mentioned." Mina frowned. "At least, I think I mentioned him. I'm sorry. I'm still getting over being a bit frazzled from worry over Noah. Doc said he'll be fine, but it hasn't really sunk in yet, you know?"

"Of course," I replied, adding a few nods. "It will take a little time before you accept the new normal, but I imagine seeing him turn into a wolf will help a bit."

Mina laughed. "Oh, yes, I'm sure. He hasn't shifted yet, and Buddy said he may not for quite a while yet. Apparently, while born shifters can shift from birth, turned shifters at Noah's age sometimes don't have their first shift until after puberty."

"Wow. Did not know that."

The arrival of a young boy and a German Shepherd running in from the backyard interrupted whatever else I might have said. The second Rex got a sniff of me, he let out a heart-wrenching whine and rolled onto his back, exposing his throat.

Wow... so *that's* what it's like to have animals afraid of you. I needed to remember to mention it to Karleen.

"Hey," Noah said. "What's wrong, Rex? Come on, boy!"

The German Shepherd let out another whine as he glanced toward his charge, but he didn't move otherwise.

"He's reacting to the presence of a stronger predator, Noah," Mina said.

Noah turned to us, his face scrunched up in a frowning question. "Huh? Where?"

"Me," I said.

Noah transferred his confusion to me. "No, you're not. You're Mister Wyatt, our friend. You're not a predator."

"Well, no... not a predator like children normally have to fear, but I'm not human, Noah. And Rex is responding to that."

Noah's expression settled into an almost-argumentative hardness. "I don't believe you. You've never done or said anything that scared me or my mom."

"Being strong and potentially dangerous does not mean I make you or your mom afraid, Noah. In fact, I don't ever want you or your mom to be afraid of me. But there is a long list of people who *should* be afraid of me, because I'm one of the most dangerous creatures walking the earth right now."

"Prove it," Noah demanded.

Mina frowned and entered the conversation. "Noah Vickers, you do not speak like that to grown-ups, especially not our friends. Besides, you already saw him shifted when you chose to become a wolf shifter."

"If he really wants to see it again, I'm happy to shift, but I'd hate to leave scraps of fabric all over your living room."

Mina turned to me, her eyes twinkling now. "I've heard about you shifting, Wyatt. Something about how much you shed in the Oval Office?"

"Hey, the ladies warned President Williams," I replied, holding up my hands in a 'not my fault' gesture, "but she still wanted to see me shift."

"Well, since Noah is so insistent on the matter, he can clean up the fabric scraps. It seems only fair. Isn't that right, Noah?"

The poor boy no longer seemed as enthused about the idea, now that work was attached to it, but he nodded his acceptance.

"Okay," I said. "You two might want to step back a few feet."

They did, and I looked all around me to be sure I wouldn't hit anything breakable, then touched the part of my mind that was no longer human. My clothes exploded in a shower of fabric as I flowed into the form of a massive thousand-pound Smilodon, and poor Rex flipped out. He was on his feet and hauling tail down the hall before I completed the shift.

Noah stared at me, wide-eyed and grinning. Of course, my shoulders and his shoulders were pretty much equal with each other, so he didn't have to strain his neck to look me in the eye anymore.

"Can I pet you?" he asked, his voice full of wonder.

I bobbed my massive head in a nod, and he almost danced over and ran his hand down my back from my head almost to my hips.

"Oh, wow. It doesn't feel anything like I thought it would," he said as he continued to run his hand down my spine. Then, he turned back to Mina. "Mom, just because I chose wolf doesn't mean I don't enjoy seeing a big cat. Sorry for pretending to be so grouchy, Mister Wyatt. I didn't know how else to get you to shift."

Just then, we heard a door open from the direction of the garage, and Mina's eyes shot wide as a woman's voice reached our ears. "Mina, what's up with Rex? He tore out of the garage like his tail was on fire. I hope he doesn't run far."

About that time, a woman who bore a striking resemblance to Mina entered the living room. Her eyes locked on me as they shot wide, and the color drained from her complexion. Her jaw dropped right before she screamed, which ended abruptly as her eyes rolled back in her head and she collapsed to the floor.

Ah, well... at least the carpet in the living room was thick.

20

Aside from the agents assigned to Mina, no one took much notice of a Smilodon trotting along the sidewalks of town. Mina was kind enough to tie the laces of my mostly intact but still unwearable shoes together and hang them over my neck before slipping my phone and wallet and such inside them, and I headed to the general store for a new set of clothes.

Most stores and public buildings around town had push-button-operated doors, and the rare human who visited town tended to applaud us for our welcoming stance on people who needed wheelchairs. Yes, those waist-high push plates were good for those who were wheelchair-bound, but they were especially handy when you were in animal form and didn't have opposable thumbs.

Hank watched me pad into the store, and he just shook his head and sighed as he made his way over to the men's clothing section. We went through the dance where he held up shirts for me to nod or shake my head until we arrived at the one I'd just shredded, and then, we did the same for pants. Fortunately, he knew what type of undies and socks I preferred, and which pair of shoes I needed was rather obvious.

He collected the tags from everything before leaving me and the stack of clothes.

I left the shoes in the trash can of the changing room and headed to the counter, human once more and dressed. My bank card changed hands, and Hank thanked me for doing business with him while he directed a somewhat reproachful expression my way.

Yeah... I knew I went through more clothes than the average shifter, but what was I supposed to do? Flash a kid? Not cool... not cool at all.

Just as I reached the doors of Hank's shop, my phone sounded off. I retrieved it from my new hip pocket and saw it was Lyssa calling. I thumbed the control to accept the call.

"Hey, Sweetheart," I said as I left the store and frowned at seeing another set of blacked-out SUVs sitting in front of the town's admin building.

"If you can, you should head over to the admin building," she said.

Not surprised, and I asked, "Does it have anything to do with the blacked-out SUVs in front?"

"Oh, good. You're close. Yes, it does."

"Alrighty. I'll see you shortly. Bye for now." I ended the call and returned the phone to my pocket as I headed that way at a slow amble.

Lyssa hadn't used any of our distress code words in the call, and she hadn't sounded under duress, but a little extra time to look things over wasn't a bad idea. As I approached the vehicles, I noticed both of them sported little Canadian flags on each corner of the hood and diplomatic plates.

Well, shit... I had a bad feeling about this.

A couple of individuals in suits and sunglasses stood near

the doors of the admin building, and they moved as if to stop me from entering. I should have been nicer about it, but these people had ruined my good mood from visiting Noah.

"Neighbors, about the worst thing you can do is try to stop me from entering this building. This is my town, and you're the guests."

One of the worthy souls said, "We'll need to see identification."

"You don't have the authority to demand anything from me, especially in my own town. Now, step aside."

The agents shared a look. The one who demanded my ID seemed like he wanted to force the issue, but the other agent shook his head. They stepped aside. As I walked past them, I tapped my nose and pointed at the one who exhibited a glimmer of intelligence.

I soon found Lyssa entertaining a couple suits in the admin building's conference room. Lyssa stood as I entered, and they were quick to follow suit.

"Lady and gentleman," Lyssa said, as she gestured to me, "allow me to introduce Wyatt Magnusson, Alpha of Precious and Godwin County, Consul of the Shifters of North America."

The woman stepped around the table and extended her hand, and I noticed the gentleman carried a folio.

"Alpha Wyatt, it is a pleasure. I am Charlotte McCabe, and I have been sent by the Canadian government to establish a consulate here to better handle our relationship with the Shifter Nation. At your leisure, I am prepared to present my credentials."

"It's a pleasure to meet you as well, Ms. McCabe," I replied. The sad fact was that I wasn't sure whether I wanted to laugh or cry. We had *just* solved this same problem with our own government. Who was going to show up next? The Mexicans? I fought the urge to snort a laugh, since the Mexicans were the only country in North America left. It wasn't like the continent had a lot of countries.

"Please, let's sit and discuss the issue, and we can even hop on a conference call if such ends up being needed. We've danced this dance before."

"Oh? How so?" Charlotte asked.

Everyone returned to their seats as I moved to mine, then answered. "Our own government tried to establish a consulate here, too, and I have to say I wasn't any more a fan of that idea than I am of another government moving in. First off, have you spoken with the US State Department before embarking on this particular quest?"

The two guests shared a look before Charlotte said, "I myself have not, as that would be above my pay grade."

"Okay. We'll put a pin in that for the moment. The next point... are the shifters in Canada not Canadian citizens? I can't speak for you guys, but as far as I know, all the shifters in the United States consider themselves American citizens, which was part of the reason the idea of establishing a consulate here just seemed... well... damn stupid. Not to mention that we're trying to keep the fact that we're not human out of the public eye. Having a Canadian consulate suddenly appear in what looks like a backwater town of rural Washington would draw more than a few eyes, I'd think."

Our two guests once again shared a look, and I guessed I was living up to the international stereotype of the brash and possibly rude American. Ah, well. I had claws and they didn't, too.

Charlotte opened her mouth to speak and closed it again, then glanced at her associate once more before turning back to me. "I'm not certain that anyone ever thought to ask whether the Canadian shifters consider themselves our citizens."

"Does your military have designated shifter units?" I asked.

Another shared look. Then, Charlotte answered, "I... I don't really know. That was never mentioned in any of my briefings before they hustled me on a plane to Seattle."

Lovely. Well, I didn't want to offend our neighbors to the north any more than I already had, so I decided to phone a friend, as they say.

"Okay. Gimme a second, folks." I picked up my phone and dialed Mina. When she answered, I said, "Hi, Mina. Hate to bother you while you're still settling in, but would you mind heading over to the admin building conference room? I have a bit of a situation here that I'm fairly certain should not be solved with teeth and claws."

I fought to keep from grinning when the guy on Charlotte's left went pale.

Mina responded at once, "Yes, of course, Wyatt. I'll be right there."

I ended the call and returned my focus to our guests.

"So, we talked the US Government out of establishing a consulate here," I explained. "They did however leave a liaison. That's who I just called. She'll be able to help us navigate these treacherous waters with skill and aplomb. If need be, we can hop on a conference call to D.C. and speak with someone there as well. I'm extremely good at the teeth and claws part, but I'm still learning diplomacy. It's not as simple."

Charlotte's associate looked like he wanted to run screaming from the room, and he earned some respect for still sitting there with a calm veneer. His heart rate put the lie to that outward demeanor, but he made a good effort.

"Alpha Wyatt," Lyssa said, swatting my wrist that was

closest to her, "stop scaring the poor souls. They probably just learned shifters are real mere hours ago."

I felt like asking what her point was, but I figured I had terrorized them enough. Regardless of how entertaining I found it, it was probably unwise to scare foreign envoys to the point they needed a change of clothes.

"Right. I'll just step outside and wait for Mina. The people you left out front seemed to be of the mind that they controlled who entered this building."

I stood and headed back outside, just in time to find Mina approaching. I saw her car parked down the street, and she had changed into professional attire.

"Hi," I said as I stepped between the two agents. "How's your sister? I'm guessing she was your sister, anyway."

Mina chuckled. "Yes, she was my sister, and she's doing fine. I hadn't had the chance to have 'The Talk' with her yet, and you saw to that far better than I ever could have... at least until Noah has his first shift."

I turned to escort Mina into the building, and the fellow who accosted me looked like he wanted to be hardheaded about the matter. Yes, I wanted to be a gracious and respectful host, but this was going a bit far. Maybe he just didn't like shifters. Either way, I decided a little education was in order.

I partially shifted my hand and extended a claw that I then used to scratch my head, all while maintaining eye contact with the guy's sunglasses. Both he and his associate took more than a few steps back, and their complexions suggested they might need to rotate off-duty long enough to get new undies. They didn't smell like it, but I made my point. I shifted my hand back to human and used it to open the door for Mina, and we left them on the sidewalk to contemplate the nature of their lives.

As soon as the door closed behind us, Mina looked to me and said, "You're certainly in a mood today."

"They tried to demand that *I* present them with identification when I arrived. If this were Canadian soil, I would have no problem with that, but uh oh... it *isn't*. Not unless there's been a war that America lost in the last hour or so we haven't heard about."

"Yes, Wyatt, but they're security. Specifically, dignitary protection services. They're trained to control any building one of their people visits."

I snorted. "Yeah, that works fairly well with humans, but the grade school down the street is full of kids who could clean their clocks. The first-graders and the ones in Kindergarten might even work up a sweat. It's just absurd to act like that when they're surrounded by *real* predators."

The conversation delivered us to the conference room, and I gestured for Mina to enter first. Lyssa and the envoys stood as Mina entered, and I said, "Charlotte McCabe, allow me to present Mina Vickers, United States Liaison to the Shifter Nation of North America."

Charlotte approached us and shook Mina's hand. "Madame Attorney General—"

"Forgive me," Mina said, "but I resigned as Attorney General. Please, call me Mina."

Charlotte's expression suggested her mind locked for a moment. Yeah. I felt that way when I met the president. She could join the club. "Yes, well, thank you, Mina. It's a pleasure to meet you."

"Likewise," Mina replied. "So, if you'll pardon me for diving right into the mix, what has Wyatt called me here to defuse?"

Lyssa smirked, and I said, "They want their own consulate with us, too, and I find the idea just as ludicrous as Uncle Sam setting up shop here. A government doesn't establish a consulate with its own people, and they already have an embassy and several consulates with the United States. So, I'm not sure where we go from here."

Mina pursed her lips and shot me a quick glance. I shrugged and gave her an insouciant smile, one I learned from my imp of a sister.

"Yes… well… why don't we sit and discuss this?" Mina said. "First, has your government contacted the State Department regarding your intention to establish a consulate here in Precious? Second—and I'm sure Wyatt has raised this point—are the Canadian shifters citizens of your country?"

We all assumed our seats, and Mina interlaced her fingers as she rested her forearms on the table.

Over the next several minutes, Mina and Charlotte discussed the situation, and I have to admit to feeling a little bit like I didn't belong. I mean… I didn't contribute to the discussion, and I didn't have any specific expertise they needed. More than once, I thought about trying to leave, but I didn't want to offend anyone or make them think I didn't care about the matter.

To be clear, I *didn't* care about it past the point that they no longer wanted to establish a consulate, but at the same time, we'd need them—all the allies we could get, really—sooner or later. The last thing I wanted to do was be so memorable in a bad way that they didn't give us the time of day when we needed to rally the world against the Fae invasion.

I fought the urge to sigh. Diplomacy stuff was not fun. Not fun at all.

The impact of Lyssa's foot against my ankle pulled me out of my thoughts, and I turned to her. "You thumped?"

She gave me an exasperated look. "Charlotte asked you a question."

I turned to the woman in question and gave her my best

attentive expression. "Apologies. My mind wandered for a moment."

Whether she believed that or not, she didn't react. "I asked if you were opposed to the idea of us establishing a liaison mission, much as Ms. Vickers has done, in lieu of a full consulate."

"I don't mind that at all. The fact is that we're not ready yet for the level of scrutiny two new consulates in this town would bring. And honestly, the day will come when the presence of your liaison missions will be rather handy. If you need to phone in to discuss the evolution of the situation, please, feel free."

Charlotte nodded. "Yes, that might be best. If we are transitioning away from a consulate, I'm not certain we even need to present credentials."

At a semi-glare from Lyssa, I did not comment on the need for diplomatic credentials.

"Well, in that case, why don't we adjourn until you have a chance to phone home?" Lyssa rolled her eyes at my phrasing. "Lyssa will be able to find me once everyone's ready to proceed."

"That sounds good, yes," Charlotte agreed. "Thank you."

"You're welcome, and thank you. I'll stop by the hotel and diner to let them know you're guests of the Alpha until we get all this sorted. The least I can do is feed you and give you a chance to de-stress from your trip. If there's nothing else you need from me, I'll go see to that."

No one spoke of anything, and I left first the conference room and then the admin building.

CHARLOTTE and her associate watched Wyatt leave, and it was apparent they were not quite sure what to make of him.

At least part of that was on him, for his unconventional approach to diplomats.

Once the door closed, Charlotte turned to me, saying, "Please forgive me; I do not intend offense, but your man there can be a bit abrasive."

Lyssa gave Charlotte a half-smile as she considered how to respond. "It requires more than that to offend us, and he is usually far more welcoming and personable. The past few days have been... trying... for all concerned."

Charlotte wanted more information; Lyssa could see that much, but she wasn't sure if it was wise to give it to her. At her most basic, the idea of showing weakness—even potential weakness—was anathema to everything she stood for. She had no problem with—and frankly enjoyed—being a moderating influence on Wyatt, because no one in their right mind would ever think *him* weak. The councilors could certainly attest to that.

"To help you put it in perspective, circumstances required Wyatt to take a day trip to Chicago two days ago, and Wyatt is still settling down from that." She paused for a moment, then slightly lifted a hand in a half-stop gesture. "While in Chicago, he confronted six councilors who disrespected me. I don't think it would have offended him nearly as much if they had directed their remarks to him, but he is very protective of us, his ladies. From what I understand, the Council is still working to fill those six seats."

"I... think I see," Charlotte replied.

Lyssa shrugged. "I'm afraid the matter is a tad arcane to anyone who isn't very familiar with our ways, but I assure you that the Wyatt you've seen thus far is not a complete picture of who he is."

Charlotte nodded her understanding. "Very well. If you will excuse us, we should get started on those calls."

Lyssa nodded once and stood. "Feel free to use the

conference room as long as you need. If you need me, feel free to ask the young man at the reception desk."

Mina stood as well, following Lyssa out of the conference room. As Lyssa closed the doors behind them, she began, "You're not going to believe what my agents told me. Do you know a Nina Carstairs?"

21

I stopped by the hotel and had a quick word with Melody about the Canadian people, specifically naming Charlotte and indicating she would know who her people were. Melody told me she'd handle it, and I knew she would. I had yet to meet anyone in town who wasn't on the ball, and as I crossed the street to the diner, I wondered if that was a shifter thing. Or maybe it was just an odds thing? Could it just be that only competent shifters settled in Precious? That didn't seem to hold water, the more I thought about it. But in the long run, I wasn't sure it mattered.

Karleen sat at one of the tables in the diner, and she didn't look happy. I was hungry anyway, and I knew Gladys would find her way to me, so I altered course.

"Is this seat taken?" I asked as I arrived at Karleen's table.

She just shook her head to answer 'no.' Well, now... this appeared to be a serious funk. I wonder what had changed since we parted ways. I sat and waited for her to say something or react or... anything, really.

Gladys came to take my drink order, and I told her we had a Canadian delegation in town and that their food was on me. Gladys scoffed and shook her head, heading off to get my drink while muttering something about idiots and their dumb ideas. She came back with my tea, and I ordered my favorite because it was that kind of day. Since Karleen still hadn't spoken, I decided to force the issue.

"So… what's going on?" I asked. "I thought—"

"Nadine called," Karleen said, interrupting me.

Oh. Yeah. That would do it. Nadine was Karleen's older sister by something like four years, if I had my info right. She had been on some kind of quest to re-unite Karleen with the family, which ultimately crashed and burned when one of Karleen's own brothers proceeded to give unforgivable offense. That unworthy soul left town with 'Precious' carved into his forehead, which was where Lyssa got the idea for her handling of the remaining councilors.

"She wanted to know if things had calmed down enough that I might speak with you about lifting the family's ban from Godwin County… among other things."

I shrugged. "Honestly, that's up to you. Personally, I think your brother Precious—" Karleen snorted a laugh. "—should live in fear of me deciding to hunt him down and end him for what he did, but at the same time, he's your family. You are more important to me than having his blood on my claws or teeth. What do you want to happen?"

Karleen took a deep breath, which I enjoyed watching, and released it as a slow sigh. "I… I'm not sure what I want to happen. Just so you know, *I* still kinda feel like hunting him down. That was a damn stupid thing for him to do, and I'm not sure where it came from. But then again, he's far enough older than me that we didn't really interact all that much before I left home, so I probably don't have a good read on what's normal for him. For all I know, he's a rabid idiot all the time."

"Then, he must be a good fighter, because I wouldn't expect shifters to tolerate people like that lightly."

Karleen chuckled, but it held no mirth. "Yeah… he is, as long as he's not squaring off against a primogenitor. They did try picking on me a little when they still lived at home, and every time, I kicked their asses for it. Nadine couldn't beat them, so it was a little funny when she'd run to a kid almost half their age for protection. Yeah… they were very careful not to let anyone outside the family know a grade-schooler could own them anytime she wanted. But that was before my first shift. After that, *nobody* wanted to fight with me."

That didn't surprise me at all. When she shifted to her dire wolf, Karleen made the average wolf shifter look like an ineffectual puppy.

"Well, think it over, and let me know," I said, entering the silence that had descended on our table. "I'm willing to handle it however you'd like, except for vacating your brother's ban. I was completely serious that he's a dead wolf the next time I lay eyes on him, and I can't say my feelings have mellowed during the intervening time."

A small smile curled her lips. "You don't need to protect me, Wyatt, but I love that you do."

I shrugged. "I wouldn't want anyone on the outside to think I loved you less than Gabrielle or Lyssa. If I treated you differently from them, you know some idiot would mouth off, and then, I'd have blood on my claws again. You'd think people would figure out they'd live longer if they kept their idiocy to themselves, but what can you do? A buddy I worked with a while back liked to say that you can't fix stupid, and I've come to agree."

"Well, we certainly don't want you to bloody your claws needlessly," Karleen remarked.

"I appreciate your understanding and consideration…

especially since you ladies are the ones who have to help clean the blood out of my fur." My mind went back to the first time Gabrielle and Karleen had cleaned blood out of my fur, specifically how they looked in their two-piece bikinis, and I smiled. "But I certainly don't mind the view."

A huge grin broke through Karleen's dour mood. "No, I don't imagine you would."

Gladys arrived with my food and, after placing it in front of me, asked Karleen if she was ready to order yet.

My dire wolf nodded and rattled off her favorite, and Gladys left us in peace.

"Don't wait for me," Karleen said, "but don't be surprised if I steal a tidbit or two."

I looked down at the pile of steaks on the platter and flagged down a passing server, asking her for a plate and some silverware. When she returned with the plate, I moved one whole steak over to it and pushed it and the silverware over to Karleen. She gave me her special smile, and I suspected she would be sitting in my lap if we were not in public.

Ah, well... I loved my ladies. They were welcome to anything of mine.

When Gladys brought Karleen's bison steaks, the extra plate with signs of my steak on it didn't faze her one bit. She held up one of the bison steaks and gave Karleen a questioning expression. Karleen nodded, and Gladys placed the steak on my empty platter. I thanked both of them, and as soon as Gladys went on her way, I carved off a fifth or less and moved the rest of the steak back over to Karleen. The look in her eyes definitely became heated then, and that heat *wasn't* anger. If Lyssa didn't need me back at the admin building soon, I suspected a game of 'Catch the Wolf' was in my immediate future.

~

KARLEEN and I stood in the bathroom of the master suite in the Alpha's house. We used large, soft towels to dry off the remains of the shower after a thoroughly diverting and enjoyable game of 'Catch the Wolf.'

"I've never said this to you or Gabrielle," Karleen not quite whispered as she worked her towel down my back. "But it's important to me that you understand how much... this... whatever we have means to me."

She worked the towel down the back of my legs, then moved around in front of me and worked the towel up my front. When she stood, rather than continue working the towel up my chest, she remained still with her eyes locked on mine.

"I went the better part of sixty years pretty much alone. For the first decade or so, I had Buttercup, but eventually, I outlived him. He didn't like that. He didn't want to leave me, but he didn't have a choice. He was so tired, there at the end. I think he knew he held me back. That I only stayed around that area for him. He was wrong... but not. I want to show you my cabin sometime. It's down in Oregon, near the Washington state line. Back in the wilderness. The nearest road is ten miles away. I built the cabin there, because... well... maybe I wasn't ready to leave Buttercup any more than he was ready to leave me."

I didn't want to keep her from speaking. We had never talked like this, but I wanted to hold her in my arms, and she was still wet. So, I took her towel and hung it over the shower rod and started using my towel on her, gesturing for her to continue.

"You have no way to understand what it was like; you're still in your twenties, but meeting you and Gabrielle—especially how well we mesh—was a transformative experience for me. I had given up on ever meeting anyone I felt I could respect. Most shifters—sad to say—are not shining examples of masculinity. They're small men, and I don't mean physically. Most hide it or control it to varying degrees, but they're all caught up in that game of strength and dominance, and they're not necessarily bad people. I don't want you to think I'm saying that. It's just you... well... you don't seem to care, and you have no idea how refreshing and welcome that is."

I paused my efforts to dry her and focused on her eyes, giving her the best warm and loving smile I knew how to give. "You're right; I don't. But I have seen girls and women chase men who treated them horribly, and I've never understood that. It's incredibly common among humans."

I resumed working the towel over her wet, glistening form. Karleen sighed, and it carried an odd mixture of relaxation and resignation. "It's not restricted to humans. I've seen it many times with shifters, too, and I always vowed I wouldn't be one of them." Then, she chuckled; it held a dark edge. "It helps that I never met a man I couldn't beat into a bloody pulp if I so chose. They're so obsessed with strength and 'proving their dominance' or whatever that they did not like being around me at all."

I finished drying her, even though I took my time about it and enjoyed all the places I brushed with the towel. From the hidden look to Karleen's eyes, she enjoyed getting dry almost as much as she enjoyed getting sweaty to need a shower.

I moved to pull her into a hug, but she stopped me and claimed my towel, proceeding to dry my chest. I didn't think it was so wet, but apparently, she disagreed. The moment I was dry to her satisfaction, she tossed the towel over her shoulder and somehow caught the shower rod without even looking as she melted into my arms.

It was odd knowing this woman who fit in my arms so

well was over three times my age, but the more I considered it, I didn't care. It felt right that she was in my arms, and in the long run, that's all that mattered. In that respect, she matched my other ladies, too. Each of them felt perfect in my arms, and I loved holding each of them.

"How much longer do you think we have?" Karleen asked after several moments of silence.

I smiled. "Today, or in general? Because I've heard shifters are naturally immortal."

She smacked my butt and pulled back far enough to look up at me. "Before Lyssa calls you about the Canadians, goof, but I suspect you knew that's what I meant."

I shrugged. "No idea. I honestly thought she would've called by now, but that shows you what I know."

"Come on, then. Let's pull something on and go to the great room. I didn't realize how much I've missed having your arms wrapped around me."

I gave her my best playful smile. "You know, I see the first part of that as being totally optional."

"Any other time, yes, it would be. But you and I both know where it would lead, and I'm not sure we have time for another round."

I shrugged and led her out of the bathroom to the bedroom. We each pulled a t-shirt, shorts, and undies from our respective dressers and made our way to the large room that was our refuge from the world.

LYSSA LEANED BACK and listened to the conference call. Somehow, they had both the US Secretary of State *and* the Canadian Foreign Minister on the call, with Charlotte and Mina in the room with her.

The Canadian Minister balked at the thought of having

the discussions with Lyssa representing the Shifter Nation. Not out of some kind of sexist leanings, but simply because he had never heard of her before. Secretary Perez was quick to confirm her authority, and Charlotte assured her boss that he'd much rather hold the initial discussion with Lyssa instead of Wyatt. She tried to deflect when he asked why, but the crafty old fox didn't let her. She glanced at Lyssa in trepidation, but Lyssa merely grinned and nodded. Charlotte quickly relaid a few of the key points of her discussion with Wyatt, and he treated everyone on the call to a few seconds of shocked sputtering before settling down to business.

But that was all in the past. Nearly three hours in the past, it seemed, when Lyssa consulted her watch, and she couldn't help but wonder how Wyatt had filled the time. Was he antsy that she hadn't called him yet? Had he realized how much time had passed? Did he even care?

Wyatt's approach to diplomacy shocked her sometimes. His style hovered somewhere between gunboat diplomacy and a shotgun wedding—the shotgun loaded with sabot rounds—and she suspected the Foreign Minister was not the type to appreciate that. Very few people who worked in government or diplomacy would be.

At the moment, the Foreign Minister and the Secretary of State dominated the call, going back and forth over the reasons Uncle Sam ultimately chose not to proceed with establishing a consulate. From the tone and cadence of his speech, Lyssa suspected Lucy was winning him over to their side of thought. There was a lot of, "Hmmm...I had not considered that," coming from his side of the call.

After several more minutes of listening to Lucy fence with him, always pushing the line of debate closer and closer to his side, he yielded, asking, "And just what of your man Wyatt, Miss Lyssa? What will he have to say about all this?"

Lyssa almost choked in surprise at his phrasing but

recovered in short order. "I think he'll be fine with Charlotte and a team remaining as a liaison, much as Mina has. It's good to keep steady, reliable lines of communication, because sometimes, matters arise where either shifters have an issue—or the government does—where a neutral party makes all the difference."

"Yes... well... Wyatt isn't a neutral party, though, is he?" the Foreign Minister pressed. "After all, he is the Consul of the Shifters of North America. That right there suggests a certain bias."

He had a point. On the surface, it did very much suggest that, but he didn't know Wyatt.

"Minister," Lucy interjected, "if I may say so, your question is only valid because you haven't met Wyatt. He simply *does not care*. For the sake of discussion, let's say you would bring a disagreement involving shifters to him through Charlotte. As long as you didn't try to shade the information in your favor, if the shifters were in the wrong, everyone in Precious would have to sit on him rather hard to keep him from heading up to Canada that instant to apply correction to the shifters in a rather stern manner. But... he would expect the same of your government. If the government was in the wrong, he would expect a rather expeditious resolution... with prejudice, as our courts say."

"Hrmm... I see your point." He fell silent for a few moments before he continued. "So, if there was a case of sheep farms losing livestock with paw prints that didn't match known wolves or other local predators?"

"Minister," Lyssa cut in, "that doesn't sound like an example for conversation."

"No, I'm afraid it's not. I caught wind of it through a friend over at the Ministry of Natural Resources, and the matter has become rather vexing. A number of sheep farms in Ontario north of Lake Superior have reported losses.

They're not destabilizing for the farms, not yet, but it is a matter of concern... especially when our finest trackers can't find the predators responsible."

"Secretary Perez," Lyssa said, "how fast can we get passports for Wyatt, myself, Gabrielle, and Karleen? Gabrielle might have hers; I'm not sure about that, but I know Wyatt, Karleen, and I don't have them."

"If you can me get all the documentation with pictures, I'll have them back to you in forty-eight hours from the moment it's in my hands. Normally, not even expedited service happens that fast, but I consider this very much an exigent situation with diplomatic consequences."

There was a slight pause, and then, the Minister said, "Do I understand correctly that you're proposing the Consul himself will handle this matter?"

"Does it help that I also sit on the Shifter Council?" Lyssa asked.

"Oh, my. It seems I should have done my homework a little better before hopping on the call. Very well. Charlotte has my direct line. When you're ready to proceed, please contact me, and we'll discuss how to get you into the country in a timely manner."

Lyssa couldn't keep from breaking into a grin. "Oh, I don't think *that* will be an issue, Minister, but we will need somewhere... uhm... controlled or restricted access to arrive."

More silence over the line for several seconds. Then, he spoke. "I cannot help but think I'm missing something here."

"Are you aware of the Magi, Minister?" Lucy asked.

"Yes, of course. One of the members of Parliament is a Magi."

Lyssa pursed her lips to control her grin as Lucy said, "Wyatt's family name is Magnusson, sir. His sister is Victoria, and his grandparents are Connor and Maeve."

The ensuing silence edged toward awkward before he spoke again. "Yes, well, I daresay arriving in Canada won't be an issue, then. I'll arrange an impromptu Customs check, just to make everything legal, and we'll proceed from there. Contact me when you're ready to proceed, please."

The remainder of the call was little more than the pleasantries associated with ending such a high-powered conference, and Lyssa was already working through the steps necessary to gather all the documentation for the passports. An unsettling thought hit her, and her eyes shot wide before she could stop them. Did Karleen even have a birth certificate?

22

L yssa, Mina, and Charlotte found Karleen cuddled in my lap as we sat on one of the large couches in the great room. Charlotte started to be embarrassed until she saw that we were not and had no intention of moving, even with the arrival of guests.

"So… what's the verdict?" I asked once everyone found a seat.

"Charlotte is the official liaison from Canada to the Shifter Nation, and there is already a matter for our attention," Lyssa summarized.

Something about how she said that did not give me warm, happy feelings. "Tell me."

By the time she finished sharing all they knew from their conversation with the Foreign Minister, I was *not* happy, and neither was Karleen. There was no doubt that shifters were behind the loss of livestock at the sheep farms, but to my mind, the question was *why*.

Every shifter I had encountered was at least established within the middle class, regarding socio-economic status, and more than a few of them were beyond it. Especially if they were older. Karleen was a bit of an outlier in that, but that was what she *chose*. Most shifters her age were already rather well off, financially speaking. Which brought me back to the most powerful word in the English language... possibly even the most powerful concept in existence... *why?*

I didn't see the advantage to the shifters in stealing livestock. It made no sense.

While I let that roll around in my mind, I reached for my phone and realized it was in the bedroom. I looked to Lyssa, asking, "May I borrow your phone?"

She frowned her confusion but tossed it to me all the same. I thumbed through her contacts until I found Gabrielle and called her.

"Hey, Lyssie, how goes it?" Gabrielle asked, answering on the first ring.

"It's Wyatt. Lyssa loaned me her phone. Prepare a hunting party, and I think we want a couple bears in this one, too. I prefer people with passports, but I'll take what I can get. You need to flag any who do not have passports immediately, so we can make that happen."

"What's going on?"

I sighed. "I don't have the full story to give you, but on the surface, it looks like shifters are raiding sheep farms up in Ontario for reasons unknown, and I take exception to that. If they're truly desperate with need, that's one thing, but if that's the case, they should have contacted the Shifter Council. We would have helped them without riling up a bunch of humans."

"Yeah, we would have. Okay. I'll round up the gang and see who doesn't have passports. Bring everyone to the house when I have them?"

"That works. Thanks. Love you."

I heard Gabrielle's smile in her voice as she said, "Love you too, you big furball."

I ended the call immediately dialed Vicki's number and felt surprised when Lyssa's phone identified the number as an existing contact with my sister's name.

As with Gabrielle, Vicki answered on the first ring. "Is everything okay, Lyss?"

"It's Wyatt, sis. I'm sorry for seeming like I only call when I need something, but I will need transport to Ontario sometime in the next few days. It appears we have shifters raiding human sheep farms up there, and I'm taking a hunting party up there to find out why. And before you ask, their foreign minister brought the matter to our attention."

The only thing I heard for a moment was Vicki's laughter. "It's just fine, brother mine. We have always helped each other, and I suspect we always will. I'll be ready when you call, and yes, I have my passport."

"Thanks. We may need your help to hop around to gather documents, because I know I never bothered with one, and I'm not sure Karleen did either. I'll work up a list, and we'll see if we can force it into some kind of order."

"Hrmm... why don't I just head over to Precious? I'll tell Grams and Grandpa I'm helping you for a few days, and that will give us time to put together all the documents you'll need for passports. But Wyatt, those normally take weeks."

I chuckled. "I have it on very good authority that Secretary Perez will expedite them to a considerable degree."

"Fair enough, furry bro. I'll pack a bag or three and see you shortly. Save my room for me."

Vicki ended the call before I could, and I tossed the phone back to Lyssa. "Okay. That's done. Gabrielle is gathering the hunting party, and Vicki will be here... probably in ten minutes or less... to help with all the logistics."

By the time I finished speaking, Charlotte stared at me. She had decent control over her expression, but I could see the surprise lurking just below the surface as she said, "You certainly don't drag your feet."

I shrugged. "There's no reason to, especially with the situation being what it is. I want to find the shifters and learn why they're raiding farms. If it's something so simple as needing food and not having money, the Shifter Council will handle that and pay reparations to the farms involved. But if there's more to it... well... I may only be a few months old as a shifter, but I will not countenance any of us preying on humans or their property. I suspect I'll be kicking some asses before this over, especially when they probably could have just *bought* the damn sheep."

"You're rather unhappy about this, aren't you?" Charlotte asked, surprise edging into her voice.

"Yes, I am. Regardless of whether humans at large know about us, we all share the planet and its resources. There's more than enough room for all of us, as long as we approach the matter from the mindset of cooperation and mutual benefit. Just because many of us are predators at our core doesn't mean we treat our sapient neighbors like prey or with disregard. I won't have it."

Silence ruled for several moments, while I figured Charlotte absorbed what I said. After a little while longer, she said, "And you have the authority to stop it?"

I pointed at Lyssa who shared the couch with Charlotte. "She and her co-conspirators made me Consul of the Shifters of North America. They made it a life appointment that can only transfer or be revoked through traditional shifter dominance challenge. They further hid language inside the investiture that made me the de facto *ruler* of the shifters in North America. So, yes, I do have the authority, but even if I didn't, my strength more than makes up for it. You see, I'm one of five known primogenitors, and we're not your average shifter... not by a long shot."

"I... see." It was clear to me she didn't, but if she tagged along with us, she might. It all depended on her woodcraft.

"You planning to go with us?"

Charlotte blinked. "Well, yes, of course. I'm the official liaison with the shifters. Why wouldn't I go with you?"

I looked to Lyssa. "Get with Gabrielle to evaluate her on woodcraft while we're waiting on the passports. I don't mind if she comes with us to a certain point, but not if she sounds like an elephant in a china shop in the woods on a dark night."

Lyssa nodded and tapped at her phone, sending a text to Gabrielle I suspected.

I took a deep breath and released it as a slow almost-sigh, considering what we knew and what we needed versus what we had. There wasn't anything I could do the hurry things along more than I already had, so I just settled into cuddling with Karleen while I waited.

It occurred to me that she had been awfully quiet during all this, and I focused on her and smiled. It seemed she drifted off to sleep at some point.

Damn... wish I'd thought of that.

TRUE TO HER WORD, Vicki arrived less than twenty minutes later... with four suitcases. I blinked.

"Sure you brought enough wardrobe, sis?"

Vicki looked down at the four, matching roller suitcases and returned her gaze to me. "Brother mine, not all of us have a coat of fur we can fall back on. After all, clothes do make the woman, and it would be such a tragedy if I didn't have the right clothes for the occasion, wouldn't it? Whatever the occasion turned out to be?"

On the surface, I couldn't argue with her, but still... *four* suitcases? And they weren't the small carry-on size, either. In the end, I fell back on a lesson I learned a long time ago. Challenging Vicki on her wardrobe decisions was a losing proposition... *always.*

"You do you, sis. I wouldn't want you to feel unprepared."

"Why, thank you, Wyatt. I knew you the purr-fect brother."

Even Charlotte shorted a laugh at that one, but from the mischievous twinkle in Vicki's eyes, that reaction was what she wanted.

"Right, then. I'll just take these upstairs and be right back. You didn't put Moira in my room by mistake, did you?"

I shook my head. "Your room is still your room, sis. I wouldn't do that."

She shot me a wink as she headed for the stairs, the suitcases rolling along behind her like obedient pets. Charlotte's eyes were the size of tea-service saucers when she saw it, and I couldn't hold back a grin. She wasn't prepared at all for the suitcases lifting off the floor and floating up the stairs behind Vicki, either. Ah, the joys of having a Magi sister...

By THE TIME Gabrielle arrived with the list of everyone who needed passports, all the ladies in the great room were getting on like a house afire. Charlotte got over her initial surprise at Vicki and her way of doing things, and I felt she'd fit right in. Karleen roused from her nap a few minutes before Vicki returned from setting up her room, and she and Lyssa held court over by the bar that separated the great room from the kitchen.

It turned out that Karleen did indeed have a birth certificate, but it was in Oregon. A handful of our standard hunting party had passports to go fishing in Canada, but those who liked hunting up there tended to use the fur highway. There wasn't a border agent born who'd argue with a grizzly bear or wolf crossing from Washington to British Columbia, and no one *ever* paid any attention to birds.

That thought led me to the natural question of whether there were shifter smugglers, but I didn't voice it in the present company. I'd ask Lyssa once Mina and Charlotte went on their way after our trip to Ontario. I wasn't sure if Mina would accompany us, especially given her son's recovery, but I didn't rule it out.

I watched while Gabrielle and Vicki worked out the plan for gathering everyone's necessary documents to get US passports, and soon enough, they vanished. A couple hours later, they returned with armloads of papers and set about sorting them while Lyssa ran everyone through an impromptu photo station in front of one of our white walls. As Lyssa took someone's picture, that individual went to one of the available laptops to fill out the online application and print it to hardcopy.

The hardcopy applications headed each person's stack of paperwork, and Mina surprised us again by acting as the notary the application required, with her position within the State Department also allowing her to administer the oath that accompanied the process.

The sun was just dipping below the mountains to the west when we finished all the application packets, stuffing them into white document mailers and writing the person's name on the front. Mina called Lucy and gathered the envelopes, moments before she and Vicki vanished. They returned moments later without the document envelopes.

Now, all that remained was to wait for Lucy to do her part as Secretary of State and get those passports for us.

. . .

WE FILLED the time with Charlotte obtaining as much information from her government about the situation as they had, so we could be as prepared as possible when we arrived. There wasn't a lot to go on, beyond the obvious that the parties responsible were indeed shifters. Modern wolf shifters were far closer to the natural breeds than Karleen could ever hope to be, but they were still larger and more robust than 'natural' wolves. The pictures Charlotte showed us of the paw prints and tracks, especially compared to natural wolves, were so different even I saw it.

Most of the affected sheep farms clustered around a thirty- to forty-square-mile area, which was well within the range of wolf shifters, and it seemed that—unlike normal predators—the perpetrators went for healthy and hale sheep... as opposed to the weakest or sickly ones.

Which only served to convince me further that shifters were responsible.

Yeah... I'd definitely be kicking some ass before this was over. I could feel it in my bones.

23

Lucy Perez, the Secretary of State, came through for us. Not quite forty-eight hours after Vicki and Mina placed the collection of passport applications in her hands, she contacted Mina and said the passports were ready. I honestly didn't believe they could print fifteen or so passports that fast, which made me wonder if they were *real* passports.

Vicki must have read my mind somehow, because the first thing she said when she returned with Mina and the passports was, "Yes, Wyatt. They're real and good for ten years, just like the ones you wait a couple months for."

Good enough. Inquiring minds, and all that...

ONCE WE HAD OUR PASSPORTS, the trip to Canada came together in a very short time like a well-oiled machine. The hunting party arrived at the Alpha's house with bags packed for a week. Personally, I thought packing for a week was a bit much, given how quickly we resolved the situation with Lyssa's niece, but it never hurt to be over-prepared... as long as one didn't take it to extremes.

Like a sixty-foot by thirty-foot metal Quonset hut stuffed to the rafters with non-perishable food... it's one thing to be prepared, but that's just silliness.

Charlotte called her people and gave Vicki the information she needed to open a portal. Everyone insisted I go first, and I left the sidewalk outside the Alpha's house for a landscaped courtyard. Stylish planters accented sitting areas, and a large fountain dominated the center of the design. A large mansion-like residence stood in the distance, and blocking the path leading out of the courtyard or garden was a setup that had to be temporary and hastily assembled, for it fouled the aesthetics of its surroundings to no end.

A young woman wearing a uniform that bore the Canadian flag on its epaulettes sat or stood behind a pressboard booth with a plexiglass divider that had a window just large enough to pass a hand and documents through. A metal detector arched over the paved path that led from the courtyard to the mansion in the distance. A dignified man in a suit stood a respectful distance behind the person at the booth.

I retrieved my passport from the pocket where I stashed it and approached the booth.

"Good day, sir," she said as he gestured for me to hand over my passport. "Purpose of your visit?"

"Uhh... hunting sheep rustlers."

My senses caught up with me as a slight smile quirked her lips. Oh, nice... she was a shifter, too. A breed of avian shifter, unless I was mistaken.

She verified that my face matched my passport as she asked, "Duration of stay?"

"If it takes us more than a week, we're doing something wrong," I replied.

Before she could respond, the gentleman behind her stepped forward. "Record the visa for two weeks, if you please. Alpha Wyatt may have further engagements beyond handling the livestock rustling matter."

"Of course, sir," she replied and looked to me. "Breed of shifter?"

"Smilodon."

She frowned. "I... I don't know that one."

I grinned. "Feline primogenitor. I'm a sabertooth cat."

Her eyes shot wide for a split second before she focused on her task of making that note.

"Th—thank you, sir. Pass your luggage around the side of the booth, and step through the metal detector please," she said, stamping my passport and returning it to me.

I complied and felt some slight anxiety ease when the metal detector didn't go off. Back when I worked in IT, I always set them off for something I forgot in one of the pockets of the cargo pants I preferred.

Karleen approached the booth right after me, and I wished I could watch the lady's face when Karleen answered the shifter breed question. Or Burke, for that matter. I saw she stood farther back in the hunting party, which surprised me a bit. I hadn't noticed that Gabrielle collected her for this.

"Alpha Wyatt," the distinguished gentleman said as he approached me, "I am Simon Ross, the Foreign Minister."

"A pleasure, sir," I replied, giving him a respectful handshake. "We've studied the information someone provided Charlotte. Forgive me, but where are we?"

"Ottawa," Simon replied. "The Minister of Natural Resources has a field office in the town closest the affected farms, and they are ready to receive you. I understand running the crew there through the necessities of a clearance raised a few eyebrows, but they've been briefed on your credentials and your suspicions regarding the perpetrators."

"That's good, and they're willing to work with us?"

Simon nodded. "Oh, yes… they're all onside. There was some consternation over Lyssa's insistence that they not accompany you and your people."

"That's just damn good sense for them," I said. "If you had to run them through a security clearance, they weren't Magi or shifters, which means they're soft and rather squishy compared to my people. If this involves any kind of confrontation, they'll just be a liability, and I'm not prepared to guarantee their safety. Too many variables, you see."

"Now, really, Alpha Wyatt… don't you think you're over-stating the case, just a bit? These are trained Natural Resources personnel, and most of them are veterans of the Canadian military. They are fully capable of—"

A strangled gasp took over his speech as I lifted my arm and partially shifted it to my hybrid form's arm, then extended all five claws on that hand.

"Can they do that?" I asked as the Foreign Minister gaped at my shifted hand… or possibly my claws. "Can they shrug off a bullet or a knife strike? Gabrielle Hassan is known throughout the western United States as the Huntress, and…" a sharp intake of breath over my shoulder told me the booth officer had heard of the Huntress, too, "…my trackers are grizzly bear shifters, who have demonstrated having greater scent acuity than so-called natural grizzly bears. If you're not aware, sir, natural grizzly bears have a better sense of smell than bloodhounds and have followed a scent trail for miles through wilderness. Plus, they're just damned intimidating when they want to be. I'd love to find a bear primogenitor… well… as long as she or he was friendly."

"I… I see your points, Alpha Wyatt," the Foreign Minister replied, his voice still a bit unsteady.

Now that I no longer needed to illustrate my points, I

shifted my arm back to human, but that didn't stop Simon from staring at it. I felt like chuckling. He seemed more unsettled by my partial shift than the fact persons or creatures unknown pilfered sheep from farms. But then again... he *was* the Foreign Minister, after all. Canadian sheep farms weren't exactly part of his remit.

It took another twenty minutes or so to get everyone passed through the impromptu customs station, and as Lyssa moved to stand with me and Karleen, I raised a point that had occurred to me while waiting on everyone to get their passports stamped.

"So, what happens when we go home? I mean... this is my first passport, but I'm pretty sure I need a re-entry stamp if I'm going to legally be in the United States."

Lyssa smiled. "Mina and the State Department already have that well in hand. Once we're ready to leave, Vicki will take us to a special receiving room at the Seattle airport, where Mina will be waiting at a special customs lane. Lucy is already conferring with Secretary of Homeland Security to get us passed through with a minimum of fuss. You know, when we finally come out to the world, Magi teleportation is going to throw the security types into a tizzy."

I chuckled around a partial smile. "Yeah... Miles didn't take us through any customs checkpoints when he took me to Avalon, and I'm pretty sure he goes wherever he wants without considering that kind of thing. The Assembly will have to work with the governments of the world to form some kind of arrangement, or it will go crazy fast. Well... it will already go crazy, but we should try to keep that to a minimum. I've been wondering if we should announce ourselves alongside the Magi or if we should do our own thing separate from them."

"I'm not sure it will help, either way," Lyssa said. "I don't think we can prevent the humans from flipping out over the idea that someone's friend from the grocery store can shift into a lion or tiger or wolf or whatever. That's just too high impact."

"Hrmm... I wonder if some kind of phased rollout might work, but I don't know how we'd manage that. The second one group of people puts something on the internet, the crazy will begin."

Lyssa nodded. "It's going to be almost a global stop event, regardless of what we do. And don't even get me started on the societal fallout from the Fae invasion. There will be riots in the streets, major upticks in the suicide rate. It'll be nuts... at least until they see we have everything in hand. And let's face it; the psychology of modern journalism is so focused on ratings and sensationalism that they won't *help* us keep things calm. They'll ratchet everyone up to a fever pitch and keep them there until there's something more sensational, or at least something they haven't broadcast twenty-four-seven."

"They'll probably get around six to eight weeks out of us, before the random person on the street is desensitized to the idea. Then, they'll go off in search of the next Cause du Jour."

"Cause du Jour? Really? That's a bit blunt, even for you, Wyatt," Lyssa remarked.

"Maybe so, but can you look me in the eye and honestly say I'm wrong? Modern journalism stampedes the populace from one perceived crisis to the next... all in the interests of filling their twenty-four-hour news cycle and whatever social agenda their paymasters dictate. And don't even get me started on the so-called people's right to know. The people don't have as much right to know as the journalists proclaim."

Lyssa shook her head. "You sure don't believe in the unbiased news media, do you?"

"Nope. I think it was William Randolph Hearst who said, 'You furnish the pictures. I'll furnish the war.' That was around the turn of the twentieth century or a little before it, and you can't tell me things have improved on that front since then."

She didn't respond right away, but that was all right. I was *not* looking forward to announcing ourselves to the world, especially since I was the Consul for all shifters in North America, and I hoped beyond hope we found someone who was good—no... divine—at being the face of it to the press. Because that most certainly *was not* me. I made a mental note to have a quiet word with Lyssa about finding someone who could wrap the press around his or her finger.

The last of the group passed through 'customs,' and the Foreign Minister gave Vicki what she needed for our next destination, and she promptly opened a portal straight to the center of a field office that looked more like a basecamp than the kind of permanent structure 'field office' brought to mind. Or at least, brought to my mind.

Large tents surrounded a communal campfire with felled logs for seating, and several men and women gaped at us as we stepped through the tear in reality.

"Hi," I said, aiming for affable. "I'm Wyatt. I'm afraid the Foreign Minister didn't give me a name for someone to speak with."

A grizzled veteran of many outdoors seasons stepped to the forefront. "I'm Carson. This is my field office, and I'd like to know just what gives you the right to tell us to stay here while you go off and hunt livestock rustlers."

Right... this again.

"So, the Foreign Minister said all of you were cleared for this, and sometimes, the best way to prove the point is just to show you."

Carson wasn't the only one who frowned at that as he said, "Now, just what the hell is that supposed to mean."

I shifted to my hybrid form as my response, and while the ladies looked startled and a little uneasy, more than one of the rough and tough outdoorsmen screamed like terrified children. One of them even pissed himself.

Damn... I love my job.

"Does this answer your question?" I asked in the growly voice of my hybrid. "I could show you my animal, but I don't want to ruin these clothes."

Carson's jaw moved in jerky motions like he was working himself up to a serious seizure, and the colored irises of his eyes were thin rings. Beads of sweat erupted on his forehead and cascaded down his face and cheeks.

When the jerky tremors moved past Carson's jaw, I shifted back to full human. "You all right, Carson? Talk to me, neighbor."

Still nothing.

"Vicki, do you mind coming over here? I think we have an imminent medical emergency."

My sister arrived at my side at once and moved straight to Carson. She spent a couple heartbeats looking him over before she turned to his people. "Does he have a history of seizures?"

A few shook their heads, but no one spoke.

Vicki shook her head and held out her hand. Her staff —Requiem—appeared in its dainty, unassuming guise. *That* freaked out a couple people, but she paid them no mind as she pressed the hand not holding *Requiem* to Carson's cheek. She rattled off a series of words in the language she used for her magic, and a healthy-green aura passed from her hand and into Carson.

Moments later, Carson blinked and shook his head. Then looked around like he didn't understand where he was or how he came to be there. His eyes settled on me after a short time, and the color fled his face faster than water through a sieve.

"Calm down," Vicki said, her tone carrying an authority only someone of her accomplishments and power could produce. "You're safe. My brother doesn't eat people, only mauls them if they're bad. You're not bad, are you?"

Carson shook his head 'no' with frantic vehemence.

"Didn't think so," Vicki replied. "Okay. So… it seems Wyatt's hybrid form tripped something in your brain. You were working on a rather nice seizure until I healed you out of it. Think of it like rebooting a computer almost. Not quite but close. Take a few minutes to relax and calm down, and we'll give this another go."

Vicki turned to me then. "And Wyatt? Once he calms down, don't break him again."

I personally didn't think I'd broken him the first time, but I wasn't about to argue with my sis in the current venue. I nodded my response and stepped back, turning instead to check on my people.

They milled about an area in front of where Vicki had opened the portal, and most of them looked as lost as I felt. We never thought to ask what kind of accommodations were available, and as such, we didn't plan on an extended camping trip. We thought… well, maybe expected… a hotel or motel or *something*. Honestly, we would've even been fine with a roach motel; with a couple primogenitors in the group, no insects would've remained in the area long.

Vicki arrived at my side as soon as she ushered Carson to a seat on a felled log around the campfire and surveyed the situation. After a couple seconds, she nodded, saying, "Yes, I see your point. We didn't come kitted out for camping. Right, then." She took a breath and called out to the hunting party. "Okay, everyone, kindly step to one side. I need a space with no people that's about twenty-five yards on a side."

Everyone present knew my sister, and most of them had witnessed how she had delivered fire support during the raid on the bunker in excess of what a modern artillery unit would have... once Miles shattered the Fae ward. In short, they beat feet to clear a space for her.

As soon as she had room to work, Vicki held *Requiem* up beside her as if handing it off to someone and released her grip. It hung there, not touching the ground, as if it patiently waited for her to grasp it once again. Vicki closed her eyes and rubbed her hands together, a nervous gesture of anticipation I recognized from our youth. She muttered to herself for a few moments, and the few snatches I caught sounded like she was sorting through options in her mind. After several moments, she nodded and said, "Okay. That should do."

She opened her eyes and held out her hand. *Requiem* obligingly drifted into her grasp. She extended her other hand toward the open space and recited a series of words in that language I didn't know, and in the blink of an eye, a small cluster of tents filled the space. And these weren't canvas Civil War tents, either. They weren't even professional mountaineering tents. They were full-on medieval pavillons, all different colors and complete with pennants and heraldry.

Vicki scanned the new digs, surveying her work in silence. After a couple heartbeats, she shrugged and said, "Well, it's not my best work, but we were a little cramped for time. There's a rainstorm coming in from the south, and I didn't want anyone—or their gear—soaked."

I heard a strangled gasp behind us followed by the sound of a body hitting the ground, and Vicki and I both turned to see Carson laying on the ground with his legs bowed over the log that had been his perch. I turned to my sister and put my index finger on my nose as I said, "Not it."

Vicki rolled her eyes. "What are you? Twelve?"

Then, she stomped across the camp to check on her patient.

24

The morning dawned fresh and clear after a night of steady rain that lulled me to sleep like the best lullaby. When I stepped outside my tent, I found Gabrielle waiting for me.

"Morning," I said, as I stretched.

"Last night would've been perfect to hunt," she said. It was a condemnation or chastisement, just a statement.

I nodded my agreement. "I considered that, but we should do the social politics and meet the farmers who lost sheep and ask their permission before we go traipsing all over their land. It's the neighborly thing to do."

Gabrielle sighed, then nodded. "I know. It's... just... I guess I always get a little impatient on a hunt. I tend to run off from the rest of the hunters."

"Well, as long as you come back to me, that's up to you," I remarked, pulling her into my arms for a kiss.

I loved how Gabrielle melted into my arms, snuggling close like I was the best blanket. But then, all of my ladies did that to a certain extent. After a few minutes, I said, "We should probably see about breakfast and head out."

Gabrielle stepped back and beamed. "Yes, you should. *Some* of us have been awake for a while and are ready to go."

I thought her reaction was a little odd, as we walked over to the campfire. The Natural Resources crew surrounded one side, and my people had camp chairs and such lining the other side.

Carson looked up as we approached. "Thanks for helping us with breakfast. Fresh is always better than packaged."

I frowned my confusion, and Carson grinned. "A couple of your people went out hunting before dawn. Brought back some damn fine deer. Technically, one could probably make a case for poaching, but there wolf tracks all over where we found the deer, so... I'm not going to pursue the matter."

"That brings to mind a question," I remarked as Gabrielle almost pushed me into a camp chair across from him. "What are you doing out here? I don't really know how to phrase this, but I would've thought a field office would at least be campers and offices on trailers."

Carson smiled. "Every so often, we like to run Naturalist classes for our people. Tracking, foraging, wilderness survival... that kind of thing. We already had this class scheduled, so when the reports of stolen sheep came in, we took it. Everyone here is a Natural Resources officer who might have to handle such a case, anyway."

"Fair enough. Honestly, it makes perfect sense. If the perpetrators weren't shifters, you'd be a good team to deal with it."

One of the guys off Carson's right frowned. "Just what makes you think the shifters are behind this?"

"The paw prints that *almost* match the local wolf population, for one. That the taken sheep were all healthy and able to fight back, for another. Most predators go for the easy kills when dealing with a herd. Just because a wolf shifter looks like a slightly outsized wolf, don't fool yourself into thinking it's only an animal; every shifter has full control with full human intelligence in animal form. So, take a second and think about what a wolf pack with military training like... say, the Small Unit Tactics School... would be able to achieve."

I saw the moment each person processed what I said. That thought changed the entire tone of the conversation.

"So, yeah... that's one reason shifters deal with shifters," I continued. "Another is that the strongest human on the planet might—and that's a huge *might*—be able to stand up to a shifter adolescent. Training will take you far, but there comes a point where you just have to step back and face the fact we're stronger than you. Considerably stronger, in fact."

The popping and crackling of the campfire was the only sound as the Natural Resources people internalized what I'd said. And that was good. We didn't need any idiots following us and sticking their noses into this. If it came down to a confrontation, I didn't want any squishy humans in the vicinity.

IT WASN'T long before everyone indicated they were ready, and Carson approached us where we milled around waiting for something to happen.

"I hope you don't mind hiking," he said. "We left our vehicles at a trail head about ten miles east of here. The sheep farms form something like a 'U' around us, and it'll take about a day to make a circuit of them."

Vicki smiled. "No, it won't. I appreciate your dedication to you Naturalist training, but we have things to do. Do you have an address for these farms or longitude and latitude coordinates?"

For a split second, Carson looked a little wild around the eyes, but he turned and moseyed back to his tent. He returned with a notebook, wherein he showed us all of the observations and notes he'd written thus far about the case. From the looks of the notebook, that wasn't all he used it for, and Vicki scribbled the information she needed on her own pad before nodding thanks to Carson.

When he came back from securing his notebook in his tent, Vicki asked, "What order did you use when you visited the farm?"

"Clockwise… east to west."

Vicki looked to me, and I shrugged. "If it worked for you once, there's no reason it won't work for us. Are you the instructor of your Naturalist class?"

Carson nodded. "Yeah, but Kayley can handle things while I introduce you to the farmers. We've already established ourselves with them, and if you just appear out of nowhere, that'll just rile them up. They're already a bit unsettled over the missing sheep."

Gabrielle arrived at my side and nodded. "We're all set, so whenever you're ready."

Vicki looked at the first farm on the list, saying, "I'll drop us about a half-mile from the farm. Hopefully, we won't scare anyone that way."

She lifted *Requiem*—still in its dainty, unassuming guise— and recited a series of words in that language that made me feel like my fur stood on end. The moment the feeling hit a kind of crescendo, the world blinked, and we stood on a small hill at the edge of a forest that overlooked a valley. Not too far in the distance, a series of fenced areas surrounded a cluster of buildings.

Carson turned and took his time looking over the buildings before he nodded and shook himself like a dog. "Damn. That is just unreal. We should've spent something like two— maybe, three—hours walking here."

I chuckled. "You should see what she can do when she's mad."

"Nope," Carson shot back, firmly but slowly shaking his head. "There's no part of her mad that I want anything to do with. I may be getting old and slowing down a little, but I'm not stupid or senile yet. Come on. Let's go."

He headed down the hill, and the rest of us fell in line behind him. As we walked, I scanned the area, mainly to get a feel for my surroundings, but at the same time, you never knew what you might see if you looked. It was beautiful countryside.

"We're just a little east of being halfway between Long Lake to the east and Beardmore and Tansleyville to the west," Carson said as he trudged down the hill. "Route 11 runs north from Nipigon, through Beardmore, and turns east just after Tansleyville. Small lakes and rivers are everywhere south of us, until you hit the north shore of Lake Superior. Our camp is—like I said—about two to three hours' walk north of us. Well… maybe a few points west of due north."

Carson continued to ramble on about the local terrain and wildlife as we walked to the sheep farm, and by the time we reached the semi-muddy track they probably called a driveway, a cluster of people stood on the main house's porch. They didn't look unfriendly, but they certainly didn't give off a welcoming vibe.

"Hullo the house," Carson called as we passed the arched gate. "It's Carson from Natural Resources. I've brought a hunting party that will be investigating the missing sheep."

That calmed them some, but they still carried tension that didn't make much sense to me. Then again, maybe they just preferred being out in the middle of nowhere to socializing with people. I couldn't blame them if that was the case; I've been known to disappear for a trek through the woods back home a time or two.

One of the people stepped down from the porch and waved for us to follow him. He led us to the north side of the farm, where we found a fresh section of fence. He pointed to a piece of bloody ground just outside the fence, and Gabrielle, Earl, and Paul went straight to it.

"That morning, I noticed a few head missing, and walking the fence, found a section broken and that bloody patch, there. I've never seen tracks quite like what were all over the place, and I figure last night's rain wiped out most of everything you need to track whatever did this."

Earl didn't quite control his snort of amusement, but I wasn't sure if it was loud enough for the humans to hear. While he and Paul crouched and examined the ground, Gabrielle produced an all-weather map of the local area, what looked like a grease pencil, and a compass. She headed off, following the tracks and making notes on her map as she went. After about twenty minutes and when she was just a tiny dot—even to my keen eyes—she turned and headed back to us.

When she arrived, I gave her a questioning eyebrow, and she said, "The rain last night wasn't enough to wipe out the tracks completely, and I found tracks coming in as well as going out. The trail going out has drops of blood that get fewer and fewer across the distance."

She crossed to the fence and used the top of the post as a desk as she took a straight-edge from a cargo pocket and drew a trend line based on her compass bearings as she followed the trail. One line by itself didn't help us much, but hopefully, the other farms would shed more light on the situation.

Earl and Paul stood and approached us. As soon as they were a respectful distance away, Earl said, "I think we have all we can get here, Boss. The Natural Resources people were right. The tracks kind of match wolves but not quite. We'll need to examine the other scenes to be sure, but we should be able to recognize these tracks wherever we find them."

I turned to Carson and the gentleman from the farm, nodding once. "Thank you for your time and hospitality, sir. Sorry to chat and run, but we need to head to the next farm."

We parted company with the farmer, heading west as he ambled back to the house. As soon as we reached the distant tree line, we stopped for Vicki to open a portal to our next destination.

OVER THE NEXT FEW HOURS, we visited all the farms that lost sheep. At every one, Gabrielle drew a line on her all-weather map. The trend lines all intersected at a point that looked kinda close to the highway Carson mentioned—Route 11. But just because the trend lines intersected there, did that mean the trails did? Gabrielle followed the tracks away from each sheep farm for about twenty minutes, taking headings at various points along the path. Twenty minutes of walking was *maybe* a quarter-mile at her slow and careful tracking pace, and who knew if the trails continued to match the trend lines?

As we waited for Gabrielle to return from the final trail, Earl nodded for me to meet him off to one side. I nodded and walked over to him.

"The scents all match," Earl said, speaking low enough that the humans present couldn't hear him and facing away so no one in the area could read his lips. "And you're right. Shifters did this. The *same* shifters did all of this."

That was enough for me.

"Okay, people," I said, drawing everyone's attention. "We're going to follow this trail. Keep your eyes peeled for converging trails from the other farms, but I'm doubting we'll have that right away."

Carson shook the farmer's hand and bid him goodbye, and we set off to meet Gabrielle who was still little more than a woman-shaped blotch against the distant landscape. As soon as we met her, everyone who could do so stripped and shifted, much to Carson's amazement. Vicki collected our clothes into small bags with our names on them and took most of them and Carson back to the campsite. As soon as she returned, we set off, bears in the lead.

It was well into afternoon when we arrived at what appeared to be a trailhead or roadside park. It didn't host any cars at the moment, but the trails from all the farms converged there. Earl and Paul set to searching the lightly graveled parking lot with their noses while Vicki retrieved our clothes and most of us shifted back to human.

Most of us were dressed and leaning on the thigh-high pole fence that separated the parking lot from the trees around us when the two bears ambled over to us, shifted to human, and reached for their clothes. We were kind enough to wait until they dressed before expecting a report.

"Okay," Earl began, still tucking his shirt into his pants, "the first thing is that all the trails are rather obvious in their convergence here. A hundred yards back into the tree line, you'll find wolf shifter tracks both leaving this parking lot and returning to it. We did pick up on faint hints of blood around the return tracks. So, once they were here, they shifted and piled into a couple vehicles. Based on the scent artifacts and faint tracks, I think we're looking at three to four trucks with heavy-duty off-road tires. We found a few hairs and bits of fur, but I don't know if they'll be enough for Vicki work her tracking spell or not.

Vicki shrugged. "Show me. The worst that can happen is that it doesn't work."

Paul waved for her to follow him, and they headed off.

"How often have sheep gone missing?" I asked, turning to Gabrielle. "Is there any identifiable pattern?"

Gabrielle nodded. "Every time a farm has lost sheep has been on the third night after the last sheep went missing."

"And when was the last farm hit?" Earl asked, after a non-committal grunt.

"Three nights ago."

I scanned the area, trying to marshal my thoughts. No one on Route 11 could see this trailhead or whatever it was. Thick trees and foliage blocked the view. But the foliage was not so thick moving away from the highway. I wondered if people came and kept the brush down to make accessing the forest easier. A breeze blew into the area from the northeast while I considered the situation, and without warning, Earl pivoted on his heel without warning, sniffing the air.

"What is it, Earl?"

"I might be wrong, Alpha... but I think I smell engine exhaust matching the traces Paul and I found over there. And I think it's heading this way."

I whistled and, when Paul and Vicki looked my way, gestured for them to come back.

"Okay... Earl thinks the trucks are coming back. Let's get back into the woods and wait a little bit to see what happens."

Everyone nodded, and like Robin Hood and his Merry Men, we retreated to the safety of the trees. Each of us picked a tree that was large enough to hide us, and we settled in for a wait. We didn't have to wait long.

Maybe ten minutes later, four lifted trucks with massive wheels sporting equally massive off-road tires rolled to a stop. The crew cabs were full, and a handful of people rode in the open beds of each truck. All of them dismounted when the vehicles came to a full and complete stop, and the lot of them seemed rather excited and energetic about something. They were all smiles, grins, high-fives, and back-slapping as they milled about the parking lot.

One of them climbed up to stand on a fence post and whistled to get everyone's attention.

"All right, pups," our shifter hearing plus the breeze allowed us to follow along with his speech without undue effort, "this is the night you'll become full members of the pack. It's time you made your first kills as wolves. Somewhere to the west of here is a sheep farm. You will shift and head out. Track only with your senses. Pick a sheep, kill it, and return here with your prize."

I'd heard enough. I stepped out from behind my tree and approached the fence until I was almost close enough to smack the guy's butt. A few noticed me before I reached the actual clearing, but the guy standing on the fence post didn't.

"Yeah, about that…"

The apparent orchestrator of this excursion yelped in surprise and tried to spin, only to end up falling off the fence post. He landed hard but powered through it, jumping to his feet.

"Who the hell are you?" he asked as he tried not to wince as he stood.

"I'm Wyatt Magnusson, Consul of the Shifters of North America, and I'm here to talk about this little campaign you have going against the sheep farms of the area."

The new arrivals all shared looks among themselves before the apparent leader scrunched up his face and said, "Wyatt who?"

The hardy souls gathered behind Mister Stand-On-A-Fence-Post snickered at his comeback, but it didn't strike me as all that funny. And not just because it was directed to— and about—me. Everyone in his group acted like they inter-

ROBERT M. KERNS

preted it as a joke, but I *saw* the guy's facial expression. It wasn't a joke. He had no idea who I am.

On the one side, that's cool. It's exactly how I would have preferred to live my life. I didn't *want* to be Alpha of Precious and Godwin County. I didn't *want* to be Consul of the North American Shifters. And I damn sure didn't want to be some kind of war leader charged with saving the world when the Fae finally decided to invade.

But—like the man said—we don't always get what we want.

While this guy's crowd continued to laugh and snicker at my supposed expense, I considered how I wanted to handle the situation. One school of thought suggested attempting to establish common ground and build a rapport. Find out what they wanted, what they hoped to achieve by raiding all these sheep farms. The more I considered it, that was probably the best, least-violent way to go about it. It was also the slowest and didn't seem to carry much of any guarantee that it would work.

So, I shifted to my hybrid form. Oddly enough, everyone stopped snickering... all at once.

"The Shifter Council named me Consul of the North American shifters, you pissant wolf," I intoned in the growly voice of that form. "All shifters on the continent answer to me now, and I want to know *why* you risk our relations with the government of Canada by raiding livestock. I'm willing to give you a chance to have your say, but unless you make an *extremely* convincing argument, either this shit stops now... or you do."

Just to make my point, I flooded the area with primogenitor alpha dominance, and it was only through an obvious force of will that the apparent leader remained on his feet. Everyone else in his group dropped to their knees, rolled onto their backs, and bared their throats.

228

"Just what gives you the right to come in here and tell me how to run my pack?" he blustered while the scent of fear rolled off him in waves. "We are the dominant species on this planet, and I say it is long past time we acted like it. The humans and their works should serve—"

His diatribe ended in a strangled gurgle after I shredded his throat with my claws. He collapsed to the ground, choking on his own blood, and I watched the life fade from his eyes.

"Okay. Immediate problem solved," I growled. "The rest of you, get back in your trucks and get out of here. If you want mutton, *buy it*. Don't raid farms. Especially don't raid farms in your wolf forms, night or not. If I have to come back up here to deal with anything even remotely like this again, your entire pack down to the pups will join this guy." I leaned over and wiped my bloody hand and claws on the cooling corpse, then shifted back to human and pointed to the former leader. "And deal with this, too. I don't want the authorities finding his corpse here. Any questions?"

Those not terrified past the point of rational thought shook their heads to communicate they had no questions.

"Good. So you understand the situation?"

The head shaking turned to nodding.

"Fair enough. Clean this up and go. Remember… this was your one and only warning. Don't waste it."

I turned and ambled back into the forest where I met with the hunting party. We waited until they gathered their leader's corpse, cleaned the blood, and left. Earl checked their work and pronounced that they did a decent job.

That done, we gathered around Vicki, and she took us back to the camp.

. . .

CARSON TRIED to insist that I tell him what happened, but that flew about as well as a dead sparrow. We shouldered our packs as Vicki dismissed our tents, and she contacted Mina for arrival details at the Seattle airport. Soon enough, we were back within the United States, dancing the dog and pony show so our passports showed a legal return.

As the hunting party split up to go their various ways and Vicki, my ladies, and I headed into the Alpha's house, Lyssa stopped and turned to the rest of us, saying, "Wait... what about Charlotte?"

25

Charlotte showed up in a couple days. She wasn't *quite* spitting fire, but she certainly wasn't happy. She stormed into the admin building, lucking into one of the rare occasions I was actually there, and stood in my office's doorway glaring daggers at me.

She didn't say a word for so long that I decided to fill the void. "Good day to you, Charlotte. I must say... you look rather vexed."

"Vexed? Vexed?" she retorted, her voice rising. "I'll show you vexed, Wyatt Magnusson. You left me in Ottawa looking like a fool in front of my boss—the Foreign Minister—and *the Prime Minister*. They spent half a day waiting for you to come back after the Natural Resources team reported the matter handled."

"If they spent half of an entire workday sitting around and twiddling their thumbs when they should've been handling the business of government, I'd say they deserve to look like fools. From what little I know, governments aren't toys. It actually matters whether you neglect them or not."

Charlotte's jaw clenched and unclenched, and I fought the urge to grin when I wondered, if I fed her nails right then, would she shit ball bearings? Oh, damn... maybe if I fed her coal, we could get some diamonds.

That thought threatened to slip the leash, so I pushed all of it firmly aside. I'd share them and the whole riff my mind started down with the ladies later. They would appreciate my comic genius. Well... Karleen probably would.

Still, she looked like she was winding up to have another go at me, and I wasn't exactly fond of that at all. Time to nip this weed at the root...

"Okay, Charlotte. You've had your say. You're pissed. They're probably pissed, thinking we snubbed them. We didn't, but I'm not going to spend a lot of time worrying about it. We handled their problem, and it shouldn't come back. If they feel horribly affronted, they are welcome to withdraw their mission here. Trust me... the shifters won't miss it. If there's something else—something important—you need to discuss, kindly move on to that. Otherwise, I'm sure your people are waiting for you."

Charlotte stood there, still glaring at me for several moments. At last, she pivoted on her heel and stormed out of sight.

Yes, I was a bit rough with her. Yes, I could've handled it better. Yes, I probably did not win a friend there. But I didn't work for them. Not for Canada or the US or anyone else. I was responsible for the shifters of Godwin County, and that was it. I had every intention of assembling a shifter legal team to go over every word, syllable, and punctuation mark in the investiture that made me Consul to find a way to nullify it.

This shit was getting more involved than I wanted, and I couldn't just walk into the woods and not come back. Well...

I *could*, but I hated the thought of leaving Vicki even though I knew she'd be fine. I had no idea how Karleen had done it. Sixty years without substantive contact with her family? I started missing Vicki around the sixty *hour* mark. It was rare that we didn't at least trade a few texts back and forth over the course of a day.

But then again, I hadn't walked in Karleen's fur. I didn't know the whys and wherefores that led her to abandon shifter society, so I wasn't exactly in the best position to say it would or would not work for me.

I growled a sigh. Or I sighed a growl. Not really sure on that, but it was how I felt. I needed a break. A few days before the sojourn to Canada, I had overheard a couple people in the diner talking about a lake up in the high country. Supposedly good fishing, the way they talked. I wasn't much for fish, but I couldn't remember the last time anyone brought some in for Gladys. The longer I considered the idea, the more appealing it became.

I stood and left my office. I stopped at Lyssa's door long enough to say, "I'm going up to that lake people keep talking about. I'll be back sometime."

I didn't even give her a chance to respond.

FROM THE ADMIN BUILDING, I went home, tossed my clothes on the bed and grabbed neat quasi-saddlebags someone had devised for us. Using measurements of our human and animal forms, some genius designed a harness with large bags on either side of it. We put it on in human form, but there was enough space that we could shift and carry stuff without ripping anything. The cargo harness for my Smilodon had four compartments a little larger than saddle-bags for a horse.

I started to head down to the kitchen to retrieve the cold packs, but on further consideration, I stuffed my clothes into one of the four compartments and tied a pair of shoes onto the harness. Never hurt to be prepared.

Once I had everything I thought I needed, I lined the insulated compartments of the harness with cold packs from our freezer and pulled it on like a t-shirt. It felt weird, standing there with it hanging on my shoulders. The weight distribution was all wrong. It didn't fit right. Still, though, I decided to give it a try and went out to the back deck.

I touched the part of my mind that was no longer human and 'flexed the muscle' to trigger the shift. I flowed into the stocky build of my Smilodon, and the fit of the harness felt immeasurably better. I moved around the backyard to get a feel for it and felt confident enough that I proceeded to head into the hills.

IT FELT good to escape the demands of Alpha and Consul. And while I didn't have a bear's nose, mine was good enough to appreciate the scents all around me. Pine. Spruce. Soft moss. These were the smells I associated with 'home.' It had been too long since I went for a hike, even if I was better built for hiking now.

I chuffed a laugh. It was easier to bound up the hills at a half-sprint with four legs than keeping a steady pace with two.

I reached the lake about mid-morning, and while it wasn't huge, it certainly wasn't a wading pond. I had no intention of wading or swimming, but the water was cool and nice. A stream of snowmelt might have fed the lake; we were close to a couple peaks that kept their snowcaps year-round. Either way, it was a pleasant drink.

Standing on the shore and watching my reflection ripple in the water's surface, I realized that I was totally unprepared for fishing. I wasn't a bear. I couldn't just wade into the water and scoop out a fish with my bare paws. Well, okay... I *could*, but that involved getting wet.

Fine. No fishing today. Maybe I should invest in a collapsible fishing rod if I was going to make a habit of this. I padded around the lake to a small rock outcropping that overlooked the water. Once I stood atop it, I decided it looked just perfect for an afternoon nap. The cargo harness didn't even feel too out of place when I curled up and rested my head on my paws.

I was accustomed to being a Smilodon—for the most part —but every now and then, I still forgot about my huge, curved incisors and gave myself a jarring impact when I tried to rest my chin on the floor or ground. Dirt wasn't so bad; they would usually sink into loose dirt or sod easily enough. But wood or stone? Not so much.

I WASN'T sure how long I dozed, but when I woke and looked at the sky, the sun looked halfway between noon and sunset. I stretched, flexing my legs and claws, before turning and heading back to town. I could get away with playing hooky for a day... usually... but I didn't want any of the ladies to worry.

I hadn't exactly been in the best mood when I left the admin building that morning, and I could totally see Lyssa adding two and two to get nine and concluding my abrupt statement was a cover for leaving the shifters behind.

As I trotted down the hill, I reflected a little more on the idea of having liaisons with the human governments. I didn't like it. We had gotten along just fine without them for hundreds of years. Beyond that, they knew enough to have shifter-only units in the militaries, so why complicate matters? Was it that the shifters had a Consul now? Something approximating a president or prime minister? Was *that* it?

I didn't know, and no clear answer came to mind... beyond sending Charlotte and her people packing with a note that things should go back to the way they were before the Shifter Council's asinine idea to make me Consul.

I wouldn't kick Mina out... not as such... because Noah needed to learn about his new life now, and Mina might decide she wanted to hop the fence and become a shifter, too. But I was definitely going to have a quiet word with her about Uncle Sam's mission here being over. If either Canada or the US needed the shifters, they already knew how to find us... and that wasn't by pestering me.

The major question in my mind was how to resolve the problem of Consul without making Lyssa and her friends and allies on the Council look like fools. *They* were pleased with themselves for their great idea, except the poor sod they foisted it onto didn't think it was all that great.

Helping Lyssa and her friends save face or maintain their dignity or whatever I should call it was the *only* reason I let it fly as long as I had. I needed to talk to Alistair about it, and maybe my grandparents. They might be able to see a way for me to get rid of the position without hurting anyone.

BY THE TIME I reached the outskirts of Precious, I felt like I had worked through my underlying bad mood and was back to a certain level of contentment. A lot of that centered round my hope that Alistair, my grandparents, or *someone*

would be able to help me get rid of the Consul business, but everyone needed hope... right?

As I padded through the gate into the backyard of the Alpha's house, my ears caught raised voices. There was a heated confrontation out front of the house, and it sounded like Karleen was about ready to throw down. I whacked the button that opened the back door and padded into the master suite. I shifted to human, divested myself of the harness that ended up carrying only my clothes, and dressed with alacrity.

I headed for the front door... but I didn't know the full extent of what was happening. If my ladies told someone I wasn't home and then I walked out the front door... well... I didn't want to give anyone the slightest provocation to call my ladies liars. That wouldn't end well.

So, I went back through the gate of the fence, jogged through the backyards aways and came out onto the sidewalk a couple blocks down from the Alpha's house. I saw a large collection of people confronting what looked to be Karleen and Gabrielle and a long line of trucks and vans sitting far enough from the sidewalk that Sheriff Clyde should probably write them all tickets.

I adopted a relaxed pace and headed home. When I arrived on the fringe of the disturbance and Karleen noticed me, she pointed both her arms at me like a game show hostess revealing a prize, as she almost shouted at a rough-looking specimen less than six feet in front of her.

"See? I *told you* he wasn't home, you stupid dog. Now, why don't you get your mangy hide out of my face before I take exception to your existence?"

I figured these idiots were—at most—five minutes from receiving an education they would not enjoy. I watched the guy standing so close to her clench his fists and grit his teeth. The tension in his jaw was obvious from twenty feet away.

I thought he was about to commit the last mistake of his life for several seconds before he spat on the sidewalk and growled, "Fine. We came to deal with him, anyway. Once we're finished, I'll be back for you, girlie."

Well now... this was interesting. They were here for me? I noticed multiple states represented as license plates on the trucks, and none of them were Washington state. So, they'd driven a decent distance to be here. But why? I felt very confident I'd never seen these people before in my life.

"Well, I'm here now," I said as I pushed my way through the crowd and arrived at my ladies' side. I saw Lyssa was there too, but the way the three stood, Karleen and the crowd blocked my sight of her. "So, what has you so worked up you've driven all this way to talk with me?"

The man turned to me, and I fought to keep from snorting a laugh. He was a classic. Tall. Broad-shouldered. About twice as muscular as most shifters. About two days of stubble on his cheeks and chin. And just tall enough to look down to meet my eyes and sneer while he did it.

"My friends and I... what was it she said... take exception to your decision that you rule all the shifters in North America now. And just like the Council's announcement said, we came to Precious to explain it to you."

Ah, so that's it.

"And I'm guessing your explanation will take the form of a dominance challenge?"

The dumbass actually had the nerve to pat me on my head as he smirked. "Hey... you catch on pretty quick. But you're going to have to wait your turn for me, kitty. I'll be your final challenge... if you make it that far."

If I make it that far? What on earth was this guy smoking? Hadn't they heard about Thomas Carlyle? Maybe they had and didn't believe it. He seemed pretty confident I wouldn't live to reach him, and I wondered what gave him that confidence. But either way, if they wanted to dance, I'd oblige them.

I took a deep breath and released it as a sigh. "Fair enough." I pointed toward the arena with my thumb. "The arena's over there. I'm going to change clothes, and I'll meet you over there."

"No. We'll fight now."

I snorted a laugh. "Go howl at the moon. We'll fight when I say we fight. Now, get your furry ass over to the arena, or get out of my county."

I knew it was a calculated risk, but I couldn't resist turning my back on him to walk inside the house. I heard more than one growl over my shoulder, but I didn't care. And they didn't do anything. So, either they needed their courage propped up, or they were at least *that* respectful.

It took little time to change into my exercise gear. Thin, stretchy, flexible clothes that wouldn't impair my movement. I turned toward the door to leave, but *something* in the back of my mind convinced me to retrieve the knife my grandpa gave me from the closet. I'd had to punch a couple more holes in the belt as my waist slimmed over the intervening weeks since I became a shifter, and with the buckle at my navel, the knife hung at my side under my left arm, angled for a cross draw.

With the knife on my hip, the vague, amorphous concern I'd felt in the back of my mind faded, and I felt as ready as I was going to feel. The unfortunate nature of these fights was that I had little choice in the outcome if I defeated them. I didn't *want* to kill them, but I didn't like the idea of leaving them alive to lick their wounds and come at me again. Especially if they drew a couple brain cells and went after my family or someone not quite as able to defend themselves. That would not end well for them, but I'm sure it would look like a viable plan in the heat of the moment.

I looked over myself in the mirror and worked through a couple stretches to be sure the clothes wouldn't hamper my movement and nodded. Then sighed as I left the Alpha's house, headed for the arena. I guess it was time for me to be the gene pool's chlorine again.

26

By the time I arrived at the arena, a sizable crowd of the town's citizens flowed around me, and I heard more than one person express unkind thoughts at these people starting crap where there was no need. It was nice to know the townsfolk in Precious liked me, but I also noticed Charlotte wasn't among them.

That thought brought a smile to my face. Right now, I wasn't willing to lay any wagers on which side Charlotte would cheer for, even though I knew her welcome around town would be short-lived if she cheered for whoever these people were. And honestly, the humans had no part of this. It wasn't their thing. It wasn't *my* thing, either, but I did not have as much of a choice. I didn't know any way to decline the challenge that also resolved the issue, so if these guys wanted to fight, I'd fight 'em. It kinda sucked for them that I didn't feel much leeway on the matter of whether they lived, circumstances being what they were.

I entered the arena through the participants' entrance and found all of them milling around the far end. When I reached the center of the arena, I stopped and tried to count noses. The way they kept moving made that a bit challenging, and I thought I counted them all when I hit thirty.

If they thought I was going to fight all of them at once, they were crazy *and* stupid.

"Okay," I said in a voice that carried into the stands, "figure out who's challenging me first, and the rest of you, get up in the stands. I'll fight two of you at the same time at most."

The blowhard from the sidewalk outside the Alpha's house stepped forward and spoke in an equally loud voice, "And what if *I* say you'll fight all of us at once?"

"I'll wait a day until you've had a chance to howl your crazy at the moon, and we'll try this again."

My townsfolk filling the stands all laughed at that, and I saw more than one of his people fight to hide a snicker, too. He did *not* appreciate that. He gritted his teeth and glared at me in silence for several moments.

"Fine." He spat the word like the vilest epithet and turned back to his people.

They talked among themselves for a while, before most of them jumped and pulled themselves up to the level of the stands. They quickly assumed seats on their side of the arena, and my people gave them a wide berth, making very clear their lack of welcome in my town. Only two remained. Fair enough.

"Okay, folks, let's do this. I had stuff to do today that didn't involve killing you."

The two facing me from the far end of the arena grinned and reached behind their backs. They drew blades that looked to be just a few inches too short to be called short swords, and I recognized the rune stamped into each blade that glowed silver. A fearful hush spread throughout my people in the stands like a wave, and more than one of my opponents' associates smirked from their position in the stands.

Oh, fun… shifter-bane blades.

Did I sense them somehow when we all stood outside the Alpha's house? Was *that* why I had that niggling thought in the back of my mind to bring grandpa's knife? I didn't know and, frankly, wasn't sure right then was the best time to dig into the matter.

The two fighters advanced on me with their own antici-patory grins, and I decided it was past time to show them *my* secret weapon, too. I shifted to my hybrid form, kicked off my shoes, and extended *all* of my claws as I struck a pose and roared my defiance to the world.

More than one of the newcomers looked a bit less sure of their plans, right then, but they did not have my focus. I charged them, running full out, and loving the extra traction the claws on my feet gave me. My speed seemed to surprise them, and they froze for a split second… and it was the *wrong* split second.

As I reached about three arm lengths from the pair, I dove into a shoulder roll that moved me on a diagonal toward my right side. As I came out of it and into a crouch, my position was perfect to rake the claws of my left hand across one guy's torso, shredding him from the right side of his groin to the left side of his ribs. His scream hit an octave I didn't know men could reach after puberty, and he forgot all about his blade as he fought to keep his internal organs from going external.

His buddy's shriek jerked the other guy out of his paraly-sis, and he spun to thrust his blade at me. The guy whose abdomen I shredded—let's just call him Idiot One—was already collapsing to his feet, and it required little effort to angle him far enough backward so that Idiot Two ran his blade through Idiot One's throat because he couldn't stop his movement in time.

I released my grip on Idiot One and did another shoulder roll, this time to my left. Idiot Two ripped his blade free of Idiot One and tried to bring it around to cut me, but I caught his wrist and put my full strength into a push against the outside of his elbow. A vicious crack—followed *very* closely by a pitiful scream—echoed around the arena as I forced Idiot Two's elbow to bend in a most unintended direction. When his blade fell from a now-numb hand, I scooped it out of the air by its hilt and made a right-to-left slash across the guy's throat as I stood.

Idiot Two collapsed as blood cascaded down his chest, and I decided to put him out of his misery by driving his own blade into his heart. As the second corpse of the thirty-odd idiots fell to the arena floor, I stepped over and claimed Idiot One's blade and cleaned both of my prizes on Idiot Two.

When I stood from that, I looked at the section of the stands where the remaining fodder waited and shouted in the growly voice of my hybrid form, "Next!"

Five of the guys waiting in the stands stood, drew their own blades, and walked around the edge of the arena. When they reached a point close to me, they laid their blades on the floor and left. The ringleader of the bunch cursed them for spineless cowards at the top of his lungs and grabbed two of those who remained, pushing—almost throwing—them into the arena with me.

"You don't have to do this," I growled. "Surrender your blades, just like those guys, and I'll let you walk out of here alive."

"If you're so spineless you listen to him, I'll eat you... and your families," the blowhard raged from the stands.

I saw the turmoil in their eyes. They didn't want to fight me, but the blowhard terrified them. I lifted my eyes to the crowd surrounding the loudmouth and saw those feelings mirrored in most of his people. Fine. Time to up the stakes.

"It sounds to me like he's the one itching for a fight, but *he's* afraid to face me fresh and at my best. Kinda makes one wonder if he's as capable as he claims. *None* of the rest of you want to fight me. I can see that plain as day from sixty feet away, so I'll make you a deal. Toss the loudmouth into the arena, and leave. I'll even let you keep the blades."

A long silence extended as I watched them. All at once, almost as if they were a hive mind, the people surrounding the blowhard rose up, grabbed him, and heaved him over the chain to land less than twenty feet from me. Then, they walked out *and* dropped their blades on or near the first five.

While the blowhard scrabbled to his feet, I looked at the two he had thrown to the Smilodon and jerked my head toward the arena entrance. They made a dash for it, pausing only long enough to toss their blades up with the rest.

Good. I wanted to know where these blades came from, and I imagined Vicki and my grandparents might appreciate the knowledge, too.

"Well, it's just you and me now, Daisy," I growled at him, breaking into a smile that didn't have a shred of mirth to it. "I think we should have started here, and I'm glad I convinced those other poor sods to save their lives. So, pull your blade and let's get started."

I watched the muscles around his eyes twitch, and a strange symbol appeared in his forehead, moments before I heard a sizzling sound like burning meat. The blowhard gasped and relaxed, taking a step back as he too pulled a blade. I hoped someone was recording this and had an angle on that symbol. *That* seemed like something I should know.

ROBERT M. KERNS

He snarled at me and lunged, his blade leading the way. I was so distracted by the odd symbol—whether rune or glyph or something else—that I almost didn't dodge in time. As it was, the blade drew a line across my left forearm, drawing blood. *Ouch... that didn't feel good at all.*

Important safety tip, there; avoid sharp objects like blades.

Despite the blood and the pain, the wound wasn't that bad, and I was able to angle my hand and rake my claws along his side as he moved past. My claws didn't dig deep, but he bled now, too. Five places to my one. If this was going to be a battle of attrition, I'd take those numbers.

He gasped and danced away, the blade guarding his withdrawal.

After a couple moments of watching each other, we started a slow circle while we sought an opening. He seemed to know his way around a knife fight, which made me wonder why he hadn't stepped up to be the first opponent. Maybe he didn't want his people to see him fight? Learn his weaknesses?

I must've looked distracted, because he shot a quick thrust toward my gut. I danced out of the way and dropped into a shoulder roll to the right. He surprised me by doing his own to get away from my new position.

Hrmm... this was not going to be the quick fight I wanted.

OVER THE NEXT SEVERAL MINUTES, we danced back and forth, each of us getting a few strikes on the other. And it wasn't long until drops of blood followed our steps like we were a pair of macabre rainclouds.

As I watched, I noticed his movements slowing. Not much, but just enough to notice. And if I were going to be honest, I didn't feel in tip-top shape myself, but the blood loss seemed to be affecting him more or faster for some reason. Maybe because I was a primogenitor? I wasn't sure, but it was something to look into later... somehow.

I noticed he started dodging a lot more, refusing to commit and get close for a strike, and I felt sluggishness creeping into my movements, too. Damn... I needed to end this before we both collapsed. I wanted to be sure there was no doubt who won, and it wasn't going to be him.

We danced a little while longer, and if he realized I herded him toward the corpses of the first two fighters, he didn't show it. What's more, I thought I had his pattern of dodges down. Side - Side - Back. Side - Side - Back. He'd done that now for several sequences. Did he realize that? Was he baiting me?

Time to see.

I had him just about where I wanted him and dove into another shoulder roll to my left. He did his half-jump back, but his feet caught on Idiot Two's corpse. He went down.

I came out of my shoulder roll and leaped to pounce on him. Fire erupted in my shoulder when he brought his blade up in time to stab me... but not fast enough to save his life. As his blade slid into my left shoulder, the claws of my right hand swept across his throat, savaging it and ripping away a nice handful of meat.

I sat back on my heels as blood bathed my left side, and I watched my opponent die. The people in the stands erupted in cheers, and before I knew it, my ladies surrounded me, followed closely by Doc and one of his assistants pulling a gurney.

I felt a little loopy and wanted the burning pain in my shoulder to stop, but Gabrielle slapped my hand away when I went to remove the blade.

"No, Wyatt. Let Doc do it back at the infirmary."

"Okay," I mumbled. It took all my strength to lift my head and scan the faces of the three people I loved most in this world. I smiled as best I could. "I love you."

The world faded to black as it felt like I fell.

27

I felt... sore. I couldn't remember the last time I felt sore. Maybe the last strenuous hike before I became a shifter? I dunno. Everything was fuzzy, like trying to catch fog when reaching for a memory. I opened my eyes and saw the white *everything* of the infirmary.

"Hello, brother mine," Vicki said off to my left. "I'm glad you came back to us."

It felt like a labor worthy of Hercules to turn my head toward her voice. My sister perched on one of those backless stools that seem to be everywhere in medical facilities, and she held an emory board to her fingernails, the motion paused as she looked at me.

"Was it in doubt?" I rasped, my voice dry and ill-used.

Vicki shrugged and went back to filing her nails. "I've never told anyone this—not even Grams—but I'm a pre-cog. I mean... pre-cognitive. I get glimpses of the future sometimes. Nothing significant yet and never very far into the future, but they happen. The day the cougar attacked you... for just a split second, I saw you dead, then you weren't. *That* flipped me out. But it happened again, so I came here.

Ditched a high-society party to come check on you, in fact, and I'm glad I did." She stopped filing her nails and slid off the stool, taking the steps necessary to stand at my side. "I saved your life, Wyatt. Doc was doing everything he could, but you were bleeding out faster than he could stop it. That knife in your shoulder nicked your brachial artery, and it was flooding your chest with blood when I arrived. It took all I had to put you back together well enough that you were out of immediate danger, because those were not just shifter-bane blades. They had a nasty bleed effect layered under the '-bane.' Someone made those knives to kill shifters and create wounds that resisted healing."

She leaned over me and pulled me into a side hug. My shoulder twinged a bit, but I wasn't about to say a word.

"I love you, Wyatt. Don't scare me like that again."

I did my best to smile. "I didn't mean to scare you this time, sis. I kinda wish now that I hadn't let the other ones leave. It would be handy to know how they came into having those knives."

"Well, I don't think you need to worry your furry head over it," Vicki remarked as she bopped me on the nose. "The shifter-bane rune is one of our most closely guarded secrets, and having this many of them out in the wild constitutes a major security breach. I have already spoken with Sheriff Clyde about it, and he kindly offered to pass me security footage of the trucks. I plan to find those shifters who left and have a rather pointed word with them about the provi-dence of their surrendered weapons."

It struck me as a bit dicey whether shifters would appre-ciate being interrogated by a Magi, and I started to speak. But Vicki stopped me by putting her fingers against my lips.

"Now, didn't I just say not to worry your furry head, Wyatt? I *know* shifters might take offense at a Magi ques-tioning them, so I've arranged some help. Lyssa... well, all three of your ladies... sounded *very* enthusiastic at having a quiet—or maybe not so quiet—word with the idiots who tried to kill you. I imagine—between Lyssa, Karleen, and yours truly—we should be able to shake the tree enough to get some ripe fruit to fall."

Now, she turned and produced a plastic cup of ice water with a straw. She held the straw to my lips, and I sipped. I sloshed the water around in my mouth a bit, then swallowed, savoring the refreshing feeling of a cold drink of water.

"Why isn't Gabrielle invited to your fun?"

Vicki beamed. "Oh, she was, but they decided someone needed to stay and take care of you until you get your strength back, and she drew the short straw."

I nodded. I wanted to argue that I didn't need anyone taking care of me, but I felt weaker than a newborn kitten.

Vicki seemed to sense that and gave me a soft smile. "It's okay, brother mine. Go to sleep. One of us will be here when you wake up."

I DIDN'T KNOW how much time had passed when I woke up next, and I opened my eyes to see Lyssa perched on the stool where Vicki had sat. She tapped away on her tablet, the most adorable frown wrinkling her brow as she worked.

"Hi."

Her eyes shot to me, and she smiled. "Hey, you. Vicki told us you woke up. How do you feel?"

"Sore. Tired. Probably more, but those two overshadow everything else."

"I'd say they would. Are you hungry? Thirsty?"

I considered the question and nodded. "I could go for some water."

She lifted that same plastic cup into view, still full of ice water. I grabbed the straw with my teeth and went to town. Yes. Pure ambrosia. When I had my fill, I released the straw, and Lyssa took it away.

"I'm kinda surprised you and Vicki and Karleen aren't already off on your inquest."

Lyssa shook her head. "None of us are going anywhere until you're home in the Alpha's house. You are incredibly vulnerable right now, and while I doubt there's anyone interested in fighting you, we're on high alert all the same."

"Have I missed anything of note?"

"Well, the Canadians withdrew their mission. I think your rather pointed comments to Charlotte convinced them to keep us at arms' length. Not sure what that'll do when we need allies, what with the Fae invasion and all, but it's one less batch of interlopers in Precious."

"Now, now. You know I don't see Mina and her crew as interlopers. After all, Noah's one of us now."

Lyssa's whole demeanor lit up. "Oh, Noah had his first shift! He's the cutest little puppy. Well... not little but still cute. His coat is kind of a reverse Dalmatian; except where a Dalmatian is white and black, he's kind of a bluish-gray and black. I don't think I've ever seen another wolf shifter with that coloring, and Mina already loves snuggling with him. It's a horrible joke, but sometimes, I think she asks him to shift just so she can cuddle with her cute puppy."

"Has she said anything else about becoming a shifter?"

"No. Not yet. I saw her watching Sloane fly over the town, the other day. She had this huge grin, too, so it may not be too far in the future. I think she really wants to fly on her own. Oh... and Hauser came to us and said she wanted to discuss becoming a shifter, but not until you were back on your feet. She totally understands that now may not be the best time for that."

I nodded my understanding, hoping I communicated

understanding and not agreement that this was a bad time. I personally didn't think it was a bad time, but what did I know?

"Karleen has taken Burke under her wing, so to speak. They've been working through exercises and training. Karleen as a dire wolf is just a little more agile than Burke as an American lion, and that has proven interesting for all involved. During their training bouts, Karleen likes to dart behind Burke and nip her tail when she's not moving fast enough or if she botches a move or something. It winds Burke up something fierce."

I chuckled in spite of myself. "Well, would you like to have someone always nipping *your* tail?"

Lyssa winced. "Okay. Fair point. That's just not fun."

"Any word on when I get to trade the infirmary for the Alpha's house?"

"If you keep improving like you have been, Doc wants to see how you handle standing on your own. If you do that without too many problems, he said he'll kick you out and make house calls."

Okay. That was good. Even though I'd been unconscious or sleeping through most of it, I was tired of being in the infirmary.

"Well, why don't you go get him, and let's see how I do?"

Lyssa smiled and stepped beyond the curtain. Soon enough, I had a pretty large audience waiting to watch me get out of bed for the first time since my injury. I wasn't sure I was that entertaining, but at least no one sold or offered popcorn.

I pushed the cover and sheet back and rolled to a sitting position. The room tried to spin on me a little, so I waited for that to pass. Then, I cautiously slid off the bed, and my bare feet hit the cold floor. That wasn't so much fun, and while my legs wobbled enough to notice, I didn't fall or have to catch myself. I stood there until Doc nodded and left.

He came back with the ubiquitous wheelchair. Seriously? I could shift into a Smilodon, and he was going to make someone push me out of the infirmary in a wheelchair? But when I took a couple steps to demonstrate my mastery of ambulation, I felt the strength in my legs start to wane.

Yeah... so maybe the wheelchair wasn't such a bad idea after all.

I returned to sitting on the edge of the hospital bed and asked for my clothes. I hoped I hadn't given any outward sign that I wasn't up to walking out of there, despite being able to stand on my own. But either way, Doc didn't seem to mind.

It wasn't long until I was dressed and rolling down the sidewalk toward the Alpha's house. After a quick couple rounds of rock - paper - scissors, the ladies determined that Karleen would drive the wheelchair, and they all hovered around me like I might vanish on them or something at any minute.

IT FEELS good to be walking around the town under my own power once again. Even three weeks after the attack, I still have days where I just do not quite feel like myself. Doc assures me that will pass, as long as I keep up the diet he gave me and the exercises he assigned me. I try my best to be a good patient, but I do sneak some ice cream from time to time. There's just something about waffle cones that is absolutely divine.

Vicki, Lyssa, and Karleen are off tracking down the shifters that came in here looking for a fight. The last time they checked in, they arrived in the county where their first name supposedly lived. But they refused to tell me any more than that. They didn't want me to worry... about them or their search for info. They wanted me to focus on getting well and back to my full strength.

On one side, I appreciated that, and truth be told, I missed the feeling of raw invincibility I had just a few weeks ago. I didn't like feeling human again. But on the other side, they were doing something *I* should probably be doing, and I wasn't sure how I felt about that.

At the end of the day, it was probably best not to let the trail get *too* cold, but that didn't mean I was okay with them being off on their own, despite all the evidence that they could handle themselves. At least, Vicki took Grandpa's knife when they left. That made me feel *a lot* better.

Moira still avoided me... at least when I was in my human form. She seemed to love running her fingers through my fur, though, and grinned like a kid at Christmas while she did it. She either had a beloved pet she missed or had never had one. I *was not* her pet, but I suppose anything furry kinda sorta blurs the line.

Mina dropped by the other day to check in and ask how I was. While she was there, she told me that Rex came back after a few days, and he and Noah were even closer friends, now that Noah could shift. Sometimes, it seemed like Rex wasn't quite sure how to handle his person becoming a pup, but so far, he seemed just to roll with it. She confessed that she loved to watch them romp and play. When she asked, I promised to visit and see it for myself.

I wasn't sure what the next step was, beyond healing, but I knew it would come whether I was ready for it or not. So, I might as well be ready. It was time to speak with Doc about kicking my exercises up a notch. It was time to get better.

WHAT'S NEXT?

Have you read "Lone Wolf," Karleen's origin story?

If not, sign up for my newsletter to get it:
https://kfplink.com/tps

Book 4 of the Primogenitor Saga is coming soon.

ACKNOWLEDGMENTS

There's an old saying: it takes a village to raise a child. I don't know if that's true or not, but it certainly seems true where publishing a story is concerned. You would not be reading this were it not for contributions from several people.

Did you like the cover? Dolton Richards (doltonrichards.com) is an awesome artist, and what strikes me as hilarious in its irony is that I've known of him *for years*. He's a friend of two of my closest friends.

No story should reach the public without passing through the scrutiny of a quality editor or editors, and TF Poist is one of the best.

I'm sure there are many who will see this next paragraph and think, "Goodness, he's acknowledging his parents and grandparents *again*?" My greatest regret is that I cannot hand my grandfather, Bob Miller, a paperback copy of my novels. So, yes... the Acknowledgements page of *every* story I publish will have the paragraph that follows. Consider yourselves forewarned.

Without my grandparents, Bob & Janice Miller, I honestly don't know where I'd be today; my grandfather taught me to read and love reading, and my grandmother taught me to develop and exercise my imagination. This story (not to mention my life in general) certainly would not have happened without my parents, Vernon & Judy Kerns.

THE WORLDS OF ROBERT M. KERNS

For a complete and accurate listing of all publications, both
currently available and forthcoming, please visit Knightsfall Press.

Knightsfall Press - Books

https://knightsfall.press/books

SO... WHO'S THE AUTHOR?

Robert M. Kerns (or Rob if you ever meet him in person) is a geek, and he claims that label proudly. Most of his geekiness revolves around Information Technology (IT), having over fifteen years in the industry; within IT, he especially prefers Servers and Networks, and he often makes the claim that his residence has a better data infrastructure than some businesses.

Beyond IT, Rob enjoys Science Fiction and Fantasy of (almost) all stripes. He is a voracious reader, with his favorite books too numerous to list.

Rob has been writing for over 20 years, published his first novel in 2018, and has no plans to stop any time soon.

Connect with Rob at robertmkerns.com.

facebook.com/RobertMKerns
amazon.com/author/robertmkerns
bookbub.com/authors/robert-m-kerns